WHAT BOOKS PRESS

AN IMPRINT OF

THE GLASS TABLE

COLLECTIVE

LOS ANGELES

THEY BECOME HER

REBBECCA BROWN

WHAT
BOOKS
PRESS

LOS ANGELES

Publisher's Cataloging-In-Publication Data

Brown, Rebbecca L.

  They become her / Rebbecca Brown.

  pages ; cm

  Originally presented as the author's thesis, University of Louisiana at Lafayette, 2007.

  ISBN-13: 978-0-9889248-7-1

  ISBN-10: 0-9889248-7-0

  1. Bacon, Delia Salter, 1811-1859--Fiction. 2. Authorship--Fiction. 3. Women authors--Fiction. 4. Plot-your-own stories. 5. Biographical fiction, American. 6. Post-modern fiction. I. Title.

PS3602.R7227 T44 2014

813/.6

What Books Press
363 South Topanga Canyon Boulevard
Topanga, CA 90290

WHATBOOKSPRESS.COM

Cover art: Gronk, untitled, mixed media on paper, 2014.
Book design by Ash Goodwin, AshGood.com.

THEY BECOME HER

PREFACE

DEAR READER:

I shall voluntarily make it known that I was unable to visit the archives that contain Delia Bacon's work as frequently as I would have liked. To be frank, I spent a mere few hours perusing the collection, as I had an important engagement that required examining the cultural significance of the world's tallest rocking chair. However, the inability to thoroughly explore Delia's documents wasn't entirely my fault. I discovered that another writer named Rebecca Brown (at present there are two that avidly publish) was also investigating the life of Ms. Bacon in order to write a fictional autobiography. The parsimonious curators of the manuscript collection wanted to ensure we were never in the same room at the same time. Unfortunately, I never came in contact with nor was introduced to this brilliantly prolific, world-renowned author. I have spent many an evening since heaved over with heartfelt sighs.

I also recently discovered that a woman who was not Rebecca Brown used the nom de plume "Rebecca Brown" in order to publish a work about the history of women mountain climbers. Cheers for the necessity of such a book (the world has been kept waiting for too long); however, although I regret saying it, I do believe Rebecca Brown was attempting to ride on the coattails of someone else's success. Yet another author by the name of Rebecca Brown who has written a novel about coping with the death of a family member has recently been brought to my attention, and I do not have the heart to accuse her of exploiting the name. I commend her bravery in these difficult times. Of course, all informed and conscientious readers are familiar with the critically celebrated author also named Rebecca Brown. Not a day passes in which I do not think of her cleverly titled work: *Buns and Puns: A Humorous Trek Through the Creases, Cracks and Crevasses of the Famous and Not-So-Famous*. Imagine the disappointment one feels upon discovering that others are more apt at creating memorable titles. Damn luck that I couldn't think of such clever nomenclature for this particular work.

Perhaps it would help vindicate my seemingly helpless case if I were to explain in more detail what occurred during my (albeit short) visit to the archives. The first obstacle to my success made itself apparent quite early on in my quest. I had written the curators in order to obtain permission to physically handle the copious tomes of delicate, moth-eaten and moldering material. I felt fortunate to have located these manuscripts, and was pleased at the amount available for grimy fingertips to wear and impair; there were over three hundred items collected and kept within the climate-controlled, dimly-lit, earthquake-proofed conditions of the building. I alternated between feelings of bliss and terror when I seriously contemplated the amount of material I might encounter: over one hundred letters in Delia Bacon's tightly scrawled, virtually illegible script; long-winded, biblical chastisements and famous hymns written by Delia's brother Reverend Leonard Bacon; notes to publishers from Nathaniel Hawthorne detailing his perception of Delia's madness; journals blurry with ink-stained tears; medical records; pages and pages of vital material that would surely produce pleasure within the heart of any aspiring biographer. I found myself, however, the victim of unavoidable circumstances, and couldn't feel the full extent of joy with which the avid researcher must undoubtedly be familiar.

Because of incompetence in which I took no part, my letters of application for use of the archival materials were lost. Reluctantly I do admit I spilled half a latte on said correspondence as I walked swiftly to send these letters to post, and I had to ask the postal manager to allow them to dry under an eave near the building with which pigeons unhygienically roost. I am now aware of the futility of explanations of import regarding certain irreplaceable documents to your local, not-so-friendly postal worker. There will always be indolent employees who choose to disregard their obligatory civic duties. The earth would cease to turn without those who ignore the magnitude of material they are duty-bound to deliver. This is, of course, an indication of larger societal ills of which there is not enough time nor space to discuss.

The employee I conducted my "unprofessional" business with apparently did not retrieve the dried letters from their place underneath the roof. But for the sake of consideration of all potential alternatives, I will not ignore the idea that the United States Postal Service may not be entirely at fault. The manuscript curators very well could have been the culprits; it is about time their reputation as the gatekeepers of culture is seriously reexamined. Who knows at what level of bureaucracy these important documents were lost?

Alas, this is not the place for frivolous accusations (although I feel obliged to inform discerning readers of a lawsuit pending with the Skull and Bones—may they meddle with my work no longer!), and I will make a vast effort to maintain dignity and remain focused on the task at hand, which is to describe the countless entanglements within which I found myself while researching this colossal project. I will describe the impediments presented against me, with hopes that the reader will understand my unforeseen plight. What toil and turbulence have been endured to present to you, worthy reader, this crucial work!

Once I physically arrived at the archives, I was treated with a certain amount of disdain that cannot be described as anything less than pure, unadulterated detestation. Perhaps my neon nylon jogging suit was not professional enough attire to sit in a room with other academics nosing their way through books. Or maybe it was the unfortunate and strange sickness I had caught on the train prior to my arrival. Because of a deplorable financial situation (why, oh why is there a lack of intelligent patrons willing to support the production of brilliant, necessary work?), I had to spend three days aboard the rumbling, nausea-inducing Amtrak. On the train, I was frequently accosted by a railroad employee (who shall remain nameless, but I will note that he looked as if he could have leapt out of a mine shaft circa 1857—with a bald head and beard that suggested a combination of elfishness and lunacy I have only heretofore encountered in dreams) who would not leave me alone for a moment to contemplate my impending work. One night after a dinner of rubberish chicken and powdered mashed potatoes, this man offered me a piece of his uneaten dessert: a chocolate cake that looked as if it were made out of synthetic materials. Being the polite and gracious passenger that I am, I took this gift and ate it without hesitation. Before I realized my mistake, I was pitching back and forth in the forbidding Amtrak restrooms. I'll leave the details of this harrowing experience to the imagination of my readers.

At any rate, this sickness followed me to the archives and caused me to run in and out of the reading room in unpredictable fifteen-minute spurts. I don't think the others present appreciated the frequent sound of flushing that perhaps ruinously interrupted their work. Ah, well. If I have learned anything from this experience, I have learned that scholarship must go on, regardless of disruption.

Thankfully and thoughtfully, considering my desire for a renewed and healthy constitution, the institution provided an afternoon tea to which all present were invited. This afforded those working a chance to mingle and scrutinize the relevance of each other's research. I usually avoided attending these frivolous displays by leaving as early as possible, but on the day before my last at the archives, I decided to join the ranks of my colleagues by having a cup of tea with these local wits.

I sat myself at a table that contained a group of historians who were all too content with ignoring my presence and talking shop about the latest unsuccessful biographers in their field. Although I do believe they were trying to be friendly by passing me a napkin when I accidentally dropped a chocolate wafer in my lap, I still could not participate in their insular camaraderie to the extent that I would have liked. One day the world will open its welcoming arms and invite me in, but in the meantime, I must work diligently at proving my seriousness and value as a scholar. I am confident I will meet these intellectuals once again and say "E Pluribus Unum," or for those of you who require an interpretation: we came, we saw, we conquered.

To the reader: my sincerest apologies. I have had to invent material where it was not readily available to meet my investigatory needs. While some uninformed critics may refer to this as shoddy research practice, I prefer to characterize it as a fusion of innovative methodologies with a mastery of boldness and bravura.

Yours truly,
RB

ALSO BY REBECCA BROWN:

3 Way Split
Annie Oakley's Girl
Becoming a Vessel of Honor
Buns and Puns: A Humorous Trek Through the Creases, Cracks and Crevasses
of the Famous and Not-So-Famous
How to Teach Online (and Make 100K a Year)
He Came to Set the Captives Free
Prepare for War
Standing the Watch: Memories of a Home Death
The Children's Crusade
The Dogs: A Modern Bestiary
The Evolution of Darkness: And Other Stories
The Gifts of the Body
"The impact of bankruptcy on dissolution of marriage in Arkansas"
The Haunted House
The Last Time I Saw You
The Terrible Girls
Unbroken Curses
What Keeps Me Here: A Book of Stories
Women on High: Pioneers of Mountaineering

Hartford, CT. Institute for Living. Archive #CF1857BAC. 322 items.
Contents: Correspondence. Notes. 1 Journal, Leather Bound. Patient Diagnosis
and Psychological History.
Collected by: Miss. Elaine Lawrence, RN. January 1859.
Document #CF1857BAC-1

    As nurse and primary companion of Delia Bacon during her final years at our
institution, I have seen to it that her manuscripts remain in our facility. They may
one day be of use to the larger community. In order to avoid legal entanglements,
Miss. Bacon designated the institute sole ownership of any written work composed
during her residence. She admitted to me personally her desire for me to do with
her writings as I saw fit. Therefore, her work completed here must remain in this
institution until one hundred years after her death, wherein they shall become
available to the public. Until then, they shall dwell within this institute's walls
and vaults.

———

New Haven, CT. Yale University Beinecke Rare Book and Manuscript Library.
BACON, LEONARD. 1802-1881.
322 B-1. 1 item (35 p.); 6 in. Journal dated from 1857-1859.
322 B-2. 66 items (92 p.) 3 folders: Letters: Correspondence with sister, Delia Bacon.
322 B-3. 1 item (86 p.); 8 in. Journal of sister, Delia Bacon (1811-1859).
322 B-4. 10 items (15 p.) 1 folder: Letters: Correspondence with Elaine Lawrence.
322 B-5. 1 item (60 p.): Typescript copies of correspondence between Leonard
Bacon and Yale Alumni.
Document #322 B-5. p. 53

    Mr. T Woolsey:
        My sister has returned to the country and has been admitted to the
Institute for Living. It is there I hope she lives out her final days in peaceful
isolation from those long-plagued spirits. I shall not renounce my desire to save her

soul from damnation. As protectorate during her institutionalization, I have legal domain over her. I have befriended a nurse named Miss. Elaine Lawrence who shall see to it that Delia no longer pollutes our community with her preposterous theories. She has caused me pain long enough. In brotherly love I shall personally oversee her detention.

Yours,
Reverend Leonard Bacon

———

Washington, DC. Folger Shakespeare Library. Folger MS Y.c.2599 (1-318). BACON, DELIA. 1811-1859. Document # 317, June 1857.

it was a mmrble mmt when you at the Avn. The signs of it are in the strt whether you understand them or not. There reason in those reasons whether you observe them or not. You have forded the Avn. You have untied the spell. Theres reason in the whole. You have crossed the Avon twice. You crossed it in the E. & you crossed it in the West. You crossed the old in the N Haven. The E in the West and you crossed the New, the West in the East. History rest in me a clue & run a right spirit millim me.

ONE

*I have only to ask that I may not be condemned for failing to fulfill
the conditions of a species of writing which I have not attempted.*
Delia Bacon

WHEN MY FATHER LEFT, I found myself in a fretful fire for Jesus.
My brother Leonard loved the Lord and I couldn't bring myself beside him
except by wanting the words and the writing. I wished I could eat those words
and watch them drip slowly the length of my skin. They would become me.
Words full of fire and fervor issued forth from our community corners and the
boxed-in white wood of the churches to set the old reeling. During sermons,
the mothers would sweat as if they were birthing and the men fanned gnats
from their hat brims. To want to eat the words, write the words, wasn't much
like other women Christian and wanting. I was not and am not a very good
Christian. Leonard told me when I was young I was full of sinner desire.
Everyone loves Leonard. As a youth he had palpable fires for pulpits. He
charmed the people from the boxed-in white wood of the churches to set their
shriveled hearts reeling.

Although a sinner, longing, I loved the revivals and the way the city burst
from the spit-fired mouthings. They reminded me of my father. He had fled
to the wilderness, had tried to move westward to create a new colony where
everyone would worship full of the fear, but who knows what evil was sent
to harm him: Indians, bears, beatings, disease, scalpings. He returned from
the wild shook and poverty stricken, and died soon after to leave me. I hardly
remember. I do remember that his hair was always clean and smelled of cedar

shavings. He wouldn't hold me, but when he walked in from a long week of wandering, I could taste the smoke of his fires. My father issued forth from a long line of Bacons somehow connected to Sir Francis; we are most of us esteemed. We are most of us Christian and wanting.

When my father fled to the wilderness, church fathers from the boxed-in white wood gave him money and permission to take all the land he needed to convert sinners and brown-skinned Satanists that howled with the moon little devils. Wherever witches would breathe, he would deliver the faith that rocked and saved souls. My father died when I was a tiny, tucked in girl. I hardly remember, yet there are papers that prove it.

My mother had to move away after my father died because she couldn't afford us. She found another woman to keep me. My mother took all of my other brothers and sisters and left Leonard and me in Hartford. Leonard studied at Yale Divinity School while I alone with another mother learned reading, some writing. My real mother complained about my other brothers and sisters as mouths to feed like nests full of dirty birds rattling the eaves with their cheeping. Leonard wrote to the others of how I grew and blossomed like a pig in the clover. Leonard, my brother smartly opinioned, likened me to a little pink piglet.

My real mother told him he was to watch over me like a good father, and he took this to heart with an intensity that pierced. He was as slim as a horse post, and just as sturdy; nothing tottered or rendered him weightless. He always knew he'd make a pillar of society—he was correctly Christian and wanting. He could talk the devil from witches without water or whip. He loved reading Shakespeare and sniveling. At Yale, his hands were constantly in a pile of books and he would quote and look down his angular nose at the men and women that gathered around him. All of the ladies loved how on fire he was for literature and the Lord. He had a knack for knowing.

When I was ten, I discovered writing. Miss. Williams, my other mother, taught me how to turn scribble and scrawl into meaning, my fingers pleasurably palsied and rawed from the practice. I wanted so much for these words to become me. I would take small scraps of paper when no one was looking and lick them, examining the ink drip lengths of my skin. Sometimes I pinned word-coated scraps to my worn thin dress and watched how they blurred from spinning. Nothing thrilled me more than messages. Sometimes secrets are divulged, sometimes private. Sometimes you should never let anyone see without looking.

The first letter I ever wrote was addressed to Leonard. I told him how much I thought about God and wished to be visited by the spirit so I could strike away all sins; how I wished to convert witches who played with fire and found frogs and devil doings in the forests behind tree cover. I wanted to form my mouth around words like Leonard so I could become the words and then light all the carriage wheels on fire with love for the Lord, but I knew I could not correctly feel it. I could not set the young hearts reeling.

I wrote:

I abused my own spirit and thought Him forever forsaken me with all of the dark hours He clout down upon me, but He awoke me from my awful slumber of stupidity and I thought I will never be unhappy I love you Leonard and miss you mother.

I was ecstatic to form the words from head to mouth to hands that scrawled the paper because I couldn't get sentences out fast enough before another would jar my brain like lightning striking the trees and the witches that wrapped themselves round them. In Leonard's response, he criticized my lack of punctuation.

All the women think my brother Leonard a handsome commanding man. When his first wife died, his step was full of the springtime gestures of bloom despite mourning. He knew his first wife's mouth had turned to dust, quietly uncomplaining her place into heaven. He told me:

Sister Delia that mouth of yours will crumble. Keep it closed, obedient. Keep it rightly tight against desires. Behave correctly. Only then might you earn peace and the Lord. When your body turns to dust you may not be worthy. Be good. Remember. Obey your brother, as I am now both father, mother.

I didn't mind when Leonard's first wife died in fever and sickness. I was still young enough to miss the palms of Leonard's hands patting my head like a plump little piglet in clover. Although each of his wives knew about cooking, proper mending, sewing, I was never like them. I would rather belittle my place through a book. When I tried to learn to stitch, I poked my fingers with needles that bled droplets that dripped through my bindings. I could never evenly place the flowers and coverlets the ladies would set on their laps Sunday mornings. My stitches were too large—grotesque and visibly bulging.

Once I learned how to read and write, Miss. Williams, my other mother, would not look over me much longer. She remarked on how I blustered with a broom like a goose shaking feathers of no help to her, but I knew she liked our teatime conversations. Sometimes I miss her porcelain cups, thick soft rugs, her study; I miss the globe on the bureau tilted toward heaven and England.

Miss. Williams loved me, maybe more than my mother, because she allowed me to stay longer than the other girls while I grew. Before I spent my final year in her pretty parlor, I was sent for by my real mother who wanted me to stay with her again although she was the one who loved leaving. I convinced her of how much I could not be needed; I had a life to learn in Hartford. On the fourth of July, I satisfied her with a visit and picnic.

My brothers, sisters and I ate sandwiches, drank lemonade and listened to the band triumph to music. The birds flew everywhere like great joyful explosions, chittering like the flitting children: my other sisters and brothers were Alice and Francis and Julia and Susan and David. They would run from the band to the grass to the matted down dust tracks to the stages while the birds dove in and out gathering broken bread. The sun gleamed through the streets' trees, men were stiff in their linens, and women whisked their dresses over their ankles. It was a beautiful day fit for Princess Victoria, and the sun shone on while I blossomed like clover.

Alice, a sister I once slept near, sat listless in the sunrays on a patched quilt while the horn thrumped thoughtfully our nation's independence. My brother David and I argued the heavy horses: Clydesdale or Danube, Belgian or Breton. I didn't know much about horses, but I liked the way David scrunched up his face to contend, a thousand tiny rivers. Sister Julia drew her painting the day around us. Susan and her fiancé fanned themselves treeside and looked as much in love as allowed for, except he kept checking for train times and looking at his grease-coated son diving after dog hides. My tiniest brother Francis was hard to keep track of through all of the this and that of celebration. Francis's cowlicked hair stood straight up as he'd run between the fingertips of the older children who'd pat him. But the Lord cannot keep all his eyes on the little children. When Francis chased after a bird into the street, the clatter and dust clouds roared and clanged like bells tied to the horse manes tromping their heavy-hearted heels down on anything that ran before them.

Francis found himself underneath a stage wheel limp, reeling. His body was bent and broken like a bow. He was bleeding. He had been rolled over, the horses clopping his frail bird bones. His head lolled about his shoulders and sighs shuddered out of his body. All of the ladies covered their mouths and gasped their eyes away. The men took their hats and waved them, respecting the ground.

I looked at little brother Francis not away. I went to his side lying coated with sticky and grass blades. A fly landed on his lip and then shooed by my ear with unaware insect song. Nothing seemed to notice. The horses pulling the stages were glad to stop and chomp weeds. The sun still shone happy fourth of Julys down upon the New World. I wondered what was missing. Francis's eyes glazed at nothing in particular. Finally, I looked away. This may have been where I lost the Lord. I couldn't care anymore about what Brother Leonard told me of down flying divinity from angels beautiful as every sunset.

Back at my mother's house, we mourned as we mourn, some weeping, others pacing. I did nothing. I went to the dreariest back room full of my mother's poverty and looked into the mirror. My dark hair glistened nothing spectacular. My eyes looked back at my dark eyes looking at my dark eyes back and I heard no lofty or loud voice calling.

I could not stand to be at my mother's much longer with the sadness of Francis hanging my head and the loss of the Lord I had wanted to believe in and no one doing much except turning to dust, breathing in, exhaling mourning. I gave up looking for the light of the Lord and could never again desire anything except words and the wanting reflected back through my eyes in the darkness. In the good book, a mess of families makes a mourn of everything.

After Francis died, I promised myself I would begin, truly writing. I went back to Hartford passionately filled with my own fire. Miss. Williams was plump with the life heart that wisdom thumped, and because I had to leave her, she enrolled me in a school for girls taught by Miss. Catharine Beecher. Miss. Williams told me after I finished I could then start my own school. She said women were necessary teachers, because men only taught temporarily to move to higher positions in clergy. She told me if I became a teacher I would always keep learning and become myself writing. Girls weren't attending universities and there was a need for them to be trained. If I decided on a path of continual study, my words might set the young hearts to reel. I might make a better book than Leonard's Lord writing.

I was an exceptional student. I especially loved when the whole room full of girls was spent writing. I loved the sound of the scratch of word to paper, how it filled the silence with a special sort of susurration. I also enjoyed standing in front of the classroom and speaking. When it was my turn for discourse, the other girls' eyes would glimmer as they stared agape. Miss. Beecher told me I had a particular public presence, that I was a better speaker than her sister, my classmate, Harriet Beecher.

In school, I pretended I wasn't eating words to make them all become me. I followed directions correctly so the world would not disown me. In private, I would often take a word I learned and make it do my bidding:

Apostle: I ran to the post stumbling over my dress quickly apostle to discover if Mr. Alexander MacWhorter had sent news.

Lunatic: Mr. Jeremiah Day's head had taken on a severe shaking when fall had come upon us and it rocked to and fro lunatic.

Tiresome: My boots were coated with dust and tiresome from walking back and forth the mountain.

Germ: Shakespeare was the stable germ, cleaning horse waste from the floors before the uppers moved him fameward.

Often I would bid these words into places of poetry and later send them to my sister Alice. I could trust her. She was as silent as a stitch and liked to spend days dreaming. I could talk for hours and not get a blink's response. She never judged, and was simply sister Alice. With her, I never had to hide.

*

Leonard says if I write sentences again like a simple sister, he will tell Nurse Elaine to release me. That is why I am here now and writing abandoned writing. I have been in this institute to long to let out. I am ready to be bothered by books again, but Leonard has penned me in. I must tell how I became this way with words before my mouth sifts. It began at the Beechers', but now I have to keep secrets. I know in hearts are desires both full and void; I know how feelings can shake a night lunatic.

*

Like Leonard, Miss. Beecher taught us to edge ourselves ever-so-slightly lest we get put where our mouths won't work. She once had a maddening romance. Her fiancé Mr. Alexander Metcalfe Fisher died in a shipwreck and she too lost her lust for the Lord. All us ladies adored her so, although she would never tell us her love stories specific. We learned of her lover through girls' mouths passed year to year why her eyes often vacated a body that moved with the strength of volition. Her deep-set eyes darkly triumphed despite the loss of a lover to the viscous waves of the sea.

We loved romance, our favorite book's pages filled with lovers that palpitated our hearts to bursting. *Corinne.* I wanted to become her, poet-priestess of Rome with long flowing hair who would recite poetry when Apollo journeyed down from heaven to award her the laurel. I slept with the book underneath my bed, hoping Apollo would try to steal it from beneath me and I would wake and catch him stuffed in a jar. I hoped to attract a man as incredible as Corinne's lover Oswald, who was dashing and daringly English. The first time I read the ending, and Corinne dies of fever, writing verse, awaiting Oswald, I cried for days to end.

One day, Miss. Beecher asked me what was wrong. Unexpectedly I called out "Corinne!" The other girls and I had promised not to reveal our secret readings, but I could not help it. Sometimes words cannot control escape. Surprisingly, Miss. Beecher had also read this romance and we talked about it just as we spoke about Shakespeare, Byron and Shelley. We stunned with pleasant shocks these moments.

Miss. Beecher spent time preparing us. She loved literature and language and would praise our compositions, especially if they were calmed with tactful fury. She admired the poetry I composed, particularly the poem I wrote for a deaf-mute named Alice, who was taught to read and write despite hardships. Her favorite lines:

Whence came that gleam of thought so bright,
like the lightning streak on a cloud of night,
to the soul of fancy dear?

I pretended I was Alice and wrote a different version I later sent to my sister Alice. The rearranged lines read:

Whence gleam came lightning streak cloud bright,
thought fancy soul like night, dear.

I discovered a power in reform, another way of doing with words. I could take sentences someone else had written and put them in orders making sense to me beautiful. Sometimes I would imagine the birds tweeting "I love you", or "you love I", or "love I you", or "I you love", depending on my mood. Sometimes I would take phrases from books and do some slight reshuffling. For example, this sentence of Thomas Hooker's: *The foundation of authority is laid in the free consent of the people* can become: *Free of consent, foundations of people laid in the authority.* Shifting produces circulation in-between words. I keep this pastime sometimes a cipher, a secret.

Every year with Miss. Beecher there was a contest for the best student composition, and I was certain during my last year I would take the prize. I had been complimented exceedingly for my first oration "A Plea for the Native" in which I commend my ancestors for mercilessly slaughtering the Indians. I also made sure, like a true orator, to consider all sides of the argument. I focused on how important it is to preserve those remaining for culture and conservation. With slight hand movements enthusiastic, I could wring and manipulate concentration; the class loved my speech and I was able to convince them to change their opinions about Indian extermination. I knew I could do the same with a story.

The only real competitor I had in class was Harriet. I didn't think her and Miss. Beecher's relation would get in the way of my winning the competition because I was obviously the better mind; however, I was wrong. This was when the schism between Miss. Beecher and I opened like an ocean swallowing lovers. Harriet and I were the top poet-priestesses in our class, yet the other girls told me I had something distinctly superior. The better girl, I did not let this affect Harriet and my friendship. Sometimes we would read to one another beneath the drooping birch trees. We were almost simply sisters.

On the day of Miss. Beecher's judgment, I wore my prettiest dress and combed my hair tightly back so my eyes and their darkness might shine more winningly bright. I perfumed my hands with powder. When I received my prize, I wanted to fragrance the air with my victory. When Miss. Beecher announced simply sister Harriet's name, I could have slid through my chair and underneath the floorboards to where worms and insects scurried about waiting for death. I ran directly home and did not see any of the other girls, my eyes deeply moist with darkness. It was a mistake. I knew I shouldn't have let anyone know how I rearranged, resounded, unfixed.

Harriet had written a five-act verse drama with expected rhymes and characters similar to those in *Corrine*. She even named her play *Cleon* to make it sound more ancient and important. Miss. Beecher must have marked through Harriet's pages and told her what to do correctly: this is what sister would do, this is how sister would write, this is what sister should rhyme, this makes you a winner. It isn't fair, this fixing.

Miss. Beecher chose her sister's work despite us knowing it was not as well-written and full of intrigue as my story. I had submitted an early draft of "Love's Martyr". In it, a woman must submit herself to the natives who of course scalp her and offer her body to their many-hearted gods for the good of our nation. "Love's Martyr" is full of action and romance and convention, popular enough for audiences of all ages. It concerns itself with a vital time, and the heroine is a noble sacrifice.

Most of the other girls agreed my story should not have lost, and I encouraged them to help me start some rebellion. Because Miss. Beecher encouraged independence of thought, I told the other girls the next time she wanted us to participate in discussion we should recite poetry and familiar expressions. I felt that this might reinforce her poor choice and she would realize the true winner in me, Miss. Delia Bacon. Even the name has the ring of a victor. I shall write it once more: Miss. Delia Bacon. It shall one day be remembered. It shall rise and be called blessed.

Harriet also secretly told me she thought my story superior, so a few days after the contest, the girls sat quiet and at my prompting recited any number of sayings. There became a jumble:

While we are engaged in the important struggle, it cannot be thought impertinent for us to turn one eye into our own breast, the iron hand of tyranny and oppression, when in the course of human events, it is only in the creation that all our ideas and conceptions of a word of God can unite, these are the times that try men's souls.

Miss. Beecher did not understand what was happening until she took the youngest girl outside and prompted discovery. The youngest being the youngest gave away our secrets. Miss. Beecher realized her mistake and apologized to me after dismissing the class. Because I am who I am and will be who I will be, I forgave her. She told me women who know how to properly hem themselves in, even if they move against the rest of the world, will never be humiliated. Humiliation, she said, is an emotion ladies cannot choose to exist. That year was the last of Miss. Beecher's competitions. She, too, would one day learn not to trust solely in the wisdom of her words; she, too, would end up in this institute for the living.

I continued my studies in the fashion of men's colleges and was soon proficient in Grammar, Chemistry, Geography, Rhetoric, Philosophy, Ancient and Modern History, Arithmetic, Moral Philosophy, Geometry, Natural Theology and Latin, and was ready to start my own school like many of the other young women. And this was just the beginning.

Now I am closing book-like ends and would like to complete it.

Please. Let me out. Can't you see I am wanting?

I'm sorry, Brother Leonard. My words will work and I will re-love the Lord. My sentences are reforming.

Dearest Leonard, you said if I were to write again whole and complete you would tell Nurse Elaine. Let me back to your loving embrace. My punctuation is fine and fixed. It is you I want and require forgiveness.

The nurses' hands I can't bear except for Nurse Elaine's. She has given me a journal leather bound and a pile of papers to leave letters for later burning so I can watch my old ways flame towards heaven.

Only Leonard, Nurse Elaine says, can save me.

I see hands writing and words burning into the soft skin of fingers. I ask you for forgiveness. I am sorry. I am sorry. I am sorry for what I've done. It is just that I could not leave those bones alone.

———

When I was younger I used to stare at the spaces before spaces where there were red, white and blue sparkling dots that move towards you. I used to see them especially prevalent in front of the sky on a bright, clear day. I've heard these are blotches of the universal energy field that point the way toward alternate universes where everything is alive simultaneously with many possibilities going on. An early edition of *Omni* claims these little lights are leftover from time spent in the womb when you didn't have fully formed eyelids but thin, viscous layers that are see through. I used to stare at them glowing like Fourth of July picnics. Maybe I was just bored, or maybe this is when I began to enjoy amassing the disparate—collecting little lives and lights.

Rebecca Brown was born at the bottom of a hayloft in the Midwest but left to find her true calling fighting cults seduced by Satan. She often hears the voice of God, who sounds to her like Ted Koppel. She spends her days with her husband John in Arkansas after being kicked out of California. The two pray on bended knees, contemplate breeding sheep, and write books about damnation. Rebecca promises to fight for you in the war against hell on earth. Be saved now little children. Profess your love. Listen to Rebecca.

Rebecca Brown was born in the West with a condition that coiled the bottom of her body serpentine. As a Lamia, she is supposed to have an overwhelming hunger for children, but she has no such appetite. After the surgeons separated her serpent half into two twin mirrored limbs, she liked to contemplate losing one of her new extremities and imagine it living a life of its own. Would her lost limb travel? Could it be sewn onto someone who likes to set sail for distant countries? Would the leg like to gamble? Rebecca is fascinated with missing appendages and avidly follows stories of arms accidentally removed by farm equipment. While she should also have removable eyes, it is her father who is missing these orbs. The replacements drift toward the corners of rooms.

Rebbecca Brown was born at the beginning of a book that delves into the life of a historical figure named Delia Bacon. She often vacations in the mountains and enjoys the privileges of a schizophrenic who can travel through time. This is quite liberating, although it is difficult for her to hold down a steady job. She has been going to workshops for the last ten years in order to learn how to write. In them she has learned that in order to produce effective fiction, one must develop round characters that are full of life and engaging. She has also learned that a successful story must have a clear plot consisting of a beginning, middle, and end. She is currently working on a novel about three contemporary authors with the same name who are each interested in a woman who in the mid eighteen hundreds was the first to suggest that members of a secret society headed by Sir Francis Bacon were the actual authors of the Shakespearean texts.

Rebecca found that her hands were itching again and she couldn't stand it. She was always washing dishes and her hands couldn't handle the soapsuds. She thought of pans, spatulas, forks, and the plastic containers she wouldn't throw away. Dishes piled up in her head until they formed a dirty mountain that looked similar to how she imagined the grimy kitchens in hell. Her sink was filled with coffee mugs and if she stared at them any longer she thought she might scream and holler like souls burning up with torture. She knew she had to clean them, everyone knows who cleanliness is next to. Her hands screamed at her so she decided to press them together to tend to the itch and pray.

She stared at the stucco crags of the yellowed ceiling. She had the opportunity to look up for awhile without thinking about much except fire and hell and damnations. Although she would not admit it out loud, especially to John, the thought of hell began to bore her. She was becoming uninterested in demons and torment and brimstones. John, however, would not hear her through. He was always making plans to leave somewhere new for preaching. He loved hymns and humming them in Rebecca's ears while she slept or knelt.

Everything was quiet. She wondered when God might speak to her again. Two months had passed and she hadn't received a word. She missed the sound of his deep and intoxicated voice. The Satanists had even stopped planting firebombs inside of her stereo system, and she missed their preoccupations. She was lonely. She thought about the possibility of writing another book. Her others had done so well, translated into many baffling, babbling tongues. There were so many sinners to speak to, so many who didn't know the law or lore and love.

An alarm started buzzing from the bedroom. Once there was a time when God told her to get rid of her alarm clock so she would wake to the sound of his voice. Back then he woke her at all hours to talk with her about all manner of things such as his love of peaches and anthills. He would tell her not to go to the grocery store because Satanists were hiding inside plastic toys in boxes of cereal. He told her he liked her hair pulled back behind her ears. He also told her who would burn and who wouldn't, and to spread the word. He was the one who told her she should be a writer and copy down his thoughts. She listened avidly to his voice, recording everything he'd say, until one day when he simply stopped speaking. She bought an alarm clock to spite or incite him, yet he still did not respond.

The alarm kept buzzing. She rose from her knees to turn it off.

She maneuvered through the bedroom. John was sleeping and snoring, swallowing air as if he were about to choke, even though the buzz from the alarm was like an Arkansas mosquito swarming in to suck. John believed alarm clocks a ridiculous waste of time because he never woke to anything except his own vigorous quaking. He didn't mind when Rebecca threw their last clock into the large bonfire filled with other Satanic appliances because God had told her so. He didn't mind either when she bought a new alarm clock and toaster to replace the ones that had melted in the flames. John spent his days focused on preaching, mostly gone.

She turned off the alarm and roamed into the living room. She couldn't think of anything else to pray for, so she sat on her hands and thought of a dusty road she lived on as a child.

The dirt was soft and felt like fine silk slipping through her toes. The consistency of this dirt was one of the finest extravagances she had ever known. It left a fine film on her skin. It powdered and covered, a smooth gray shield against the sun. She would bury her paper dolls in it because she liked the way they would rise curling from under the rain like Jesus sailing across the water on his tiny feet. Their paper dresses confettied in the warm showers that would sneak through the heat near the end of summers. She would paste the wet strips onto her dress and watch how they whirled as she turned on her heels. She loved the way the dirt smelled when the water patted, the way it sounded like skin when it rubbed against pews.

"Rebecca? It's late. Fuck." John stood in the doorway and spit into a cup. *"That light shall glance on distant lands, and heathen tribes, in joyful bands…"* Rebecca? Do you hear me?"

"Yes. Sorry. I didn't want to wake you up."

"Next time do as you're told." John stood and stomped off his sleep. He could make a hole straight through Satan's heart.

"I'll make you some coffee." Rebecca was glad to have something to do.

John plodded toward the shower and Rebecca went into the kitchen to stare into the sink. The glasses, so many glasses: big mugs, small mugs, mason jars of mugs, mugs! She decided that she must wash them before she prepared anything for John. Suddenly, there was so much to do. After she finished, she might also dust and rearrange her ceramic angel collection. She wrung her dry and itchy hands. She turned on the tap and waited for the water to steam.

This was one of her favorite chores, despite the aversion of her cracking hands. The scraping of the food residue made her feel as if anything could be cleansed, even caked-on grease and grime. Washing dishes made her think about the comforts up in heaven. The soapsuds were as white and iridescent as angel wings, and sometimes in them she saw the eyes of saints and spirits. They blinked at her quick and moving fingers, and they were pleased.

While she washed, she often made up songs: *Rebecca, Rebecca, oh where have you been? I've been to the bottom of the tallest trash bin. Rebecca, Rebecca, why did you go? I went there to watch the griminess grow. Scrub, scrub the filth away, you have to keep washing till the pain goes away.* She should, like John, write, recite and sing hymns, except one of the last things God told her was that her inside voice was best, and she was much better at writing prose. She rarely sings out loud, except for when she is at church. God told her singing in church was permitted because her voice would be drowned out by all of the other worshipers, and she knew God knows best.

Rebecca dried the mugs on a towel with a cross-stitched picture of a house that said "home sweat home." She heard the shower stop and remembered that she hadn't started John's coffee. She filled a teapot with water and set it to boil. When she turned, John was standing in a towel, dripping.

"Forget it. I'll stop at the 7-11 next to church. Fucking Satanists. Soon they'll start buying more chains, then what? They're destroying everything. Only Armageddon will make them stop. *Though now the nations sit beneath the darkness of o'erspreading death, God will arise with light divine on Zion's holy towers to shine.*" John placed one palm on his skeletal forehead in a gesture reminiscent of thought. Rebecca grabbed his other hand with her blotchy fingers and looked toward eyes that looked inward. He let her linger for a moment before pulling towards the door.

———

Rebecca is half snake, half woman, and has the scale and tenor of a poet. There is a name for women like her, but it has not been in use for centuries. She is made from myth, elusive, filled with vast seduction. She is bold with desire not fit for human hearts. Perhaps it is because she is ectothermic— needing heat from rocks or stones or meat.

Shortly after she was born squirming and screaming, she was split down the center to form two legs from her now absent tail. Despite the two quite normal kneecaps and knobby, unsleek feet, sometimes she sheds. Sometimes she still shucks skin in sheaths of unique fabrications. Her apartment snows with fragments of these floating motes, and she must sweep them away before Elaine finds them and thinks the dust abhorrent. Elaine is irrefutably neat, yet she doesn't mind the few tufts of fur she finds now and then from their Doberman Sophia. Sophia was a present from Elaine on their third anniversary and had arrived wrapped in a bow just before Elaine began her doctoral work in psychology. Rebecca believed it a gesture both sweet and disgusting.

Rebecca was walking Sophia in a nearby park, waiting for her to do her business. Sophia's flanks tensed and pulsed, tensed and pulsed. The twitch and pull of Sophia's musculature caused Rebecca some anxiety. She knew she needed to write another book, but had not yet discovered a story worth pursuing. When a narrative compelled her, she knew she must spend time tracking, meticulous and deliberate, bound to the tale to the point of suffocation. The story must be sensuous, delectable, as elegant as well-wrought limbs. It must embrace the void of lovers who were once there then gone.

The memory of absent lovers reminded her of what it was like to live a life lipped to the rim of a bottle, futilely sucking like an ouroboros, but it had been years since Rebecca drank anything strong enough to subjugate her. She spent her last sips determined to quit even if she had to break her own back to slink through the lengths of it. Never again, she promised, never again. So far, she had stuck to her word.

Sophia finished expunging her waste in a healthy and tremendous lump. *Bitch*, thought Rebecca, and let her off the leash to run.

Elaine was currently in Connecticut finishing research for her dissertation as a fellow at the Institute for Living, and before she left she had promised to keep in constant touch. She was studying to be an art therapist and was especially interested in how women's institutionalization in the 19th century may have thwarted their creative pursuits. Rebecca and Elaine often talked to one another about the books that these women might have written had they not been bungled behind bars. Elaine believed, as did Rebecca, that women who were not allowed to explore their anxieties with their own nourishing inventions would suffer interminably at the hands of others' dangerous whims. Elaine and Rebecca would talk late into the evenings about what the world would be like had the women explored their fears and longings as prolifically as men.

Despite these regular collaborative exchanges, what kept desire sweltering between the two was selective omission. Elaine didn't know about Rebecca's once serpentine half, but enjoyed the way Rebecca could acrobatically curl around her, her hunger concentrated in acts of enfolding. As for her sometimes shedding, Elaine believed that Rebecca had a serious case of eczema. As for her flexibility, she believed Rebecca was multiple jointed. Elaine understood that some women were sensitive enough to peel and bend and burn. What she didn't understand was why Rebecca insisted on laying fully flayed on the warm summer rocks by the river with skin as touchy as hers.

Rebecca met Elaine at an English Department Christmas party. Rebecca did not usually attend these types of gatherings, but that particular Christmas found her all alone. Old skin had recently peeled from her thighs and her fresh pink flesh itched. She was cold and wanted to wrap her legs around something as hot as blood or stone. As soon as she arrived, her emptiness muttered and spewed—ancient engine—and was gone. She noticed Elaine's calves trailing under a red velvet skirt sliding across the back of her thighs. Rebecca's skin flushed into fire and her eyes vertically slit as she watched Elaine manipulate the party without any self-consciousness or pretension. Rebecca found Elaine both repulsive and exciting, as cunning as a rat. A few cups of punch later, Rebecca asked Elaine out. Elaine said yes, and later that night Rebecca removed more of her unnecessary flesh.

Sophia circled a grove of pine trees and wove her sleek physique in-between. She pushed her nose into the cone-littered ground snouting for sticks until she found one thick enough to give to Rebecca for throwing. She dropped it at Rebecca's fictive feet. Rebecca picked up the stick, threw it and watched as Sophia chased desirously after. As she tossed and Sophia ran, Rebecca thought:

bodies unburgeon themselves from their skin as sleek as melting. the heft of desire turns itself inside from out. we make love immobilized by sun and night. you, like blood, let me.

Desire. A lover is gone. Missing. Found. Rebecca planned and associated:

moments align like gestures in places your body understands. maybe i am here without reason. maybe that is why i coil at and strike you.

Sophia was panting. It was time to go home. Rebecca looked forward to an evening spent possibly writing. As she walked, she noticed the sun shuddering on the shoulders of trees with a lackluster light that might later weigh heavily upon her.

TWO

The curse of having lived in these wilds cleaves to me in all things.
Delia Bacon

NURSE ELAINE TELLS ME to write it how it wants to be written, not how I want to write it. She reminds me I am strong. She looks at my hands and calms them when she whispers stories of what happens in the cities, how women newly refashion their steps. She won't tell me used-up tales from books; she knows I know most of them and will not believe any of them. She wants to leave here, too.

She knows Leonard. I imagine them speaking each to each, and they speak of me.

Leonard is not allowed to see me and he will not let me. The only place I am is here, somewhere, between. My hands no longer command it.

Nurse Elaine, trust me, for you.

I continue. The doctors believe this the most radical of rehabilitations, and I do it again in secret when the walls aren't tumbling down. I do not know what will become of me, pressed between the pages of this book.

*

I was ready to start my own school. I left for New York with my sister Julia, who could draw and paint the world around us. We took nothing but one trunk full of a few dresses, some art supplies and books, our mother's silver spoons and two slim coats for the evenings. We didn't speak much on the journey except to compare our coats. Hers had shades of blue and cream and was tightly stitched, mine was green silk worn with holes from aging. We had nothing between us but blood and the desire to do. Julia silently sketched the landscape while I busied through my books.

Queens was marshy and full of crawling, stinging things. We were told to beware of spiders, flies, and creeping insects with teeth as sharp as tomahawks. Julia and I chose a worn-down lodging house, and with the little money we pooled, we had enough for the first month's discomforts. Everyone in town knew of our coming.

Miss. Williams and Miss. Beecher had established Julia and my reputations as intelligent and bright young women aspiring. I was only seventeen and Julia was four years older, but one would never know because she always did what I told. Although Julia could not recite from books with eloquence, she was capable of piano playing and coloring sky tones to match the air's weight. Her familiarity with art would provide our students shrewd cultural eyes while my loving of language would open their intellect to historical accuracy.

We planned to room students as boarders in order to make a modest profit and later send for our mother who would keep house. Our mother could cook and clean and stitch, and was especially practiced at cording, boring and crewel work. Her boring needles worked endlessly in and out of soft fabrics to produce tablecloths and dresses. Her crewel work was thick and conspicuous and made firm placemats. She could teach the young women how to produce heirlooms like me. All births and baptisms could be properly sewn, passed from hand to hand and trunk to trunk, in endless cloth-formed communications. The young ladies needed to know methods and modes with precision, all forms of writing. They needed to know that tongues take their place through many secretly spoken vibrations.

We had hopes for our school, but when we first brought our trunk into empty mildewed rooms and realized we had no other furnishings, we were exhausted with optimism and desires that dampened. If Julia and I were to carry on with our plan, we needed to obtain a few tables, a couple of beds and pans for a kitchen to eat. While Julia and I often went without provisions in order to tend to preparations, it would not be proper to see our girls hungry.

Because our mother was not yet there, we worked for weeks on the unpleasant work of sewing curtains and bed sheets from old fabric we found in the back of a building, and we also arranged for a man to upkeep the house and grounds. We made friends with wealthy patrons who also wanted to see ladies properly prepared for living and they promised to loan us money so we could begin. It was not a problem finding students who wished to attend. The town and nearby county were teeming full of girls hungered for learning and fathers willing to pay the necessary tuitions, and we had students before we had anywhere to seat them.

I wore holes in my green silk coat through the exhaustion of our preparations, and when I went to speak with people for money, I felt I could not cover up enough. Although I was ashamed, the manner of my speaking was always pleasantly appreciated. I could strike a sentence glorious. I would say:

The girls necessarily full like the tree of life wouldn't benefit from Milton's mastering of Eve in the garden, though they should read all books…they need to place themselves properly to serve our community's great men with their intelligence…

and the potential patrons would hand me their pocketbooks. They seemed not to notice the holes in my coat.

I was treated especially well by the King brothers, John and Charles, who were heart-patteringly nicknamed Beau Brummel and Charles the Pink. Mr. Charles King was courteous and brotherly with arms as big as beer caskets and Mr. John King was handsome and tall with waterlike blue eyes that reminded one of seasides. They used to bring us freshly seasoned meat and would joke about the marsh weather or overwhelming presence of beetles this year. As much as I enjoyed discoursing with Mr. Charles King, he would not be my first love. I had no attachments then except to false men in books. And Leonard. Of course, brother Leonard. I shall never forget it.

Julia and I borrowed money, yet I still did not buy a new coat. We bought tables and boards to write on and other items for the house to entertain guests like the Kings. The brothers stopped by frequently with tales of their adventures to the city where fashions, commerce and news spilled with people's business. The brothers were always welcome and pleasant.

Julia and I and our ground's man kept readying. We lovingly acquired two green parlor chairs with gilt flowers and white buttons, two mahogany tables, three yellow dressing tables with looking glasses and a carpet which did not run the length of the stairs, as we prepared to invite students into our meager, affectionate halls. I was nervous about our beginnings. We had brought mother's silver spoons along in our sparsely-packed trunk. When I became ill or anxious, I would fill my mouth with her slender silver, the metal tart and speckled with age or love. The silver comforted somehow where no words would wander.

I remained nervous and still I refrained from buying a new coat. Things were rarely terrible, yet something inside of me did not sit right. I joined a church to ease my will and trust in others, not exactly trusting of the Lord. I met people and talked. I made associates and was not conflicted about going solely for these connections, because my thoughts were independently worn. Although I was occasionally ill, my desire to affect the minds of young women as bright as their brothers remained strong.

I no longer thought of eating words. I began putting them on paper filling endlessly the nights. While our days were consumed with cleaning and preparing for the coming years, in the evenings I worked around stories of romance. I grew increasingly happy, so much as I had never been before.

Julia called our place "the Castle of Delia," although it did not resemble lush buildings from tales and I, only sort of Cinderella, still had not bought a new coat. Sometimes in the early evenings, despite the warnings of others about the many insect things, we would sit outside and enjoy the sunset before we continued preparing for the pupils and I wrote through the hours of night. One evening, a terribly tiny insect bit and sucked my blood. This insect, as small as a needle and just as crewel, forevered my bones full of fever.

I became ill. Terribly ill. So ill Julia could not care for me. No one seemed to know how, not even the local physician. They let me sweat and brim off the bed all night. My brain bustled wistfully fevered and frenetic and I cried to mother or Leonard, but Leonard was nowhere to be. My mother was present through my distorted image reflected in spoons. This sickness formed my face to twitch one side up and scrunch my right eye into its socket. This sickness from the tiny bite, this sickness when I called and no one could assist, infected me forever.

*

Nurse Elaine tells me if I had not been bitten by an insect with tiny tomahawk teeth that evening, I would not have had to stay here for so long. She says my sentences would not break like old women's faces crackling. She says I should not speak of fever lest my emotions excite and cram up thoughts.

*

I did not buy a new coat.

*

The nurses try to fill me with calm. They tell me to think of wind breeze when fevers stop my thoughts or else they will place me under the weight again. They tell me if I don't pacify I will never be let out. I must continue a calmly sort of writing.

I do not want to go under the water. I do not want to be fed medicine with their not-so-silver spoons. Calmly, I can tell you, correctly, how the writing wants to be when I felt my fever first. This is what the writing wants.

*

I spent three weeks in bed calling to the night and Leonard or the Lord but nobody listened. I saw things through my fervor: books filled with pages full of worms and bodies made of paper and women witch-burning books and laughing the laugh freely. I saw mother mending silk green coats out of beetle wings. I saw Leonard praising the Lord from the pulpit and smiling, his teeth made of tiny urns and breath filled with ashes. I saw horses trampling Francis flying into feathers on a nearby tree to whistle me future I love yous. I saw the sky break apart when down came the fingers that formed the mountainsides pointing to the heart beating England. I saw ships and traveling on them. I saw men made of schoolbooks, thumbing through fictitious men leaping small and running into the wild to turn green and rupture father. I saw things not of this time, drops and tunnels. Clean white boxes and glass shards. Women with no legs and letters. Scratches stitched across the flesh, blotchy arms. Dogs mutilating streets with meanness. Looking glasses and spoons reflecting back darkness looking back dark and then darkness looking back.

This is what I saw alone and fevered, if I tell all stories true. Once the words are gone and unfettered, they will set them on fire and I can watch them rise the ashes. I am not like the others. Please let me be or out.

*

I did not buy a new coat.

When I woke from three long weeks of sickness I was mostly the same, except exceptional, surviving the fever that almost rested my mind, rocking to and fro death and mother like. The sickness stayed with me slightly yet I can sometimes suppress it. With control and constitution, I can stuff it under waves.

Weeks passed, and Julia and I were able to begin. I taught the girls and had no noticeable problems or patterns, repetitions, except I did not like the time that was not spent writing. Our venture was modestly successful and we made enough money to pay back the lendings. We were planning to send for mother, almost a family perfect, but first I bought a new coat.

Two years passed. We taught and I wrote; I wore my new coat.

We never earned enough to send for mother, and I soon realized it wasn't feasible for me to remain there either. We barely kept afloat, and I less liked teaching. The ground's man became uncomfortable with what we could inadequately give. We had to say goodbye to the King Brothers, our students, and leave the marsh. Although I held a vague resentment for a land that produced insects small enough to infect me, Julia and I may have been a little bit like happy there. I had worked through the nights on a short story collection, and this manuscript would one day set me on my course. I believed Providence had finally found me.

When I told Leonard what I did, every free moment spent with pen, he told me I should quit my scribbling. He was envious that I had sent one of my stories to a competition hosted by the Philadelphia *Sunday Courier*, and that it had beat a work written by a writer as renowned as Edgar Allen Poe. Although my name remained anonymous, I was more satisfied from this achievement than when I stood in front of a classroom with those little ladies' eyes fixed admiringly upon me. I was awarded one hundred dollars for my story. I was successful, a writer, and had done it without the shrewd vision of Leonard looking down his nose.

I knew I could make my living this way even though Leonard told me it was not fitting for a woman naturally weakened with intellect and insect fever. At seventeen, I had started my own school. At nineteen, I was an award-winning writer. Leonard warned me women must not become inflated with literary pride so much they consider teaching beneath them. However, I wrote:

Six hours a day of the most exhausting of labor—teaching stupid girls to write compositions—is worth more than $120 a year. I would rather adopt the *retirement system than take my meals with 150 girls at my elbows.*

I returned to New Haven, Julia just a few miles near, and asked Leonard if I might stay with him to study. When he said I could tend house like his dead wife Lucy if I kept my mouth uncomplaining and closed, I decided it best if I kept away from the taking of this place. I found a lodging house and filled my room from floor to top with all matter of books.

I was to take a year or so for retirement, then begin to teach a new course. I studied subjects the male students were learning. I read tome after tome on Vegetable Physiology, Mathematics and Elements of Ideology. I taught myself everything I needed in order to be as learned as the male professors who roamed the halls of Yale with Leonard dead as ghosts. I also began to send my story collection to publishers. One day, I am still proud to note, it was accepted. This book held me by name like a mother.

I told him so.

Leonard advised me to learn more about publishing rights, but I was too excited to see my name lengthen those bony spines. What mattered to me most was that the words I toiled over through fever and fire were everlastingly issued. The words I worked furiously for would move freely about the world unconfined but for a binding.

Yet Leonard was right, and I did have problems with the publisher, who set my book to print while keeping most of my returns. Leonard said *I told you so. I told you so.* I lost money that could have been earned had I paid attention to Leonard's warnings, but I couldn't listen to him over and over *I told you so. I told you so.* I likened Leonard to the bored repetitions of a goat.

Despite what he may believe, I am satisfied with my publication. Leonard memorized someone else's words and made up silly hymns to spit forth from the pulpit. He saw women with shawls leave a little bent and wilted under the effect of his voice and deeply fiery gaze and he would rise, inflated. He saw men regret last night's liquor and yesterday's sinful thinking and he would puff up like a sail filled with the storm of violent weathers. He saw bodies break under the pressure of those tides.

I was just as good as he. I was also an excellent speaker who would quake hands enthusiastic and see admiration in an eye's flash, but I enjoyed how much different it was with writing. On the page, I could affect from a distance. I couldn't see the people glassed over or bent and staring. This way, I could be left alone. The words that roll off the tongue are different when waiting surprise-like alive through books. Notice what happens when you read these words that are mine and mine alone:

moment a fainting, death came, the forms of savage warriors from her eye, insensibility succeeded, long excitements of feeling.

Did you feel the rush and swoon? The long excitement of feeling? And you were not even looking. I did not have to quaver my hands in a feigned gathering of energized agitation. I am tired of these eyes sometimes upon me that watch for ciphers splintered from my hands.

My favorite character is Helen Gray; I made her. Helen resists her family's desires for her to flee from the war and remains in a home which will soon be attacked by Indians because she is waiting for her lover the British soldier Maitland who eventually goes mad at the sight of her unwarranted death. Helen's menacing and powerful brother Mr. George Gray prevents her initial betrothal because of an argument he had over the outcome of a battle with Maitland and Mr. George Gray hates him because he is more successful and looks better in his battle clothes. Mr. George Gray is always getting in Helen's way, but she loves him despite his interference. However, she loves Maitland infinitely more. After all, he is her lover. I mean, brother. Maitland, that is, her lover, not her brother, who is George.

Helen's mother leaves without a look and George too, and Helen remains in that house because she cares more about the beauty of true love than an uncaring family. Helen's sister is the only affectionate member, and she is happy for Helen's reunion with her one true love. Helen remains in the home and the Indians come. She is terrified of them; she waits in a white bridal gown while they hoot around painted up with warfare. She eventually dies at the hands of these plotting natives, muttering incoherent final words in Maitland's too-late arms.

You can see why I would win in a competition against Edgar Allen Poe. I wrote this before I knew Helen would become me. Inseparable, somewhere, them and I, in-between. These words prophesied my family's fall apart.

When I was writing, I was full of romance, inseparable from true love. Sometimes wrong men not from books would try to love me. As I studied by reading, devouring every word, Yale professors paid attention. I don't know if they wished to tame and narrow my weaving wind-like conversations or their true intentions. I was becoming known for a wildly wondrous tongue.

I befriended a Mr. Samuel Morse. I think he might have loved me, but

I did not encourage him except to fascinate over his odd and interesting inventions. He told me of his plans to create a new kind of code in which people communicate in secret taps and clicks. He also told me how Sir Francis Bacon and members of the old aristocracy had used ciphers to convey private matters. Mr. Morse was the ultimate Renaissance man and shared a mind with those times.

As he invented the telegraph, I listened to his pauses and ticks. He knew everything from electricity to sculpting and we would talk about the nature of secret meetings. He told me of societies that went back endlessly before time and moved culture along by their sides. Mr. Morse said at Yale the men were forming an association like the ancients. He opened another world to me and knocked where the truth leaked from skulls and bones.

When I started teaching again, Mr. Morse often visited my class along with other thinkers to speak to the girls. My students especially loved him because his information adored them, but I couldn't love him except as a friend and what he'd tell me. He was too eager to run his hands over everything and make it all progress.

Another man named Mr. John Lord came speaking around my schoolhouse door. He was a history teacher. Lord, how I was always surrounded by history and the Lord. If I did not want to hear it from the pulpit, I had to hear it in the name of this burly, broad-spaced suitor.

Mr. John Lord did not look very lordly. He was unpolished, crude, raw. Despite his cumbersome appearance, I respected him for his intelligence. He was known for having a brilliant, historical mind, yet one would not know by suffering him a glimpse. He had an overabundance of facial hair that would twitch when he contemplated the intricacies of battles. He would also make strange pig-like noises when he paced the floor as he lectured on the forming of this our wonderful nation. He was a true specimen, intimidating and grotesque in his gruff, furuncled way.

Imagine my shock at his marriage proposal. I believed us friends, colleagues, he an informed lecturer for my students. I knew he thought me egotistical, so I could not understand why this buffalo of a man would want me for his wife. I also knew he appreciated an opinionated woman who liked to word with battle, and thus, he apparently came to love me. Imagine my surprise when he bumbled through billows of hair to ask me for my hand. I shall reproduce it as truthfully as I can.

"Miss. Bacon, you know how I [cough cough] have been patiently early every day to visit with you before my lecture about the French Revolution this week [hack hack mustache rising, falling]? Seeing, dear lady, how you are especially fond of yourself and that deep toned voice of yours you will not yet let lull any man to sleep [snort hack], I find myself in need of a companion for evening time discussions of war," he harrumphed through bursts and starts of phlegm rising, falling.

"We are not all in need of companionship, Mr. Lord," I replied.

"Well, Miss. Bacon, seeing as you are often busy preparing for your lectures [cough snort], I was thinking you could become my wife and thus have access to my library [cough cough cough snort wheeze]. And in this manner [harrumph wheeze], you would not have to expend so much energy except on meal preparations of course [wheeze wheeze wheeze cough humph humph] and the occasional mending and dish washing, or whatever it is you women do to keep order in the home." He spat out the window to punctuate this brilliant offer, then gazed at me droopily before lighting a pipe.

"Thank you, Mr. Lord, no."

Thus, our courtship was over.

Leonard didn't like Mr. Lord, nor obviously I. Leonard didn't want me to marry because he still entertained ideas of me helping maintain his household after his dead wife Lucy. I told him to send for mother, but he would not stop insisting I oblige. We bickered, fought and could not argue our way out of letters. I wished to be close to him because of love, but I was never far enough away.

*

I love you, Leonard. I promise.

If you let me out I will sweep and sew and tend to anything you may need. I do not want to be submerged under water once more. I cannot stand the pummel and the plunge. It is too much to remember.

Nurse Elaine and I walk around the gardens. She is like my sister, has the same soft hands and flints of golden in her eyes. When she speaks they sparkle and I know all is right. It is beneficial.

I can't stand to be without words, as much as they may have fractured people say. My body paragraphs by the belly full. I have been eating words again secretive before the night bell when they put me under the water when I am well enough to read. I swallow and they glisten down my throat.

My words sometimes seem to unsentence on their own.

*

Although I was teaching again, I maintained my focus on my writing. I finished another manuscript, this time a full-length play, but I gave it to Leonard for commentary and he kept it. It was my only copy. I wrote it before the days of my student secretaries who listened while I lilted lectures out.

I did not know what Leonard might do with this writing, I did not know what. He held and hid my script while Miss. Ellen Tree, the actress, waited for her part. I had plans to watch my play performed in New York, but it was too late to be delivered. He kept it from me; he kept it from becoming.

Leonard was angry that I wouldn't keep his house. The ladies were on fire for his love for the Lord, but he still entertained ideas of me living like some sisterly wife. I couldn't. *I told him so, I told him so.* I had plans all of my own.

*

I write my letters and watch the words rise up. I love Leonard. *I told him so.* I promised.

They place me in a basin. They dump water and more water over my head and feet higher to cleanse me from all thought. The doctors believe enough water will return my sentence. I do not know if I believe them. When they pour, my hands are wrapped to my waist. Sometimes it streams so long and it is difficult to breathe. I gasp and thrash. Nurse Elaine stands near. The flint of her eyes reminds me of passions, zeal of fire.

She is the one who waits while I write. She says the water is working. She tells Leonard how this comes along.

I feel I must be ready. Once more and I am raining.

I told you so. I told you so.

———

I once received fan mail intended for Rebecca Brown. It was written on a sheet of notebook paper in pencil, scrawled almost illegibly. Here are some of the more memorable lines:

youre book helped my husband he is in jail and he didn't mene to hit his cousin with a bottle (drinkin) but he was at the bar five minutes when that dam girl came and they started fights. but I listened to you said yoga is satan people shouldn't sit like that worshiping the devil thank you for telling me my husband for hitting leonard with a bottle is possessed and my children will be saved soon they keep messing with the trailer tho and one of them sat the grass on fire but I gave them your book about becoming a vessel and I love you peace and The Lord you are my favorite writer Rebecca without your books we would all be damned and burn.

As a writer, I was confirmed. I was glad someone respected my work.

When I was in college, I received a telephone call from someone trying to locate the writer Rebecca Brown. Imagine my thrill at being twenty and having had only published a measly poem or two in my university's literary magazine, I hear this:

Hello? Is this the writer Rebecca Brown? If not, please disregard this message. I just wanted to tell you how much I love your work. Your last novel is such a beautiful and poignant book. It changed my life. I am glad such striking prose like this is being published. It makes a difference. If you can, and if this isn't too strange, please call me so we can talk.

It is a great feeling to receive such acclaim for work you have not written. I have reveled in my newfound celebrity for some time now. Although I am not me, it sure feels great to be me.

I don't know if it has been a benefit or a hindrance knowing about other authors with the same name writing at the same time as myself. For one thing, I happen to know I was published in a fairly renowned journal because the editor assumed I was the other Rebecca and had decided to try my hand at poetry. The editor went so far as to change my bio from "Rebbecca Brown's poetry has appeared in" to "Rebbecca Brown's stories have appeared in." Pretty careless, I thought, for a journal of such repute. I don't write fiction. I am a poet. I've always found it difficult to sustain longer works.

Despite my awareness of these fictional shortcomings, I once tried to write a novel. The title was *The Autobiography of Nothing*. In it, three different narrators living in different places and times tell their stories with three obvious stylistic differences. One character is simply referred to as "the girl who was named after nothing." Another has no name. Another has a name, but I have forgotten it. Really, all three are the same.

I often wonder if the other Rebecca Browns receive fan mail for me, or if they receive phone calls that wonder at my ability to express the human condition so poignantly.

Send all inquiries and fan mail to:
—Rebecca Brown. 322 17th Avenue E; Seattle, WA. 98117.
—Rebecca Brown. 322 E Lee Avenue; Rudy, AR. 72952.
—Delia Bacon. Room 322. Institute for the Living; Hartford, CT. 06108.

I'm not listed. There's one of me in Randolph, NY but that's not me.

Rebecca could sleep all day if it weren't for the sun. The sun always made her feel as if she must do something: wash dishes, clean the bathroom, scrub the toilet, dust the ceramic angels, deny Satan, pray for forgiveness. The sun shone brightly like the gleam from God's teeth or the perfect bleach. Which reminded her, she must buy some laundry detergent. John's underwear were forming a monument to Moses in the middle of their floor.

Rebecca whistled loud enough so her keys would respond and when they heard her, they beeped. She loved this device and had bought it for a dollar. After a quick consultation with God, he told her it was not against his will. She would never lose her keys again, and John could not blame her for making them late to church.

Rebecca thought of the house she lived in as a child where she cut paper dolls and watched them rise up through the dust. She thought of how she once lost her keys while running. She was eight or maybe seven and hurrying to meet her little brother Francis at the bus. After she picked him up, she took him home and realized her keys had fallen through a hole somewhere between her pocket and front door. When she went back to find them, they were lost and gone.

She began to panic because she did not know what to do. She had to watch Francis until her mother and father came home, but they were not scheduled to arrive until five, and it was only three. No windows were open for her to shimmy through. She started to cry and so did Francis.

Rebecca said:

Stay here. Just wait. Just sit. I will be right back. Don't cry. It will be okay. Later we can play Jesus and Mary.

She ran frantic kicking up the dust like a beating back to the bus stop and the keys were gone and if Francis did not eat and mom and dad came home she would have to face the corner head down while a belt snapped Amens across her backside like jaws and she would be sent to bed again hungry fainting Jesus. She ran back home careful to avoid the neighbors who were mean with a big dog and gun to shoot balls that flew over fences. She had to run quick to make sure Francis did not want to pet the dog. She hurried up, quicker than a rush.

Francis was not on the porch and she screamed: *Where are you, where are you?* She ran around the house and he was nowhere and she kept running enough to think she might tornado herself up to heaven but she had to stop to breathe and look and her tears fell in the dirt patting like rain falling somewhere close. She imagined he might be dead, crushed somewhere underneath one of the rusted vehicles that spread throughout the dusty yard. She imagined his tiny arm fluttering beneath an axle like a felled bird's broken wing.

Suddenly she heard him; he, too, was close, whimpering and breathing. She knew then where he was. He had climbed under the porch and when she crouched down, she could see him through the peeling skin-like paint, dirty with mud cheeks streaming.

Francis, come out let's sit on the porch where we can play.

For an hour she tried to coax him. She knew she couldn't climb under because she would dirty her dress and then she'd really feel it. Francis cowered for what seemed all afternoon. He would not move and pretended not to hear. He sucked his thumb and looked eyewide as an owl.

Finally, finally, he crawled out. He was coated with dust and cobweb but Rebecca was so happy to hold him and they sat like that on the porch near the metal rusty swing and cried themselves sleepy until their parents came home and found them like that dirty as usual.

Rebecca could sleep all day if it weren't for the sun but now she must get some soap. She whistled to hear her keys again. She walked outside and got into her car.

The nearest town is a shopping center. Most of the local stores constantly switched owners or closed. She looked at the thick foliage that sometimes lined the streets. There aren't as many trees in town as near her house in the Ozarks. This was Fort Smith, after all.

In Easymart, she roams the aisles staring at the orange and yellow smiling, plastic faces. God once told her Satan had his hand in most everything and she should not be tempted, especially by bright colors and jingles that sounded nice and appealing. God told her this store was infected with the devil, that it was hell itself; he said you could tell by the presence of hundreds of screaming, tormented children. God also said if you had the constitution to ignore Satan, it was all right to shop.

Rebecca found her desired items and waited in a line. Although she knew she should not do so because she would tempt a fate in hell, because God had ignored her for so long, she read her horoscope from a tiny booklet placed near the register. It said:

Your passion is on fire, don't let it burn! Keep cool and drink lots of water. You have the power to influence others. Have you ever thought of writing a book?

She thought of her previous books, but knew she needed to find a new way of condemning the immoral that would teach sinners more than just a lesson. She wanted to write about someone who let the devil flow through her mouth in waves of wickedness with no one to believe in. She wanted to write about the only man who might save her. Rebecca tried to imagine this character so she could lock her up, but she needed God. She needed John.

She dropped the horoscope booklet as if it had sullied her fingers. Soap, she had forgotten to buy soap.

With a jerk of neck and flick of the tongue, Rebecca noticed that her mailbox was piled high with flyers for take out, Carbon Copy Plus, and Barb's Spa and Beauty, which spilled messily from the metal box. Rebecca hated junk mail and tried tirelessly to make it stop. It reminded her of her oft abandoned drafts, which she would sometimes tear in fits of dissatisfied fury until they made mountains of wasted pulp. She pulled the advertisements from the box and shred and shred, unconsciously pacing around her porch. Her legs wobbled as if she were made of rubber. She shrank lower and lower with serpentine velocity, her legs bending and bonding. She perceived nothing except rip and tear and slash. Her tongue flicked quick against her lips. Suddenly she stopped. The neighborhood air was filled with unusual silence. The children had all gone. Their toys creaked, abandoned in the yards.

Unnecessary textual waste unnerved her, cracked her composure like rodent bones, but she knew there was no way to avoid receiving, or sometimes creating, the superfluous junk. While her and Elaine often spoke about the relative therapeutic value of unwanted compositions, the way Rebecca treated her own undesirable material bothered Elaine, so Rebecca usually began a project internally on her own.

Rebecca had previously focused her ire on the post office and emailed them regularly, asking them to please remove her name from whatever list she was on, or to please add her name to whatever list would prevent so much paper waste and proliferating propagandistic forms, feeling that she often hypocritically contributed to this painful system. Elaine always tried to reassure her that when it came to her own writing, she was wrong.

As a last resort, and during one particularly long bout of creating what she deemed to be her worst novel yet, Rebecca had even tried befriending her mail carriers to prevent the unwanted flyers and advertisements from appearing, but nothing worked. Any time she felt she made any headway, someone would quit and routes would shift. First there was Charles, who she would invite in for coffee or water, whatever he took. Charles was a nice man somewhere in his seventies who liked terriers and stamps. He once had a wife who liked to cross stitch houses on dishtowels with the words "home sweat home". Although they had spent quite a lot of time together, time when she should have been writing, this was all Rebecca really knew of Charles, and soon he had retired.

The woman who succeeded Charles came sporadically. Rebecca tried to time her afternoon tea at exactly the right moment for the woman's arrival, but she was rarely correct in her approximations. The woman would cross the porch with eyes downcast and shirk from Rebecca's toothy *afternoon there*. Although in her postal uniform, she pretended to look lost. Rebecca eventually gave up trying to befriend her local postal workers when she finally began to devote herself to a satisfying draft of her novel. Mail deliverers came and went and Rebecca tried to accept that people and wasted papers ebb and flow, ebb and flow.

Rebecca noticed that her father had sent one of his inadvertently rambling letters, which she always enjoyed receiving and didn't consider to be a waste at all; the art of letter writing, often marked by beautifully awkward syntax, was something Rebecca cherished, as she did the power and pleasure of rearrangement, intentional or not. Rebecca's father's current helpmate and scribe wasn't much for proper punctuation, sentence structure, or revision. He would write each word by rote, adding ums and huhs, sighs and space for pauses. Even if her father had two operational eyes, he probably wouldn't have been much for proper grammar. He grew up working in the oilfields and had lost both orbs in a tragic fight fit for the old times.

He was rowdy and lost sight young. Sam grew up in middle California and liked to frequent bars from the time he turned fourteen. The waitresses at The Broken Spoke knew his name and liked to pat his head with hands that smelled of rosewater and Lucky Strikes. One afternoon after they served him one glass of whiskey too many, he picked a fight with a man passing through who holstered a bee-bee gun to shoot birds from their nooks. In the parking lot, the man shot Sam's eyes into bloody gulfs.

Although completely unnecessary, Rebecca's father had replaced his original eyes with glass nearly the same color as his real eyes, and with age the colors had faded. The doctor told him not to leave his eyes on the windowsill in the direct sunlight lest they lighten, but Sam didn't heed much advice from doctors. Ever since Rebecca was young, Sam had amused her by taking out one eye after the other. He would make them wink from inside his closed palms. He liked to pluck them out and punch them back in to Rebecca's delight. He told her although he didn't have eyes, he could see numerous things all at once.

Rebecca read:

Becca. Can you turn the radio off? I can't hear. Glad to hear your new book is at the local library where. You saw it? I might have you read to me if you have time. I hear it is a good one. Calvin?

I've been working in the garden planting seeds Calvin brought and I don't have free time as yet but wanted to write a letter by hand or Calvin and tell you I love you proudly. Dad.

Rebecca knew she should visit her father soon, but that she probably wouldn't get around to it until the semester was over and she had time away from teaching. Rebecca arched around a sofa cushion and stared at the empty spaces in her apartment. Although she was not there, Elaine seemed to move through the rooms in shifts of breeze. It was freezing. Rebecca opened the curtains and stretched her legs in the rapidly fading rays of light. She was almost finished commenting on the last of her student's papers, but wasn't much in the mood to continue the often exasperating process. Sophia was curled in her doggie bed snoring. Rebecca didn't expect a phone call from Elaine, because she usually spent her Tuesday nights with other graduate students discussing the foibles of contemporary psychology. Rebecca hated the moments that were emptied of distraction and didn't feel like moving from the departing heat. She thought:

you swam those years across me and I followed the paths of your snaking. the water slicked you back. despite a mouth full of fur and loathing I could feel you again if I waited through the floods of this wanting.

She couldn't help returning, recurring, and wondered when she would hit upon a project that would compel her to pick up a pen and act. She thought of Elaine and all of the archival delight she must now be in the throes of. Rebecca followed the winding weaves of her thoughts, trying to hitch upon some new character or idea that might fill her full of a compositional rush. Her thoughts slowed as she lay in the waning heat. These were the plagues of her lives.

THREE

Can our humanity's darkest extremity wring no love from the invisible?
Delia Bacon

I HAVE WRITTEN letters apologizing that I cannot bear to send. Sometimes I slash and tear them. I have written to Leonard begging for freedom and love. I have written to mother, sorry she has left me, buried beneath flowers, earth and stone. I have written to myself in former times and future times, warning myself of what's to come. I have written to everyone except for Alexander, who I wish I could unknow.

Leonard believes I should not relive certain experiences or create others that might cause my hands or face or heart to shudder, tic deleroux, but these moments are most revealed. They appear and I write them. I cannot keep these secrets, enclosed like some dumb tomb.

When I first learned of the men and their meetings, I did not know what they wished for. I did not know they imprisoned those who challenged their ancient orders. If before he was free with ideas of sin, slavery and redemption, when I discovered the men, Leonard became guarded, grave, inwardly consumed. The Skull and Bones were selective and important. They were elite and they were few.

Alexander once revealed to me that he was a member, too. They are chosen in secret and inscribed by numbers—powerful, invisible, deadingly literary. Most do not know how and when they speak. But I know. They know I know and will not let me out.

Hysteria, Leonard says. *Fever*, which cannot cause forgetting.

Nurse Elaine says repeating events can be reliving and reliving events repeating. Everything doubles. Triples. I do not want to be reborn, alone in a world without water. I must be careful. I must continue.

*

I remember Alexander.

*

The water is violent as it pours when we breathe and thrash to gasp. There are fishers of men who yank and pull the lines. It is them I must forget. They are an ancient organization. I will not abide by their rules.

Some say if it weren't for Alexander I would not be here, uncontrollably forced. Some say if Alexander had not ruined my trust, I would retain their love. Some say Alexander is now a fisher of men, exculpated from all bonds.

*

I splintered at the sight of him.

*

Nurse Elaine assures me I am whole. She has never loved anyone other than her father, taken by a wilderness like my own. He disappeared and she was left with brothers who taunted her with sticks. When she speaks about this, she touches my hand and looks at me with her shining, fire water flints.

She believes after I write of Alexander the water treatments will not be as cold. When I see water I think lovers and seas and lovers in seas that drown in them and how when the water first poured, I felt I was being fished from the seas of men as it stormed through the night I was raining. Alexander was with me the first time I took the water cure, and he will be with me my last. I told you so.

Nurse Elaine tells me to allow myself. This I remember, and then let go.

*

When it rained, and it rained often in New Haven, the streets closed up their watery shops and I studied alone in my rooms. I was still young—not just girl and not quite woman—unmarried with years of teaching already behind and beneath me. I found work instructing at a girls' post-educational school and Leonard preached nearby at the First Centre Church. He also taught at Yale Divinity School. I admit sometimes there was lonely.

When it was not raining and I passed along the avenue, women nodded politely and lowered their eyes and thought me esteemed. When I strolled, they would tell each other the great woman lecturer was *there, over there, with the dark eyes and hair sometimes slightly gleaming*. I could huddle them in like men, jealous and frightened. They would whisper in tones I could sometimes hear:

Her speeches are better than tonic, full of elegance, fire and fury!

Some called me prophetess and came to hear me speak: pastor daughters and mayor's niece, lawyer's cousins and banker's wife all crowded my lectures despite rain or heat. After they listened, they spoke about brilliance and what they learned, the wonder.

I was not reading minds like false performers, or presenting parlor tricks. I read every book I could run my mouth through. I read the dead into existence, breathed them into being and spoke of their lost lives. I read English Literature and Shakespeare, all the men's subjects, my new and forbidden fruit. Something suggested the past was not merely past but alive and knocking around like a repeating father's ghost: *remember me remember me.*

At Yale, men formed a secret society called the Skull and Bones. Leonard pretended he wasn't paying attention to my developing theory and tried to blind the evidence all around. While he professed to busy himself with writing and anti-slavery issues, he was always somehow near these men eager for a look.

No one else in history had articulated a theory quite as progressive as mine. After I roundabout suggested it to a misunderstanding and peculiar Leonard, after I said *Suppose Shakespeare didn't write those books?* I saw fires from pulpits burning yesterday's danger clanking to keep those secrets. I then decided to keep my discoveries private until I could work them absolute. From Leonard's miens I knew there might be danger. I locked myself away from living distractions so I could encounter and cognize any number of names and lists or formulations. I didn't want to risk further exposure or too-early Leonard-like condemnation. It would be best to focus on the secrets of the past before I dangerously revealed the presence of the future.

I boarded a room at the Tontine Hotel. It was large enough to where I would not feel caged from too-long hours spent working, reading, writing. In it I had a number of papers and quills, a desk and a small nook of sleep space. I enjoyed the Tontine, and felt the joy of self-imposed, bookish concentration. I could work as many hours as I wished, and was without worldly interruption, except for a tiny nest of warblers outside my window in a willow tree, but I often welcomed their sweet and solitary song.

I spent hours reading, reading, reading. Information jumbled together, often contradicted and sometimes tore apart. Words circled and inside became out. My mind felt more and more caged full of the feathered beating of birds, flapping wings incessant so I had to claim and calm them. Headaches began to plague me. I discovered something so exciting and terrifying that filled my head with the disorder of droving, gabbing birds.

In the evenings as the sun went down, I took short walks to ease my aches and let the birds out near their natural habitat of quiet, outside spaces. I had to move about, yet when I was invited to participate in any number of social events, I would always politely decline. If I were to attend these enclosures, I knew the birds would become so excitable I couldn't sit still and I would hear beatbeatbeat through and through and through. While I studied alone they were not as loud nor consuming because I listened to them beatbeatbeat and allowed them freedom from outdoor flying.

I studied as far into the night as candle would allow me. I often saw people pass under the moonlight as spectral as mists or ghosts moaning *tomorrow and tomorrow and tomorrow* and *frailty thy name is woman* and *done to death by slanderous tongue*. Sometimes I would see one man in particular who would glance up at my window and tilt his head in what I thought was a pleasant, welcoming nod. When he moved his head a little to the night, the birds would start singing a low-toned long. When he bent under a shaft of the moonlight they twittered. Although I could not clearly see the man, I fell in love with the idea of him as shadow, but it was too dark for me to see what he adored.

The birds and their word-covered wings kept beating. They subsided when I realized the theory that was to become my life's work. It started so simply at first.

William Shakespeare was not a writer.

When I finally said it aloud and wrote it a hundred times on various scraps of paper, my head stopped pounding violently full of bird flutter and wing, and I began to take earlier evening walks to let each bird one by one fly back to the eaves. Soon they had mostly gone and I was planning. Chapters came fledgling formed. I was pouring through plays, locating references, and studying other Renaissance writers who were intellectually attuned. I began to search for proof.

Rarely although sometimes I missed the oft exasperating companionship of others, and happily one evening I was invited by a fellow boarder to join her for supper because she was worried about what she called my "unnatural seclusion." I did not tell her I wasn't exactly alone because I had my words, not unnatural at all. I agreed to join her because something in the morning air told me this night the moon wouldn't be especially full and I couldn't see the shadow man who preferred midnight walking. The moment I agreed, I was unnaturally alone.

When I arrived downstairs to meet her in the dining area, the midnight man was sitting at a table nearby with his head tilted a little to the night. He was not shadow, but had a face full of flesh and blood. I felt a bird fly back from the eaves to rest inside my chest. It nestled soundlessly. I knew it was not going to be like the other birds with their loud wings whipping.

The young man looked at me from across the room with eyes like midnight and the solo bird building a blood-filled nest in my chest fell to sleeping. I heard from others' passerby greetings that he was a Mr. Alexander MacWhorter. People were drawn to him, especially women, and they would stop at his table to charm with a laughter all too much like dribbling. The women would titter and shield their mouths exclaiming *Oh Mr. MacWhorter, Mr. MacWhorter!* They didn't help themselves.

It became impossible to pay attention any longer to what my fellow boarder said. I began to notice the patterns fastening in the walls. I heard birds warbling, insisting on their song. I became impatient to be introduced to this man who I felt surreptitiously glance across my back. He must have noticed or known, because he rose from his table and walked towards me as slow as a trickle.

The fellow boarder concerned about my unnatural seclusion had no idea the room had begun to melt, and yet kept prattling on. My clothing started sinking into my skin in liquescent phantasms. While she spat on excitedly about committees and recitations, something rolled inside me to turn syllables out of the emptiness of new wounds. Speech simmered silently from the vastness of my bird-hearted body. I wanted to call to this Mr. MacWhorter in a voice high-pitched, preening, but I knew he was made of more than this kind of trilling.

He was now more than moon lit below me. I stood from the table to greet him. The room was molten through the floor. With shock and a penetrating heat I am sure he was shaking.

"Miss. Delia Bacon. I've heard a lot about you. I've heard you have some interesting ideas about literature and history, and are especially interested in the famous Bard." He looked at me as intent as if he were reading. "I would be honored if you might meet with me sometime so that I might hear your thoughts." I had to keep my hand pressed on the table. I swooned, and I was not that kind of girl.

"Mr. Alexander MacWhorter, I would like to introduce you to my companion, Miss. Delia Bacon," the insignificant boarder concerned about my unnatural seclusion after-the-fact imparted.

"Pleased to make your acquaintance," I said. "I would be honored to share some of my thoughts. Perhaps later this evening…" I wondered if he noticed my dark eyes and hair sometimes slightly gleaming. I wondered if as much.

The inconsequential boarder nervously moved between, shoving her shoulders in. "I don't think it would be appropriate for the two of you to exchange ideas alone," she blathered, "I am willing to accompany you during your conversations."

"Thank you," I responded, looking at Mr. MacWhorter's tailcoat, which was brilliantly fitted, faintly rising and falling. "While I appreciate your gesture, I believe I am mature enough to have an unchaperoned conversation." The now indistinguishable boarder must have said something about returning to her room.

"Mr. MacWhorter, I would like to extend an invitation to my private quarters any time you see fit. That way we might carry on our conversation uninterrupted." The bird in my chest softly lifted its feathers and heaved, lifted and heaved. When Alexander MacWhorter left, I knew it would be a long time before it would silently slip to sleep again.

*

This was how we met, everything then now seemingly different. I've written this for my former self:

Dear Delia, Alexander is one of the men who knows the E in the W, a fisher of men, a Skull a Bone, he will tell you and you won't take it. Do Not Believe. Watch him ruin you will. he knows your knowing and wants to take your love you know.

L and A pretend alike. Do Not Trust HIM or them. Leave those Bones alone.

Nurse Elaine will take this letter. She promises she will not reveal it. She tells me to warm my hands in the fire, the one that contains the words I write and sometimes burn.

On Valentines Day long ago, my preschool teacher called me to the front of the room so I could pass out cards. I remember all of the other kids cheering and shouting "Rebbecca! Rebbecca!" as I joyfully put each note into their cubbyholes. I cannot shake the memory of those kids as they screamed, their faces blurring together in an encouraging, enthusiastic mob. They chanted with recognition as I flung each pink, red and white card into its consecutive nook. I had spent a painstaking number of hours inscribing each card with barely-legible young names scrawled across all those envelopes. I had signed my name on each with zest, with what I now know was love. I wonder if my former friends have kept these cards or if they have been lost, covered in ink stained tears.

When I was young I had a crush on Joshua Fowler. He was my friend throughout elementary school, and I remember how we danced. He was the only boy in my ballet class who also liked to tap, and could play the Charlie Brown theme song on the piano with great aptitude. Bobby Thatch used to tease him and push him in the grass, but Josh could do anything better than or at least equal to most of the boys and all of the girls in my class. He was the fastest dog-paddling boy across the pool. His hair was as soft as Emily Sand's, who had the finest locks. Joshua Fowler was a boy of many talents, and I made sure to draw a scraggly heart on his Valentines Day card that somehow looked more like a mushroom. When he came over to my house to dance to Olivia Newton John's "Physical," he always brought dandelion weeds. Sometimes we blew them together. Sometimes I blew them alone. When I was young, I learned to enjoy the pleasure of ambiguities.

When I was young I had a crush on Bobby Thatch. He didn't enjoy my attentions and would run around the schoolyard and collect bees in his lunch pail to release dangerously close to my juice box and peanut butter sandwich.

He always said he wanted to watch a girl take a bite out of a bee and see her tongue swell up big enough to get stuck down her throat. Bobby had big blue eyes for charming. If you were not careful, you would fall inside, and then he would sting you with one of his lunchbox bees. One Valentines Day, I saw him chasing Emily Sand, and he pushed her onto the concrete and she skinned her knee. He then kicked asphalt rocks on her shoes and ran away. I knew then he didn't love me, but I used to stare at the back of his head during math. Eventually he disappeared and I never saw him again. One day he lived down the road and the next he was no longer there with his lunchbox buzzing. When I was young, I appreciated Bobby Thatch's lack of ambiguity.

When I was young I had a crush on Emily Sand. She had beautiful curly hair that tumbled around her back in waves and ripples. She was the most beautiful girl in the entire school and her mother always bought her socks that matched perfect dresses freshly pressed. They lived on the hill with others who had swimming pools and we, being at the bottom, never got the chance to play. One day in the cafeteria, Joshua Fowler accidentally spilled his fruit cup down Emily's tresses. Emily ran away crying and I followed her to the bathroom where she sat locked in a stall. Only her shiny shoes poked out. I took off my bright blue plastic watch and slipped it under the door. She stopped crying. She never knew it was me. I wasn't sure if she even knew my name. When she passed out Valentines Day cards, she never addressed them personally; they were written by a discerning mother. I was disappointed. My father tried to comfort me and told me that some little girls couldn't write a name as long as Rebecca. I wondered why I was given such a difficult name. Sometimes when I was young, I felt the flush of ambiguity.

John would be home and Rebecca still hadn't cooked his soup. She rushed to pull vegetables from the refrigerator. She was also going to bake some cookies and needed shortening to grease a pan. Suddenly, she thought of Satan. She decided she should quickly anoint her doors with the oily Krisco to impede the frequently flying-in demons. She had coated all the door handles not too long ago with motor oil, but you could never be too careful. *Always plan for the future*, that's what her mother had once said, *You don't want to wake up burning in hell today.* She couldn't remember the last time she spoke to her mother because she had some time ago died and was more than likely in hell despite her well-intended advice.

Rebecca figured she had about half an hour before John arrived. She lined the vegetables on the counter and lined and chopped, lined and chopped. Since John was so good at reciting verse and she wanted to please him, Rebecca decided to make up a hymn of her own: *Where oh where has my little God gone oh where oh where has he gone? He told me once my TV to pawn, oh where oh where has he gone?* On and on Rebecca joyfully sang, humming songs in her indoor voice, punctuating each beat with a chop. Before she realized it, John was standing behind her. He touched her arm and she dropped an onion into the boiling water with a lumpy splat.

"You scared me. The soup will be ready. Soon." She is breathless. She stops singing and begins to pray. She wished John had noticed the Krisco, then maybe he wouldn't be angry. He would commend her for a job well done. "Don't worry. It will be ready. Soon, I promise, soon..."

John grabs her wrist and twists. He is a good Christian. Rebecca will always believe it. They work together. They are a team. They speak together, write together, pray to save all souls. John edits her work, says he must fix her sprawling prose because it is no good. From the floor she kneels while the soup hot with fire is spilling. John looks at her and twists, twists. He quotes from Isaiah: *Is not this the fast that I have chosen? To loose the bands of wickedness...Is it not to deal thy bread to the hungry...that thou hide not thyself from thine own flesh?* He is all hands covered with oil and she is pierced beneath his nails.

When she was little, Rebecca's father used to work on their car all day long on the weekends. She could always find him in the garage lying on a black oily rag placed underneath the car to protect him. Sometimes when he knew she was there he would ask her for a "Phillips Head," "Ratchet," or "Flat Head," as if she knew what these things were. Because she was always eager to help, she would hand him whatever shiny tool was nearest. Inevitably, the tool would deafeningly hit the ground.

No, no, no. That's not it. I'll get it myself, little shit. Go play with your brother.

Sometimes her father came out from under the car and hovered over her. Sometimes she could hear Francis inside watching cartoons. She longed to hear him laughing.

Sorry. I didn't know.

Her father would pace steaming as a bull and eventually he would slide himself under again coated with words her mother said were dirty.

The weekends would ease themselves into pleasant evenings. After the oil was scrubbed off his hands, her father would add grease to his hair for shine and sit in their rutted chair. Sometimes she would ask to sit there too and they would be there just like that with his hands smelling like cedar shavings while her mother rolled dough in the kitchen. The aroma of onions and something like soup filled the house during those anticipatory afternoons.

John is finished sermonizing. He stares into the corner with crooked, glazed-over eyes.

"Sorry. I didn't know. Just give me a minute. I can make more." Rebecca grabs a towel and starts wiping.

"I'm going out. Don't wait. Pray I'll be home soon." John walks across the soggy swill. His boots leave black marks. Rebecca needs to anoint devotion back. Her hands are dry and cracked.

———

Rebecca was famished. She knew as soon as she had food, Sophia would wake from her dog dreams to keep her company by searching for fallen scraps. Rebecca opened the refrigerator and looked shiftily at a container full of rotting reddish glop thick as blood with clots. Her mouth filled with fluid from a desire for flesh that this dish would not slake. She knew the brackish paste was not anything she truly wanted; Elaine must have forgotten to finish her chickpea stew before her departure for Hartford. While Rebecca knew she should discard it, she wanted to leave it in the refrigerator as a keepsake. It somehow reminded her of Elaine's supple skin swathing the back of her neck like spidery silk.

When she was younger, Rebecca liked to play massacre with the neighborhood boys, careful not to press her thighs too tight around them when they twisted the ground in a huddling mass. The girls did not like to play with her; a rumor had once been started that she liked chewing the heads off of baby dolls. They imagined her gnawing and eating their own, licking the plastic bones with a tongue too pointed to be perfect.

The boys, however, were braver. They picked Rebecca for their teams because she was determined to be a winner. She didn't care about dirt or dresses or dolls and was especially gifted at battle. She intensified these matches by smuggling her father's ketchup packet collection to the games for the excitement of life-like blood. Sam couldn't see Rebecca's bursting pockets with his glass eyes as she left to play daylong games of destruction with her boy friends.

Rebecca and her friends took turns squirting the goop over each other's bared chests, and when they rolled around in the dust, the ketchup would clump and blotch like scrapes and cuts. They blasted each other with invisible rifles and cannons—each team an army blown up with Heinz-streaked guts. Their parents never knew the extent of this violence, how some of these boys heard stories about fleshly disasters from late night television they were not supposed to watch. Some of their fathers or uncles or cousins had been in wars, and these boys gratuitously told tales in which people lost limbs, half of their ammunition, their newly corrugated bodies. Rebecca liked listening to them talk—their eyes wide as mortars as they punctuated each word and wound with explosions of spit into the dust. Rebecca did not have an uncle or brother who had been to war, and she envied her friends' closeness to this particular kind of destruction, this secret sort of society she could never be a part of.

Rebecca and her friends fake fought each other until they were tired or swarms of flies found them and landed to dine on their sticky sweetness. At the end of the day before the creek was too cold, they would run into the chilled water and splash the sacrificial evidence clean. During this time in the water with the boys, Rebecca finally felt anointed. There was usually enough time for them to dry on the rocks together in the last rays of light.

Rebecca's hunger got the best of her fatigue and she decided to order a pizza. With a full stomach, it would be easier to deal with a night seemingly beset with the heaviness of Elaine's distance and the inability to begin a satisfying new project. For a moment, Rebecca thought of how nice it was not having Elaine around to complain about her cravings for meat still red and muscled, practically raw and newly wrested from bone. Elaine was a vegetarian and tirelessly enjoyed criticizing Rebecca for her fleshly cravings and compulsions.

Rebecca placed an order for a Meat Madness and decided to wait on the porch for some kid to drop it off. Last time, the delivery boy was one of her students. She wondered if she would see the spiky posts of Waldo's hair ambling up her walk. He was an aspiring writer who probably wouldn't spend much longer in school, as he was enticed by the crabbing boats that set sail for quick money in Alaska. His impatience for the end of class always irritated Rebecca. If his story was not being discussed, he would stare at the clock lethargic, mouth agape. He was one of the finest fiction writers in the undergraduate program, but Rebecca didn't think he cared much. There was something in his gaze almost accusatory, almost as if he was afraid of her.

Rebecca sat on her porch and waited. It was a nice night. The stars were beginning to eke a dim existence throughout a newly darkening sky. She could see them if she focused long enough through the light pollution. She thought she saw a star that might be a flickering Cassiopeia. She wondered if Elaine was looking at an even darker sky, or a sky filled with hundreds more constellations somewhere on a far-off coast. Rebecca thought of the time her and Elaine had once fallen asleep in a field underneath the moonlight, how under the guise of stars her dark eyes had sparked like flints, her hair slightly gleaming.

FOUR

Why you'll be chronicled, there's nothing on record like it, that ever I heard of;
I am well-read in romances too. We'll have a new love-ballad made and set to tune,
under the head of "Love and Murder".
Delia Bacon

PERHAPS IT IS MOST DIFFICULT to talk about Alexander because
I keep imagining his mouth full words that lull me into romance. I should
not have invited him to my room, but I couldn't avoid it. His hair waved like
mountains meeting the skyline for the first time. His eyes were deep, filled
with questions that probed. It was impossible not to want him.

When I tell Nurse Elaine I miss Alexander, her eyes turn glass up and she
stares into the corners. She pretends she does not know what it is like to love
another like Alexander, but I think she is false.

Leonard never understood. He would rather take wives for their hands. When
I was young I told him about the boy who peeked at me through Miss. Beecher's
schoolhouse window. He pounded his fist on the table and the forks fell and spoons
jumped. His face twisted like a froth jawed dog's. He could have bent me like a switch.

Although I cannot speak to Leonard about love, I will write it. Leonard
boils, clenches his fists, and stops his ears. I run the risk of lapse. I fall with the
knowledge of this different kind of fever.

*

Mr. MacWhorter wasted no time in visiting me at the Tontine. I heard a
knock a mere two hours after we met. The exuberance with which he pounded

sounded like the start of a tumultuous symphony composed about the ocean. I could feel him expanding behind the door like a seed that fights against nature to keep its growth from the burst. When I let him in, he appeared younger than I had first noticed. I wasted no time for questioning.

"Mr. MacWhorter. Please come in. What is it that you spend your time studying? From the way your eyes look intently, you must be interested in learning a great bit of everything. Why is it you wish to speak with me so urgently? You seem to carry an important message only I might decipher. How old are you? Who are your parents? Do you enjoy Yale and your midnight walks?" I wobbled slightly through a nervously audible voice. My questions were the only thing to still me from my beating, beating, heart.

"Miss. Bacon. Please. One question at a time." His eyes were cavernous. "I have heard so much about you." He unconsciously stroked his hair away from his forehead so his eyes took up more space. "I've heard of how you lock yourself in your room for hours reading. I've heard it has been some time since you have ventured into the sunlight of society. People are worried. I worry. I'm twenty-four." He took a seat boldly by my window. His silhouette sharpened against light that kept leaving. His eyes were eating up the room.

"You are so young! Fortunately, I am a decade older. I can teach you many things." I felt safer knowing he was so much less alive than I. Yet, there was something about him that couldn't keep me calm. "But, unfortunately, I am not interested in having another pupil. I wonder, Mr. MacWhorter, if there is anything I could possibly learn from you?"

I sat down at the edge of my bed and studied his strangeness. He was like a leaf blown forcefully in. He was water flowing the moon into midnight. He was a bird pitching its noise through the emptiness of flight. He caused me to lose my organization and mix my metaphors and every time I tried to define him, he shifted elusively away.

"I doubt you could learn from me considering the vastness of your interests, Miss. Bacon. I've heard you are more intelligent than most men. I could, however, take you walking. Sometimes I like to gaze up at the moon." He stared deeper and for a moment I felt I did not exist.

"Mr. MacWhorter, please. I am serious." I squinted a crooked eye as if to peek through a telescope.

"I'm studying the new theology, Miss. Bacon. I also study Greek and Hebrew and am fluent in both. I know your brother. He's a great man. Highly respectable." He waited for my response, but I fixed myself firmly and gave nothing away. I continued to regard him. "We often meet. At least once a week. We have many things in common. We attend the same meetings."

"Did you come here to talk about my brother? Or moons? That's enough." I was able to turn myself solid from the pricks of light I was certainly perceiving.

"Miss. Bacon, you mustn't be impatient. I am not looking for a teacher. Trust me. It's just that I don't have any sisters with which to confide. I want to speak to you like a sister, Delia, if you would only let me." As he glanced at his boots I was able to blink back with a flicker the weight of his look. The sound of my name in his mouth needed me.

He continued with eyes averted. "When I was a young boy, I wished every night before I fell into the luscious land of sleep that I had a sister with which to share stories. I wished for her to make up tales of intrigue so I might become scared and ask to hold her hand. When I went for long walks in the woods, I would speak with any creature that would allow me, pretending I had found a sister lost once upon a time in the thickness of trees. I spoke the longest to the bright and pretty birds. I wanted them to light down from the limbs and land on my hand where I could pet their yielding coats and coax them into singing. If I really had a sister, I would hold her hand and take her to see the robins, warblers and blue jays. I would shelter and keep her warm. I would protect her from the dangers of the wolf. I'm sure your brother does just as much." He looked at me and the bird in my chest opened its wings; I couldn't breathe for its expanding.

"Leonard and I are very close. He loves me more than a husband or father, I suppose." I began flipping ferociously through pages of the closest book.

"I understand. If you were my sister, I would love you just as much." He looked at me and knew I was through looking through. "Miss. Bacon, do you ever wonder if God is lonely?"

This question made me start. I had never heard anyone else so bold as to ask something of this our Lord I still didn't quite trust who takes the little brothers sleeping.

"I haven't thought of anything of the sort. I can't believe supremacy becomes loneliness." I was beginning to fear. This young man was pushing me into a corner with his looking and I shriveled toward the back of my bed. The bird in my chest opened its beak but no sound came out. It was choking on its own melody.

"I was thinking God must be lonely, being one and all and everything in it. Do you think God has a companion?"

"God is his own companion. He doesn't need."

"He needs our love, Miss. Bacon. Ours." He reached out his hand. "Delia. I want you to be my sister."

Against everything I felt conflicting, against the impossibility of advance, against everything I knew from the end to this beginning, I took his hand. This was how I was born another brother.

When he walked out of my room, I broke into a million spaces of emptiness. I never felt loneliness until his flesh fused to mine, that terrible longing. It was as if he had swallowed me, simple as a stone, solitarily wonderful and warm in the safe of his stomach. I had never known this of the world. I desired his eyes to look me over, consumed by the weight of them. I wanted to turn myself into a book he would read, the words becoming his through the deep thickets of his eyes. He would skim pages with his fingers and touch. The thought of him looking at a tree or horizon or anything else shook me with a fundamental quavering. I wanted his eyes only to read me for myself.

Alexander and I met almost every day after and spoke deep into the flesh of our evenings. He talked of his studies. He spoke of a Dr. Taylor and lectures on the place of man being evil in a schema of good. He spoke of a Professor Gibbs who taught him to master the Greek and Hebrew tongues. Alexander said power and authority lay with older times, which men once easily controlled. He spoke of fishers of men. While Alexander's eyes concealed the presence of each room, he asked questions. He asked about the education of women and was interested in my discovery of ciphers. He was curious about Shakespeare and the types of men to befriend him. I spoke, we spoke, and he listened.

When I asked Alexander's professors about his character, they spoke highly of his intellect. If he was spending much of his time with Dr. Taylor and Professor Gibbs, and they approved of his thinking, he must be worthy of seeking me. These were my fine scholarly friends who did not dally with just any young man with passion in the eyes. Mr. Alexander MacWhorter was known throughout the college as an intelligent, ambitious man on the upward rise. He had come from a fine line of MacWhorters who had once made a modest fortune. He shared every quality with the best boys in books: good looks, manners, eloquence, education, and eyes drawing in. We spent days walking together, reading verse and dallying under trees narrowly avoiding the rivulets and trickles of sap. There were never such eyes as ours discoursing. They pulled and pushed in and out, breathing together, breathing. When we read poetry, I watched the light move shadows through his hair. We studied Milton, Wordsworth and Shelley and he told me when I rolled words in my mouth it was sweet and tastefully rewarding. He said he could almost see my tongue touching each syllable, that the syllable wanted to be touched. He told me poetry became me.

Although then I would not admit it, I desired to become his sister or mother or lover because all I wanted was ever more. I wanted to be turned into light, so I might fold over his skin with warmth and enter his eyes to see me through. I wanted to turn to wind so I could travel through his mouth and into his heart to see how strong it was beating. I asked God to change me into these things so I might abide him. Anything to be close to Alexander but God, that lonely ghost, ignored me.

Soon enough, because New Haven was so small, rumors began to circulate. People whispered that I wanted to be near Alexander so I might one day wed his money. They alleged that if we were joined in conjugal bliss, I wouldn't be without fine silk coats or manuscripts to line my bookshelves. They looked for any indication that our skins might touch, but we were careful and stayed in public eye to eye a distance. Alone, he would venture close enough to gently touch my hand, and this was enough. They did not know that we were almost mirrors, cracked and looking glass.

They said I was too old to spend so much time with a man more than ten years younger, they said the grey strands peering through the darkness of my hair must have been to him a shock. What they did not know was that after we read, after we attended lectures, we discussed how we might effectively impart this information to these same gossiping people's progeny. We united not under the guise of pleasure, but for future edifications. It was not desire for finery or bliss, but our learning that led us together.

This is what I wanted to believe. I didn't know he had a mastery I could never be afforded. I didn't know he met with the men who all concurred. Because he was always listening, he was the first person I dared fully elaborate my Shakespearean conspiratorial theory to, as he had quickly earned my trust. I didn't know he would retell my every description to the men who would detail my thoughts in their record books.

At this time, Leonard was again wooing, preparing himself for the pulpit and a new lady to love. I didn't need him to look me over anymore like he said our Lord always would. His ever-discerning eye was nothing like the draught and draw of the beautifully forged eyes of Alexander. Yet, despite his courtship, Leonard must have secretly seen me. I wasn't aware of how thoroughly these men stripped my flesh with their bones.

I trusted and felt safe in the swallow of Alexander's eyes and told him all of my secrets. I told him I did not believe an ignorant stable boy such as William Shakespeare could have written such historically accurate plays. He was, after all, the son of a butcher. I doubt a butcher had as much a mind or fervor. How shrewd can you be if you spend your days chopping meat? I can picture little William's father, sheep blood running from thumb to shoulder. His mind must have sludged from the gristle, uncivilized gunk. How could little William have learned such tragedy, such beauty and romance, such cultural critique, by watching flesh torn gruesomely from beasts?

America needed an appropriate literary icon of its own. It was high time this country placed glory on the head of a genius, prophetess, born of the land that breathed new life into the wilderness. Someone, perhaps, who could make the words become them. Think of the Bible, think of Aristotle, think of Shakespeare, think of me…

I had thought of several potential authors for the plays, all of whom I discussed with Alexander. There were too many powerful men hobnobbing with kings and queens at the time for some rake to have shaken the literary world as such. Sir Walter Raleigh, for example, a favorite of the Queen, is a likely contender. He was a poet and a fighter, and knew the complexities of war. Sir Francis Bacon, master of thought and letters, revolutionized the essay and knew too much to be ignored; it was Bacon who initially devised the cipher in order to keep secrets in the hands of the powerful and deserving. Or perhaps Edmund Spenser, who was in league with the feelings of the Queen. These men are full of minds that could make such language wring and rend the page, not some horse-shoeing manure shoveler. There was the Bible, there was not Shakespeare, there were others, and there was me…

I thought Alexander believed me. He also had speculations about the shrouded past in need of new deciphers. He was working on an interpretation of the Bible that supposed continuous revelation. He believed that depending on the tense of "Yahweh," the name foretold the coming of the messiah. For him, the New and the Old were one long line. There was no such thing as before and after coming together not just then or only now. Alexander and I took the skeins of history and wove them into the presence of beginning. Alexander looked through roots, I wondered at misuse. We agreed that each word was like a tree hiding rings of age on the inside. I didn't know he was placing our intimate history in other private books.

As much as I didn't want to be bothered by the triple-tongued town, after weeks and months I could stand it no longer. Against my heart and wishes, I told Alexander his visits were too frequent. His response was to tell me I was the only one who properly curbed his loneliness; this alone I understood. He said he needed me to reflect. Despite the talking of the town and the meeting of the men and my dishonest request for us to be divided, I promised still to see him.

My mother came to visit and I asked for her advice. I could not be without, I said, we are whole alone together. I told her how Alexander's eyes made the past our future present like courtiers charming queens. I told her of the others who thought I wanted his money, even though I had done much for the teaching of their daughters. I asked her how they dared question my intentions. My mother began to fret and pull at the corners of her garments. She wrung her hands with lifted eyes.

"Is he interested, Delia, in making you his wife?"

"Mother, I don't know. I don't know if it is important. We are companions of the mind. I know he loves me as any brother would cherish a sister, but I can't decide for certain. There is something with him that is different." I sighed, not being that kind of girl, and my mother saw this indicative of something worse.

"Delia, he is not your brother. Wasn't Francis enough?" The reminder of Francis limp and reeling under the coach wheel was enough to make my tears well. Sometimes I tried to forget about Francis, but each time I thought of him in order to push him away, there he was.

"Mother. Please. I am interested in Mr. MacWhorter in a way in which I have never been interested in another man. I think I love him more than a brother." I did not know what I was saying.

"How dare you utter such thoughts! Francis is dead and Leonard is your brother and protector who gallantly took the place of your father when he died. Break all of your connections with the man. He is too young, and you are much too intelligent to get caught up in matters of the heart."

My mother seemed slightly sad, but I couldn't be certain. I was surprised at her conviction. Often I didn't know if she wanted me alone or with a husband with whom I could read meanings with well into the night. She hunched and left the room. I knew then what I must do.

I went on a brief trip to visit my sister Julia, who would advise me nothing like my mother. She knew all of the painfully eager inflections, having once fallen for a man who would not return her love, and she advised me to tend to my seemingly insatiable affections. I watched as her willowy hands painted the intricacies of a garden. She spoke of nothing worse than not following what the heart often demands.

I wrote to Alexander to inform him that I would remain at Julia's until I could return without thoughts of him pressing me so penetratingly into bird wing and bee season. I told him I had to be away to clear my head out like a rug shook clean in the springtime. I told him I believed it best we did not see each other for a while. I believed it. He returned:

DB: I promise to love you in death, life, and beyond forever as I love you in the past I love you now. I love you purely, most appropriately and passionately. I am inseparable without you. My love is like a brother's, and you my cherished sister. I will protect you until you exist no longer. How will I go on? Dear Brother, A.

I responded:

AM: Please do not follow me any longer to the grave or near as I must be alone if you love me as a brother, let me go, let me go without Leonard I am better without. The people will stop speaking and although I return your love purely you cannot be my brother, I have more than one enough.

He replied:

Miss. Bacon: Since I cannot be your brother is there some other relation? I cannot be without you always. Lovingly, A.

I was assured. I now had evidence to tell my mother he wished to marry, but something told me to keep this information private. It must have been the sleeping bird. I had forgotten it was nesting. Since Alexander and I had been spending so much time together, it mostly kept quiet and went days without rustling, but when I received Alexander's final letter it beat against my chest again. Something was not right. When I returned home from my visit with Julia, even the sky was tinged a sickly different tint.

When I saw him again, Alexander did not mention the words in his letter proclaiming love. In fact, he ignored our every exchange, the importance of those letters, acting as if I had never gone or written or wanted at all. In a fit of fury one evening I threw his lies into flames and watched the orange fire lick the language into dust. I waited for something more, but Alexander gave me nothing but his way of looking and absorbing all in sight. Sometimes I would try to find his proposal in the abyss of his eyes, but nothing appeared except my searching. The bird in my chest rattled, thrashing, and gave birth to a bunch of baby birds that hatched somewhere high in my head and wouldn't calm, so often prattling. I waited for Alexander to make me his wife while the town talked, but he didn't, and those baby fowls kept violently fluttering, a nest of dirty birds.

Distracted, I could no longer think or study. The birds flew back and forth, in the evening whistling in Greek and Hebrew, Alexander. They would not give me peace or solitude. I never wanted those flighty, noisome births.

Someone suggested I take Dr. Wesslehoeft's Brattleboro Water Cure. The local physician said my headaches were not caused by birds but by studying too hard, or Leonard's attitude, or Alexander—who never mentioned marriage again, not one word. I left for Brattleboro and made sure no one would follow. I left all my books.

*

Nurse Elaine is pleased. I must spend time at rest. Tell Leonard I am not to be read. I do not allow them to place me there again.

The men cannot condemn me. Alexander was never my lover. He did not speak of every line and curve. They cannot see me when I am underneath the water. From above they peer, drowning out my words.

There are dangers involving matters of the heart. You run the risk of:
— using cheap, clichéd dialogue for the love scenes
— recycling terribly predictable metaphors in order to describe the love object, such as comparing them to water or the moon or any other entity of mythic proportions
— having your characters constantly look into each others' eyes

— falling into abstractions to describe situations instead of admitting
the underlying banality of each lovelorn event (these circumstances are
only significant to those involved – and possibly not even then at all)
— getting lost in the idea of the other at the risk of losing you

I once was involved with a man who wanted to keep our relationship a
secret, and because I thought I loved him, I complied. He said he was like
music and I was like writing and we fit perfectly together. Our conversations
were fragmented and beautifully abstract. There are a few moments I cannot
forget although I thrust myself in the ocean to be pounded free of memory. We
often went hiking through the Santa Monica mountains on a bike path near
the sea and could see it beautifully below. I loved spending this time together,
beautifully abstract, and it seemed he loved spending this time together, too.
I found myself secretly falling in what I thought was beautifully abstract love.
He told me once or twice secretly he was also in beautifully abstract love, and
once he called me by the wrong name: *Delia*. I often wonder about our secrecy.
Maybe he never loved me beautifully or abstractly at all. I cannot be certain
because of the improbability of both memory and love.

I once was in love with a woman I met with in secret because we decided it
would be best if we were veiled. We kept what we shared behind closed doors.
We met in hotel rooms, restrooms, bedrooms, any room, in secret. Wherever
we could get away from the scrutiny of others, we'd go. I found myself falling
in beautifully abstract love. She told me once or twice secretly she was also in
beautifully abstract love. We used to walk together in the evenings through the
busy streets, people unknowing underneath the secret wanting of our surface
skin. There are things no matter how often I plunge underneath the water I am
unable to misremember. She married and moved on.

I once was involved with a man who told me if I wanted to be closer to God
I should let him read the sacrament of my body. He told me I was eternally
dirty, a sinner. He told me there was nothing I could do except let him sanctify
the burning of my bones. He said if I gave myself to him I would be filled with
the full light of God and glory to the highest. He said our meetings should
be secret. He said if anyone found out, he would oust me from the warmth
and loving friendship of our congregation. He was a powerful man who from

the light of a room would take my gaze up with it. We remained together in secret meetings prayerful of lust that dangerously brought us close to hellfire. I began to concentrate more on his hands than the Lord and his word, and I knew I could no longer stand to walk the churchyard without wanting to touch beneath the protective layers of his clothing. I fell in beautifully abstract love. He had to move far away and join another congregation to end our closeness. I was increasingly afraid my husband or his wife would find out. I can't forget the intensity of his flesh. When I hike to the stream to walk my feet through, the chill sends shivers that remind me of his after love.

When she was little Rebecca liked to pretend to drive a chariot. There were a few old cars in her dusty yard and sometimes she would sit in them and imagine she was steering the galloping horses among the clouds into heaven. Most of the time she would imaginatively dash through the yard and run over everything and anything in her way. Metal and dust would cloud up until everything was a huge tornado. She would watch the twirls spin around her. Sometimes Francis would drift by and he was always laughing, even in the dust. Sometimes her mother and father would swirl by and pretend not to see her, even though she would offer them her hand in case they wished to stop. They never took it.

The water eddied down the drain. Rebecca was washing dishes from a soup she had sipped alone. She become bored again, as she often was. She stared at the ceiling. She prayed. She gazed out the window. Nothing moved or spoke.

Hello? Hello? Calling on God, calling on God. God, please pick me up.

She longed for his voice in her loneliness. Did she do something wrong? She decided she would do something wrong so he would give her his attention and she could write another book, although John warned her not to do this on her own. She found an old television set on the top of a shelf in the closet. She took it down, twisted in the wire and turned the knob.

A talk show flickered on. All of the people who appeared were in a fury fit for devils. Some of these people had stories enough to fill books and books and books. In her next work, Rebecca would have to mention demon possession and the women who were always talking too loudly beyond their place behind walls. This poor lot would spend a lifetime burning.

The topic was "my husband is no lover and my lover is no husband." There were many triangles and squares. Women who loved their husbands but also loved their lover's husbands whose wives didn't love their lovers but loved their husband's brother's wives. There was even an older woman who was in love with a man ten years her junior but his other lover was a woman whose husband was the older lover's brother and wouldn't allow it. Rebecca wondered why these people wanted everyone to know their no longer secret loves. She wondered why they subjected themselves to the never-ending eye of Rebecca and other people with tubes.

The people on the show were fighting and the audience was screaming. The older woman was getting stoned. The people shouted and someone crouched behind a chair dodging shoes and scraps of clothing. Then she, he and her got confused in one big dusty tornado. The chanting and spinning, the tumble and toil. Satanists crouched everywhere ready to pounce and there was no one to save them, not even the host, although he sort of looked like Jesus, if the Lord had lived that long.

The stoning stopped and the commercials came on. It had been such a long time since Rebecca had seen television advertisements. She was truly impressed with the secret ways in which sin and temptation were delivered. The first commercial was for a psychic hotline. The commercial said, "call me call me call me and you will know tomorrow." Rebecca knew what was really important was what happened yesterday to get you through the gates of heaven today, but she did enjoy this commercial because it had a lot of lively music playing in the background. She knew that because of the colorful allure, it must have come straight from the soul of some Satanist.

The second commercial was for a plastic cutting device that could chop all manner of vegetables, fruit and meat in any sort of slice and dice. It was the most amazing gadget that had ever been made because it cut preparation time in half. To clean it, you merely had to unscrew a cylinder on top and rinse it in the sink. It had an anti-bacteria mechanism on the inside that got rid of germs without one having to touch them. Miraculous. She thought of her hands. If she bought this apparatus, she could make soup in only a half hour and she would only have to wash a pot, two bowls and spoons and her hands wouldn't crack and split from the soapsuds. She must remember to ask John for extra money so she could buy this wonderful contraption.

The next commercial was for lawyers who would fight for you even if you were dead and burning in hell and couldn't do anything about whatever sin it was that killed you in the first place. If you let them, the lawyers would give you money. All you had to do was call for a free consultation and within moments they would send their team of cleaners to your house. Rebecca copied this number down. She might need more warriors to fight with her against the impending hell on earth. These lawyers promised to fight for just about anything. These lawyers promised to fight for her.

Rebecca tried to think of a reason she could call the lawyers now, despite the fact that there were no current signs of the apocalypse. No frogs fell from the sky, no locusts smattered the sky with their wing beats, no dead rose from desiccated graves. John wasn't around, so she could not ask him his opinion. She wondered what hymn he would quote on the day when the sun would burst and the angels of death would come riding through the clouds on glorious horseback. She thought about calling for a free consultation to find out if there was anything the lawyers could consult with her about, but decided she would have to wait until John came home and everything began to burn.

The next commercial focused on a couple on the beach. They held hands and smiled with huge teeth. The man had a ponytail. The woman did not. They kissed and the camera swirled around them. Rebecca had no idea what the commercial was for. Was it for a car? The couple must have gotten to the beach somehow, so it must be for a car. Regardless of how they got there, the couple flaunting their premarital relations in the face of the few devout would surely go to hell.

The talk show host rose again to introduce the next group. The guests were the same as before but they must have changed their clothes and faces. The same things that had happened before happened once again. Rebecca could not pay attention or pay attention and watch or not watch and always know what was to come. She liked the predictable repetition of the past. There it was, like someone knocking at your door. Someone knocked at her door.

"Yes?" Rebecca looked through the peephole and saw a face she did not recognize. The man was holding a clipboard and had newspapers under his arm.

"Sorry to bother you. Do you have a minute?" The man must have seen her block out the light through the peephole. He smiled and his teeth were bright like the man with the ponytail on the beach.

"Yes?" She began to unlock the locks. Her fingers slipped a bit on the oily doorknob while the man waited for her. He was young and wearing a green silk coat stippled with moth worn holes.

"I am a representative from the *Ozark Express* and I was wondering if you had a subscription to our paper?" The young man shifted from foot to foot. His eyes were dark and cavernous.

"No. I don't read the paper. I read the Bible. Would you like to come in for a chat? Do you read the Bible?" Rebecca was doing what was right.

"No, thank you. But if you subscribe to the *Express*, I can guarantee you will start reading the paper. There is so much to learn. On Sundays there are stories about things happening all across the world. Sometimes they even profile historical figures."

"We go to church on Sundays. Do you go to church on Sundays?"

The man turned. "Thanks for your time," he said as he quickened away. Rebecca stared at the landscape trailing behind his coat.

Rebecca closed the door. More commercials were about to begin. She wanted to see if they would advertise the amazing cutting device again or tell her "call me call me call me and you will know tomorrow." Maybe the lawyers would return and give her a reason to talk with them about inevitable doom. She knew they would return. She believed that God's voice, and John, would one day, too.

———

Rebecca sat on her porch holding an elaborately decorated rain stick Elaine once brought home from a vacation in New Mexico. She needed something to distract her while she waited to fill her belly round with food. Rebecca listened to the tiny beans oscillate through the wood. She shook the stick in percussive fits. The repetition calmed her, stilled her hunger with peaceful rhythms of primeval sounds.

The pizza boy finally arrived, pulling up in a dented truck. Rebecca saw him through the windshield glass, seemingly hypnotized by her recent rattling. He was frozen, red reflected in his eyes through the still and heady night. Rebecca fixed him in her sight, hunger welling for the flesh she knew was steaming in the box. Her mouth swelled. She stretched her jaw wide and felt a strange surge. Suddenly, she found herself overcome by an eruptive bout of laughter.

The unfamiliar pizza boy trembled at Rebecca's prehistoric chortles, but must have realized that he could not sit all night fearfully in his truck. He opened the door and moved cautiously toward her. He held the Meat Madness away from his body, as if it might burn or bite him. Rebecca noticed glints of fear reflected in a skin gouged with pimples that pocked his face with post-pubescence. At one time out of respect for an emergent manhood, Rebecca might have feigned forboding feelings. Another spell of her uncontrollable laughter sent the boy unsettling into shivers. She waited for him to near.

The first time Rebecca got into a fistfight, she had punched a boy's braced and wired jaw. The children around them on the playground stopped pounding each other with the dodge ball to laugh and point. The boy had called her "shark tooth," "lone shark," "shark skin," "shark head," and Rebecca finally had enough. Rebecca wasn't sure why these names angered her so much, but she knew she had to defend herself with the throw of a punch into the boy's sparkling metal mouth.

For years in elementary school this boy had sent her Valentines Day cards covered with an excessive amount of hearts. He also used to ask her to come over after school to reenact *The Clash of the Titans*. He would complain and send himself into asthmatic attacks because Rebecca always wanted to be Zeus and not Andromeda, who was weakly subject to the merciless scale and fin of the Kraken. Rebecca would arm wrestle the boy for the coveted authorial position and always win. He ended up eventually fearing her, as if she were Medusa.

When they both sat in the principal's office (Rebecca with a scraped knuckle while the boy's eye blued from Rebecca's boxing), he admitted that he did not mean to hurt her. He apologized to Rebecca and they were both sent home early from school. Rebecca and the boy did not remain close after this exchange of brutality, nor did Rebecca ever truly forgive him for trying to humiliate her, although for a while he tried to tempt her back into friendship by offering to loan her his favorite GI-Joes. By the time they were both in high school, they were no longer even enemies.

It wasn't until later in life Rebecca realized she could never truly be anyone's bridesmaid or buddy. Perhaps she was a lone shark, shark tooth, shark skin, pistris solus. She was more and more comfortable with shedding and shaking yesterday's skin with a conviction that new growth only momentarily prickled and itched. But still, she had spent most of her youth wobbling in the knee with insecurity, outwardly baring her teeth at anyone who came close.

Shark face. Shark head. Snake eye. Sibyl.

The pizza boy regained some courage and strutted up the walk. He thrust the pizza at her.

"Eighteen fifty nine," he glared with his bravest, big-boy face. Rebecca shoved a twenty into his fist with muscles toughened.

"The change is in my car," he said, suffocating on words.

"Then you'd better go get it." Rebecca licked her lips. She stared at the boy with eyes now made of slits.

Sophia must have woken. She commenced a subterranean woofing from behind the rackety door. She jumped up and down, knocking the hinges, cleaving almost through the wood.

The boy backed a few paces, careful not to turn from her, and sprinted to his truck like a jittery rodent. As the wheels screeched, Rebecca tore into the pizza, occasionally tossing a pepperoni or two inside the open window to Sophia. Rebecca ate vociferously, finishing half the pie quick. Her stomach bloated and protruded as if she had swallowed a ball. She was misshapen and malformed, bulging from the middle. She could barely move. She had to lie down until the pizza moved laboriously through her.

She went back inside and as she rested, she tried to think of something poetic to say to Elaine. She wanted to compose something expressive of her particularly excruciating absence, something that would scatter her memories with tremendous beauty, but her belly gurgled and bubbled, distracting her. She thought of some ideas she might use in a later work:

everything i want swims from me through the water like blood enticing. i accompany the torrents through. i try to hold the flayed edges of you that let slip. i miss your crash and flood. the warmth of hands suspiciously scarred. i am tired and this longing cannot stop. i want to be light, folded over your skin with warmth, entering your eyes to see me through. you cannot see me when I am underneath the water. from above you peer down, drowning out my words.

FIVE

Continents of hail and darkness, the polar seas—all earth's distance,
could never have parted me from him; but now I live in the same world
with him, and the everlasting walls blacken between us.
Delia Bacon

I REMEMBER THE WATER, forced underneath and between it. It pours from above a torrent, nothing like Brattleboro. This water pounds as if I were a plant forced to bend down and kiss the ground with a head broken stalk. I am not a flower. I did not have to bear these rapids freely with the cure. Here I am unwilling.

Regretfully, I have no regrets. I do not need other than myself. I understand. Leonard says there is no writing when sentences still aren't clean.

I will bear this water as the water once bore me until I break free of my own volition. I practice pretending. I wear my hair as if fashioned and fold my hands lapdown. I break shakes by thoughts. I close myself up like a coffin where no words like worms breach through. No Alexander. No Leonard.

Soon, I learned the truth. Nurse Elaine holds my hands soft, like evening baths that once healed me with warm water.

*

At Brattleboro, I reunited with the Beechers. They had been taking the water cure for some time and knew the routine and benefit. Harriet talked extensively of the cure. She had been exhausted from five pregnancies and marriage to a balding pallid man of the clergy named Mr. Calvin Ellis Stowe.

She had headaches from calomel, and was tired of doctors administering medicine that made her sick.

For ten hours each day, Dr. Wesselhoeft created a regimen that involved us in and out of different fluids. The mornings were tepid. We were wrapped in wet sheets and covered in blankets. Then we drank glass after glass of water from a clear spring to run clean the system. Next we were to bathe in a stream that chilled the bones. We were also to take numerous walks, which I enjoyed best, being used to them long and engaging with Alexander. There were stone benches placed at different spaces among the trees where we could rest and gaze out at the hills and wildlife. It was a pleasantly wooded and watery area being fed by curing streams. The place bled health in perceptible veins to alleviate my bird-beaten body.

I spent most of my walks alone, but sometimes Harriet, Miss. Catharine and I would join together. Harriet and I often spoke of writing. I told her of my book's plan and some potential interest. Wiley and Putnam's Sons told me when I finished they might find a place for this work among their American Authors collection. Harriet, of course, was jealous. She folded her hands when I talked of my success. At that time, she was hardly even known. I could see by the way her eyes squinted and body slightly tensed she was uncomfortable discussing my accomplishments. In our schooldays she had sat in front and I knew how she straightened when twinged with discomfort. I could not forget her undeserved composition in our class, and now she squirmed as a bug about my potential publishing. Or maybe she was thinking about the heft of her husband's dowdy body. Poor Harriet.

During our walks I told Miss. Catharine my plans for future lectures. I was desired in numerous areas of New England to speak to larger groups, and was promised a full-time teaching commitment in New Haven. I would never be without work, because I had recently developed a new way of speaking that did not involve recitation. Miss. Catharine was not jealous, her usual self-encouraging, but she did imply that one should not let love get in the way of a career. Although I had not told her explicitly about Alexander, she was secretly informing me I could succeed as long as I kept away from men like him. Sometimes we spoke in code. By now I was adept at reading meanings just beneath.

Like Sir Francis Bacon and his ciphered circles, we sometimes have to let what should be known remain hidden. Sometimes we put the meaning in our hands and let each other know by wrings or grasps. Sometimes we put the meaning in mouths that purse, or in eyes that blink and look. Some things cannot be rendered clearly into language.

I tried desperately not to reveal Alexander's presence through cheeks that would rouge if the topic came to love. While I looked for meaning, I did not want others to read or mean from me. I kept my secret as long as I could.

After a few weeks at Brattleboro, I had to interrupt my cure and return home to attend a wedding. I was in fine spirits when I arrived at the church. Three weeks had passed since Alexander and I had met or spoken, and I was finer alone. Yet, I could not help but to look for him through the tiny eyelets stitched into the sides of my bonnet. Thankfully Alexander was nowhere. His eyes would have robbed the church.

After a ceremony of reciting and vows, I stood on the chapel steps to enjoy this kind of sunshine. Unexpectedly, from the corners of my heart, I saw him. He rattled up in a stage, head jutting from the window.

"Miss. Bacon! I've been looking for you." He stepped from the coach like any gentleman would and dusted off his coat in such a way that made me shiver.

"Mr. MacWhorter." I tried to still myself, but the bird was beating, beating, and lost some quills that fluttered to my feet. "I've been taking the water cure at Brattleboro, and I must return. My headaches are still sometimes pounding. I need invigoration. I need the cold and time away from this kind of thinking. I was just on my way. I am taking the last train and won't be back for a while." I noticed at my feet the ground was littered with feathers. The birds were bashing their brains against my ribs. I imagined them suffering, needing.

"I can accompany you. We can talk about my discoveries and the lectures I have heard in your absence. Dr. Taylor spoke eloquently the other evening about men placed beneath angels with the will to deny turning into beasts. I've learned so much about the chain of being, and I've changed, I tell you. Let me take you." I felt myself dragged throughout his eyes.

"It's a long way. I can catch the train. You must have other engagements." He did not catch the significance of the phrase.

"I wish to accompany you. I do have a commitment to preach in Springfield, but they will surely understand if I purify with water prior to purifying their church with my good words. I've heard wonders about Dr. Wesselhoeft...Delia, without you, I have not been able to bear this loneliness. Will you accept my offer of companionship? I can afford some repose." I don't know why, but again I took his hand. It was late. I was tired. Alone. I had forgotten how much I did not want him without me.

The ride was pleasant and passed quickly. We spent it ignoring the countryside together. He asked me about Brattleboro and told me about his friend Mr. Robert Forbes, who I was warned by others to never invite to any gatherings. I did not say anything contrary to Alexander about this man. I only pursed my lips and hoped he could read my meaning.

We arrived back at Brattleboro in the late evening. I was placed in Paradise Row, the women's area, and Alexander left for where the men were sequestered. Dr. Wesselhoeft made it certain that men and women, although maybe legally joined in marriage, remain at nights a separate distance. He believed this important. The women needed to be away from their husbands' requests so the water could clarify them of complaints. The men needed to be away so water could illumine their minds. In Paradise Row, we were pleased with our division. We would stay up nights speaking to one another about the progression of our health and other issues not normally confined to secret meanings. We women remained together, in the water and out. I cannot speak for the men.

Alexander and I took our afternoon hikes together, and it was then when we sat underneath the trees looking at various grass blades and stems. Sometimes I watched the clouds pass through the swinging of his fingers. These trips were cheerful and I believed nature and water were slowly invigorating through me.

After Alexander's arrival, however, I noticed a change in Miss. Catharine. She shut her support into stone. When I began to also spend my exercise hour with Alexander instead of her, she slit her eyelids, disapproving communication. She might be turning into one of the statues that lined the facility and poured water from pots onto chisel-perfect feet. Maybe my Alexander reminded her of an Alexander lost in the waves of a violent current. Although I did not wish to hasten her transformation, I knew Alexander and my relationship had somehow become her, but my Alexander was nothing like that avaricious sea.

My Alexander enjoyed the pleasure of the land, and was afraid of journeying tumultuously across any rivers or oceans. One day we sat underneath a fir and talked of his aversion to deep water. He said when he was a child his mother had left him too long in the bath to chase away a snake that slithered through the kitchen. It was a tremendous story, full of the excitement of reptilian tongues. He said while in the water, he thought of ships and pirates and people attacking his mother being bit by a land lost serpent. That is why, he said, he did not like sitting in the freeze of a Brattleboro spring. But, he said, he hoped to overcome this fear, and thought it would help being close to someone such as me. He said I was the sister he could hold to pull him through.

A shadow fell on the back of my dress. Someone was approaching. When Alexander leaned close to brush a fallen pine needle from my hair, I noticed the skirt of someone moving just behind. He jumped, and I turned to boldly confront the snake.

"Mrs. Harriet Beecher Stowe! So nice to see you during your hour of exercise. You usually leave so quickly and I don't know where you move off. Have you been enjoying your walk?" I mustered a smile and tried to hide my shock. I tried to look like a woman immobilized in a painting, but my thighs twitched underneath the thickness of my skirt. I felt I was crawling all over. Alexander kept inching back until he leaned like a bruised apple fallen far from the tree.

"Mr. MacWhorter...Miss. Bacon. If I hadn't known any better, I would have thought I was interrupting a lover's tryst." Her black eyes searched through our garments and over our figures to find evidence of an illicit love. I laughed nervously and hoped she could not see the betrayal of my twitching thighs. Alexander studied cloud formations and checked for peals of rain.

"Not at all. Not at all. We were talking about the cure and how happy Mr. MacWhorter is to have joined us. Don't you agree he looks healthier than while in New Haven?"

"He does appear to be much more...robust. And you, Miss. Bacon! You've such a flushed look." Harriet's eyes dug into the ground around the fallen needles and grass blades, noticing what was displaced. "Mr. MacWhorter" she continued, "I heard you broke an engagement to preach, and that the Reverend's wife will not forgive you. Is this true? I should think you are healthy enough to tend to your professional duties. I, however, am truly in need of this cure."

"Dear Mrs. Stowe, of course I would not neglect my responsibilities. I wrote to the Reverend informing him of my delay and he extended his invitation for when I feel healthy and ready once again to mount the pulpit. His wife must have taken our arrangement to heart more intensely than she should."

Harriet raised her eyes, nodded slow as dusk and strolled away. Poor Harriet. Later she began to refer to Alexander as my shadow and told all the other women about how much time we spent together. They would press me for information in the evenings at Paradise Row. I was squeezed as thin as a sheet. Sometimes they whispered as Alexander passed: *there goes Miss. Bacon's shadow, see how he follows her; he's a sneak.*

I told them we were close companions, that was all; we shared ideas about Shakespeare and the Bible and names masking authority, our minds intellectually ignited. They could not truly understand, so I told them nothing of our bodies walking wistfully among the vegetation sharing the solidarity of rocks.

There is one walk I cannot forget as long as I remember, despite the water trouncing memory. No amount can rinse this moment from my thoughts. After so many weeks at Brattleboro, I was strong. I had gained weight and could climb as high as any horizon wished to peak. Chesterfield Mountain was no match for me among its foothills. The Connecticut River couldn't wash me in the grips of rushing. I was even stronger than Alexander. He was not reacting to the late night chill of footbaths like I. This gradual freezing woke me from what felt a long slumbered dream. I was ready for anything, and would go with Alexander anywhere, further. I could climb higher and longer and walk beyond, and I became increasingly frustrated at how often he had to stop.

We began the walk I remember by ambling along the grounds, and I wondered out loud about what makes the mind go. I was watching other patients move amongst the gardens in varying states of agitation. Some of the women let their hair fall and stooped low beneath the weight of it. Some of the men juddered like an earth's subtle trembling and looked as if they would shake themselves to sticks. I remembered my fever from the insect that bit and wondered if I had, momentarily, become one of these mind-lost souls, unable to clarify what was around me. I remembered most of what happened in the fervor of waking sleep, and became unsure of the real and the invented. I voiced these concerns to Alexander. He told me not to worry; he said now my mind was crisp. He believed we should thank the Lord we were so obviously dissimilar from the unfortunate ones.

We sauntered to a cliff's edge near the West River and looked at the clouds billowing landscapes while the water rushed below. We sat still as silence for many moments listening to gullies wash the stones. I soon lost where I was and felt myself surrounded by foliage that bent and wrapped my body. I wasn't sure of what was real and what invented. Were the trees holding me tight in a grip that would erase me?

I realized that the tremendous pressure grasping my midsection was not from the branches of nearby trees. Alexander had enclosed me. His arms surrounded with a pressure fantastic, and I felt myself recede into the pleasures of his pulse.

"Delia. Be my wife."

I backed away and looked at the space seeping beneath his eyelids. Everything began to disappear: the clouds, the river, the cliff side.

"Alexander," I sighed, not that kind of woman, "I am nothing else."

When he let go, all of the valley with everything in it lifted and entered the cavernous depths of him. The birds that formerly beat their wings with the thrashing, the birds that bashed against my ribcage to rush to their early deaths, stopped flittering. My head ceased pounding and my chest was not compressed. Those bloody birds finally flew their cruelly fallen feathers away.

Nothing changed about me physically, emotionally or mentally except from that moment, I contained a secret knowledge I coveted proudly and privately. I was to be a bride. The pleasure of owning this information filled me with an assurance hitherto unknown. I was ready to return to my former life as soon as the treatment concluded.

Alexander and I decided to wait to marry until he was awarded a pastorate, because this was the most responsible plan of action. He gave me a gold pen as an engagement gift, and I wrote my correspondences thereafter with the ink from the coalescence of our love.

I wrote to Leonard to tell him I missed his sermons, but I mentioned nothing of my love. I wrote to mother of the fantastic treatments, but told her nothing of my love. I wrote to Julia outlining the various trees and valleys, but revealed nothing, my love. I did not tell the Beechers or any other patient. I did not tell the trees or stones. I kept the secret to myself, happy doing so.

A few days after our engagement, Alexander and I decided to venture on a longer, more adventurous hike. I was especially exuberant, and I invited him to climb higher up the Chesterfield than we had ever ascended. I wanted to secure the most intense and intimate view. A fellow patient, however, warned us to err on the side of caution. He heard rumors of a wolf that scoured the mountainside ragged and hungry. He told us the mountain held dangers not immediately apparent; snakes hid under dried leaves that bit and left for dead.

I was not frightened, but I noted Alexander's slightly pale visage. This trip, I noticed, he had brought his walking cane, which he usually forgot. I assured him not to worry. If a wolf emerged from the woodlands, I would stomp upon its throat until it bayed at the moon and begged for my mercy.

Instead of utilizing the path the other climbers took, I decided to scale the mountain rocks sideways to the top. I thought it might be quicker because I could hop from crag to crag. I wished to feel what it was like to leap like a happy ram.

Soon I was off, grabbing bushes to stabilize, sometimes slightly slipping in my boots but laughing and shaking traces of fear off. I was quicker than Alexander, and often had to wait. We could see the Connecticut far below winding its way through the valley like a serpent. People manned the river small as gadflys and just as inconsequential. We were almost to the top when something shrilled hollow with a tongue that shriveled up. It was spook-like as a banshee.

"The wolf! We must climb down and warn the patients. Hurry! Down! Now!" Alexander clambered spasmodically down the mountainside, scrambling and knocking loose pebbles that rubbled after. I remained positioned on my rock.

I looked up and waited to see if the banshee-wolf-ghost would howl another cry. I thought if I heard it, I could read the wail of meaning in its voice. I knew it would not hurt. After a long stream of silence, I continued to climb.

Occasionally looking down, I could not see Alexander. I reached the summit and gazed out upon the valley. I understood at that moment alone is always how it should be, always and simply alone. It is impossible to escape the inevitable presence. The space within silence sounds just as the baying of an isolated wolf. The men moved boats down the river, individually guiding currents that coursed around them, alone. Birds flew overhead, diving periodically from the flock for what might have been food, alone. The food, singularly plucked. Alone.

I walked peacefully down the mountain via the trail. When I reached the bottom, it was time for my meal and footbath. I did not see Alexander the rest of that evening.

After a bottomless sleep, I woke with a terrible headache and had to stay in bed the next day, alone. Alexander was not allowed to see me, as I was in Paradise Row, alone. I rested and regained my strength and decided to embark upon another journey with some of the other patients to hunt for chestnuts.

I happily observed that Alexander was one of those in attendance and approached him as soon as I could. Although it had only been a day, I missed him immensely, alone, always alone.

"What happened to you? Were you scared by the howling of a wolf?" I poked him in the chest and anticipated the sink into his eyes.

"You're impossible. I can't believe the things you do. What made you think it was all right to remain on the edge of a mountainside alone? I told you to follow me down. I thought you were behind. Soon I noticed you were not. I don't know what you thought you were doing." He reflected me back to me looking back my dark hair sometimes gleaming.

"Alexander. There was no wolf. Don't be upset."

"I'm not upset. I must leave you. I promised a friend I would accompany him today. Try not to follow. We've got matters to discuss."

Alexander walked away and did not speak to me for the rest of the day. I searched for chestnuts with the Beechers, who must have noticed something was wrong. Perhaps they read the meaning in my avoided eyes and low-turned lips. In my upset, Harriet seemed happier. It could have been the beautiful weather with sun shining comfortably between the trees, but somehow, I felt like it was not. Harriet sprung from one maple to another, laughing and tossing her hair around the frequent shadows. Miss. Catharine stayed behind and walked with me. I was having a difficult time moving.

The next day, Alexander approached and acted as if nothing had happened. He did not say a word about our conversation or the calling of the wolf. The joy that filled me with his renewed presence overshadowed any doubt or upset I may have previously felt. He asked me if I wanted to join him for a walk, reached out his hand, and of course I fearlessly took it. We went on our own. Alone.

*

Please understand. I was not capable of guarding against betrayal. I did not understand the meaning of that lonesome wail. I did not know it told me truths of Alexander. If I could have read the solitary bay, I would have heard him speak my secrets to the brotherhood of wolf.

I tell Nurse Elaine I am ready. I will not hold my breath. I will breathe in. I will change from skin to feather to fin.

In my first creative writing workshop, I wrote a forgettable story entitled "Charlie and His Indo Factory." At the time, I was seventeen, smoking a lot of dope and also under the assumption that everyone in the class would find tales of marijuana and drug-related intrigue as amusing and significant for rendition as I. I stole the story idea from a *People's Court* episode, and because it was based on a real-life event, this made my exposition all the more relevant. What was relayed in the episode was this: an elderly woman rented out a room of her house to a young couple. Months passed, and she noticed an abundance of strange weeds growing in her backyard. The woman proceeded to pick the weeds and burn them in her fireplace, all the while swaying the day in her favorite rocking chair in the living room unbeknownst to the young pot-growing renters who were away on vacation. They returned, and in an angry frenzy, realized that she had destroyed their secret crop. The elderly landlady was, of course, rightfully humiliated, and thus the whole lot ended up on *People's Court*. I remember finding it terribly hilarious when the old woman was describing why she was suing the young couple for her feeling strange, lightheaded, and extremely hungry after she threw the plants into the fire. I thought Judge Wapner might explode, as he always seemed on the verge of combustion. The poor woman was about seventy-five years old, but the Judge did not take pity on her, and she did not win her case.

I remember only a few of my classmate's comments on my story; some asked if I wanted to get high after class (this was how I met my first lover), and others wrote helpful expressions in the margins like "funny!" or "hahaha". I tried to keep these comments in mind when I worked on revisions.

My professor had a completely different response. He critiqued my work as being rife with cliché, and said I spent too much time with erroneous description. How this wounded my poor young writerly heart!

I now know not to begin stories with sentences like:

Charlie could sleep all day if it weren't for the sun. He rolled groggily out of bed and onto the dirty floor. He had not gotten much sleep last night because he had gotten drunk at the local Karaoke bar, The Broken Spoke. His vomit breath could set old Miss Peabody's house on fire like the wolf howling flames tattooed across his arm.

I have vowed to never make these amateurish mistakes again.

The first poem I ever wrote is a short, twenty or so line poem written in free verse. In it, the speaker addresses a former lover who has disturbed the speaker's melancholic sensibilities. It has no formal title and I usually refer to it as "Number 1." It begins with the following lines:

Sometimes you look to me
so very much like a whirlpool.
You spin around and around
until I am dislocated.

The poem then interestingly shifts to describe "you" as a lifesaver within this whirlpool with the potential to save the speaker from being "dislocated." What a thoughtful transformation from an object of destruction to an object of liberation! However, true to the lover's capacity for continuous letdowns, the speaker notes in the penultimate line:

and then I find out you are not [a life preserver].

The final line sums up the situation between speaker and lover. It functions as a final blow to the unreliable lover:

you are just a floating plastic baggy from Albertsons.

Note the use of contemporary, concrete details. This is an example of how one should "show, don't tell." I never did circulate this poem for critique, but when I've read it aloud at various open mic nights, I do believe I've heard the audience sigh "ahhh," as they often do at the end of a particularly moving poem.

In the first song I ever composed, I use the "f" word too often for it to be as Christian as it should. This was when I was young, before I truly found my place in the kingdom of heaven. I used to say the "f" word occasionally because I sensed a power in it, and now I worry I might never be forgiven.

The song I wrote is called "F--- Off." It is a love song. There are three part harmonies in the outtro, where the words "f--- off" are repeated over and over with increasing volume. In order to document this beautiful refrain, I recorded my voice singing the song on one tape recorder, then played the tape back and sang over my vocals while recording the song again on a second tape recorder, back and forth, until I arranged the harmonies. This was before I knew Satan hid demons in electronics. I used to worry I would burn in hell for such profanities, but this is just not true. I've discovered how to prevent burning, and that is to offer everything to God, to know that one especially righteous can be saved from impending doom.

My name is Rebecca Brown. I am Rebbecca Brown. Call me Rebecca Brown. I am Delia Bacon. Maybe the end is near? I am beginning to believe in Rebecca. I am worried about Delia. I am worried about you, too.

————

It has been three days since John left and for three days Rebecca has wanted to ask him for money to buy a chopping device or advice on what to say to the lawyers so that they would join their army against this hell on earth. For three days Rebecca has been watching the television, the same commercials over and over, knowing they will be there tomorrow, but tomorrow she did not want to stay at home alone. She knows it is John she must obey. God usually tells her so. Although sometimes she thinks she should leave him, she is afraid he might follow or send Satanists after. She believes there is no success without him. God says this is so. Sometimes she prays for ignorance, but what would she do without his revisionary voices?

Sometimes she takes long walks up mountains in the middle of the woods. The dirt is clotted with insects, and is not extravagant like the dirt she remembers the fine silk of when younger. It is stickier to her toes. These walks hold her in their grip in the strongest sort of tug. Sometimes she is able to hear God more clearly once she arrives at the top. Sometimes on her way up she thinks about what she has or has not done.

When she was small she went on camping trips with her family to the mountains in Northern California. She had never seen so many trees before and the immensity of them made her feel as if she could not breathe. There were too many spores giving off green. The air was clean where mountains seemed to squeeze. There was always so much to do before they settled into singing hymns by the firelight while Francis shook the tambourine.

Rebecca climb down that hill and get us some branches. Your mother is going to cook. Make sure Francis does not follow you down the ditch. I don't want him to get hurt.

Rebecca hates gathering wood. The trees bend and scratch her. She carries the pile in outstretched arms but it is impossible to avoid the abrasive kindling. When she walks up the hill, she loses her balance and slips. The wood falls and she stumbles on it. The green is drowned in blood but she must not forget the kindling or else her father. She climbs up the ditch. Francis starts crying because she is scratched and scraped. She wipes the blood with her shirt. Her mother empties the car then turns, noticing her swollen blotchy arms.

God damn it Rebecca, can't you do anything right?

Her hands itch and bleed with surface splotches radiating from her palms.

You'd better clean yourself up before your father gets back.

Later when he tramples through the trees with a dead wolf slung over his back, he does not notice her.

Look at this. Look at her wagging tongue. She must have been sick. Tonight we won't be bothered by her lonesome howling.

He rubs the matted fur. It is sticky and dark. He makes the mouth open and close and says: *You are gonna skin me. You will do what you are told. I told you so. I told you so.*

He peels the matted fur with a knife and Rebecca watches. Her clothes are crusty with blood. Her father strips the flesh and finally looks at her.

What the hell happened to you? You're dirty. Did you slip, you big dummy?

He drags her by the arm and yanks her down into the ditch. There is a stream with water and it is colder than ice cubes with tea. He pushes her in and waits.

Get all that nasty shit off.

She does not cry or else she does not notice because she is wet and shivering. She cleans herself as best she can but she cannot get rid of the bright red scratches. They leave marks on her skin that she is too afraid to read.

Rebecca wishes she could have a cat for company but John will not allow it. She once had a cat named Apostle who liked to lick his wounds, but John says animals are too unpredictable. She is tired of waiting on the couch for John so she decides she will wait in warm water instead. She is also tired of the television, so she puts it back up on the shelf. God still hasn't said one word. She goes into the bathroom to run the tap. She lies in the tub and doesn't think. She doesn't pray. She stares at the ceiling and silver faucet. She does not think about John or wolves or anything but warmth. She remembers being this warm before and floating in water but she can't exactly place it. She does not know when or where but she was and she is there again and tries not to think. She decides to listen but realizes that she can't hear anything at all.

She lies in the bath a long time and finally looks at her hands. Shriveled. She decides it is time to get out, get dressed and continue to wait for John, who she figures by now might not return. She will wait forever. She has to. Without the presence of those she abides, she does not know what else to do.

Rebecca sits sighing a bevy of forlorn gazes through a window increasingly filled with far off stars. She wishes Elaine would call. She contemplates going to a bar, but knows if she does she will fight or fuck and strangle, and this was part of a former life she did not wish to remember. She has shed that self in striations of painfully flocculating skin.

When she was in her late twenties, drinking a fifth of vodka nightly and dating a woman who would throw dirt clods at her window whenever Rebecca would try to break their bonds and knots, a friend told her about a retreat in the desert that claimed to heal all ails. Whatever the issue, the creators of this sanctuary promised a visit to this hideaway would cure through intense therapy designed to imbibe the body with newfound verve. Although skeptical, Rebecca decided she would take a chance and try it. Nothing more than what she was then doing with her life could possibly hurt. She was tired of waking in drunken clouds inexplicably coiled and decided she needed a long-deserved break from a life of inexhaustible skirmish.

She might as well have vacationed at Mount Olympus. If the magical healing occurred because of the visitor's incredulity at the ridiculousness of this particular therapeutic process, then Rebecca had arrived, hallelujah! This asylum was a haven for those interested in getting in touch with their inner stupidity—women sat in semi-circles covered with crystals and robes made of burlap meditating and burning from the blistering heat but still as the desert that surrounded. Groups of men pushed baby carriages filled with cotton balls, and every time they felt angry, they picked up a handful of fluff and blew it from their palm with a passionate huff of "I love my mom!" Counselors would huddle together in the cafeteria during dinner hour, occasionally shouting words like "love!" "fever!" "trust!" and the audience would reverberate back with an enthusiastic "We are us!" that would echo amongst the clatter of silverware and tapioca-smeared trays. Rebecca spent a week prescribed on the preposterousness of a neo-hippy generation.

Part of the healing process was to spend time with a small group conceptualizing a planet filled with a superior sort of life form. They were to make sculptures of the buildings that would be present on their planet and create visual depictions of the alien land with sticks and stones picked from the refuse of desert. Rebecca's group named their planet "Farfetchedopia," as she was placed with other cynics like herself who sat cross-armed and joking through the week at night in the climate controlled igloos they were roomed in. Rebecca's group knew she was a writer, and commissioned her with creating Farfetchedopia's national anthem. Rebecca wrote:

Farfetchedopia there you are, full of us who drink at bars. The people there all play with toys, trucks for girls and dolls for boys. Farfetchedopia where you are, people don't get hungover and barf.

Her group would often sing it loud enough to block out the incomprehensible chanting they would hear rising up from the sacred sand crevice before the morning "Get in Touch with Touch" meetings.

Rebecca regrets not keeping in touch with Jaded, Lilith, and Thumb-Guzzler, nicknames each of her group members had chosen for themselves and written sloppily with a Sharpie across stickers under the familiar "Hello my name is...". Rebecca chose the name "Snakey the Lone Shark" because she liked trying to squish all of the words into such a small space. Despite the ridiculousness of the week, Rebecca often missed her coconspirators and their shared skepticisms. Their counselor Glitter did note that their particular group experienced a breakthrough when they had to destroy Farfetchedopia with golf clubs and wuffle-ball bats to illustrate the concept of letting go. She said she could tell by the way Jaded had instinctively shared his prided Eagles lighter with Lilith to ignite Farfetchedopia's paper-mache town hall that something magical had happened between them. For their breakthrough they were awarded tiny plush cats with large button eyes, which they were asked to carry around until the graduation ceremony at the end of the day. Rebecca's group passed around a joint as they torched these childish prizes while Glitter flit about them clapping enthusiastically for a group that knew how to relish individuality.

Rebecca had eventually quit drinking, but not because of her time spent happily heating herself with skepticism in the desert. Slowly she became tired of it on her own accord, and now she didn't miss the intensification of a life spent suffering through constantly wavering interactions. She believed she did not have enough time for such frivolities anymore. She'd rather spend her time looking for subjects lost enough for writing.

Sophia was snoring in a mound at Rebecca's feet. Rebecca debated whether she should move or wake her. She decided against it and thought about the plentitudes of a love she could not forget or quite remember.

SIX

Prose is the dream, and poetry the truth.
That which we call reality, is but
Reality's worn surface, that one thought
Into the bright and boundless all might pierce,
There's not a fragment of this weary real
That hath not in its lines a story hid
Stranger than aught wild chivalry could tell.
Delia Bacon

I HAVE NOT WRITTEN to Leonard. My sentences took a worse turn; they wound and curved in other tongues speaking not related. They are like wild horses unbridled and free seeking the vast profusion of pastures. They are bloodied up like wolves. I wrote of Alexander, and Leonard no longer hears.

I am sick. I shadow myself. I am a mark at the end, storied. I try to place words in order like proper soldiers. They elude me. They are off galloping like knights on let-loose steeds. They breathe steam and fire through their noses. They are disasters.

Sometimes I recompose the fragments. I find them underneath bedclothes and in pockets of coats I wear to protect against the cold. They gather. They piece like asymmetrical quilts. They knot and weave. They warble. They say: *None the many without one; none the many without one.*

Nurse Elaine keeps my company. She understands. She has asked that I not receive the water pounding down, the flooding. I opened my mouth and choked until she saved me, pulled me floundering like a fisher of men.

I begin again. I pretend the meaning underneath tames the wildlike voices. I've found:

Birds beaks and broken as if.
Alexander breathing my breathing my eyes secret blink.
Brothers make Brattleboro go meeting men in the gallery books.
Water altitudes and longing. History is.

I have found poetry I don't remember. Lines in infinitesimal, cramped spaces; shoved in the toes of my boots. Here, revealing:

My mouth is stuffed with straw and fever or fear of letting
blood to slim insects. Once I said I am
alone and they listened to bones stacked
straight like bookshelves. This time likes
no others and the dust mites wave their spiny
fingers under microscopes that pin and defend them.
My skin sinks sallow in the corners of my chest
and my face rests right under a window.
The wind winks in to remind me I am sleeping or on
top of layer after layer of blood brick and artifact my
bones shift and settle. My skin breaks open I imagine
it leaks out. Nothing beautiful about river leading river
into landslide. I wait wordless while
the days flick off and on and no one listened.

This language comes in solitude with no one to listen except sometimes glass-eyed Elaine like a doll. I ask her: *From where do verses come?*
She says they are born.
I recite verse after verse from other times while faltering: history, bones, Alexander, Leonard, Shakespeare, sometimes yelling at the Lord. My mouth births while she traps them and defends them before they slip. I don't remember.
I don't know for whom or when I am writing. Nurse Elaine tells me to finish, this will help, letting go. She says to keep Alexander separate from Leonard. He no longer gives brotherly love. He cannot save me. She tells me so and it is so.

*

Brattleboro was no longer a haven for love blossoming and healing, but a nest of asps with tongues serpentine flicking, flicking. People talked as in New Haven and wouldn't wait until I was absent to speak. There seemed nothing for anyone to do except talk, constantly the jaws jabbing. Mr. MacWhorter. Miss. Bacon. Delia. Alexander. Delia's Shadow. They sought to define and describe a love terribly illicit.

I thought Miss. Catharine would bolster me like a familiar petticoat. Although I was healthy and glowing as never before, she made it known that if Alexander had no intention of making me a wife, she would separate us regardless of our friendship. She split up at the seams. She gave me a copy of Eliza Farrar's *The Young Lady's Friend* saying: *This is a book you need.* She told me: *Study chapter fifteen: flirtation. Read carefully. Listen in between.* She told me I was a sinner if I continued a relationship with a man under the guise of Platonic love. Because of her sisterly seeming interventions, I gave away the secret knowledge I formerly owned alone. So she would leave me and cease her bookish recommendations, I told her of Alexander's proposal to solidify our now non-Platonic love. She did not seem surprised.

Alexander also had problems with companions meddling and not minding. His friend Mr. Hamilton's favorite topic of discussion became the elderly; he asked Alexander how many new grey hairs he might spot on the women patients' heads, and lectured about older women's difficulties bearing children. These details Alexander told me while he pat my hand against worry. Wretched Mr. Hamilton would point out the younger patients to Alexander and comment about their superiorly sturdier bodies. When I was in earshot, Mr. Hamilton made no effort to lower his booming fat baritone; he resounded louder than a locomotive. I could not stand it.

I was finally relieved to leave the nattering mob at Brattleboro to return mostly robust to New Haven. I was a new woman, and would be perfect except for others' unsolicited intrusions, ready to carry on with my work. When I arrived home, however, I found Miss. Catharine had told most everyone in town I was newly engaged to my young love. I also discovered Alexander's friends were priggish and denying. They gossiped that he never had and never would make me his wife, this particularly painful information supposedly gathered from Alexander's mouth. Yet, I remained confident and calm. They were ignorant. Uninformed. Blind as sheep headed straight for a sheering. I wrinkled at the thought of Alexander's friends and their wagging tongues, distributing lies and hardships about the truthfulness of not our love. Alexander and I were scholars. Objective. The others: erroneous, misinformed. Alexander had left Brattleboro to attend to his preaching engagement, and was not due back for weeks. I thought when he returned he would make our love public and certain. He would relieve me from New Haven's babbling frauds.

I told Leonard about Brattleboro because I had to. He had already circuitously found out some details. He asked that I disclose all of our exchanges—the river, the water and the way—all the while stroking his chin with bony fingers and inhaling too deep not to know. He fidgeted when I alluded to the leach of space in Alexander's eyes.

I told Leonard because I had to. *I told him so. I told him so.* I could see he wanted to pound his fist through the eye and ear of every wall. In Leonard's gaze, the fury he spoke flamed as when he worked to deny the sins burning eternal with damnation. Although he might explode, pushing all of New Haven from the stern of his chest, he sat impatiently listening. I cried, and I was not that kind of woman. I told him Miss. Catharine's untrustworthy mouth was ruining my reputation. If the spreading news of my unladylike conduct continued at such a pace, I would never be able to lecture again. Because I might ruin, Leonard listened.

"I love you, dear sister," he said. "Of course your loving brother will assist. I am always at your side, bound by blood. I have your best intentions in mind, devoted Delia, and you, in turn, should have mine."

The community loved Leonard, impossible to not. He had everyone's best interests at heart. Leonard informed all others of my true and noble person, and the women still attended my lectures, despite or because of the talking. Leonard impressed my genuine and solid spirit upon them, and circulated the virtuosity of my vocalizations. Leonard, as always, was correct. Most everyone believed him.

Perhaps some of the women merely felt sorry for me; perhaps they believed I would be jilted. Some of them gazed at heaven with saint's salver eyes while I mouthed the making of history. They might be sad or sorry. Some afterwards gave thanks, deliberately patting my hand thin and gloved as if we shared the same kind of knowing. Despite previous attempts to render me untrustworthy, ruined, soon I had secretaries. People began to write me down, not inflicted by a supposed lovelorn suffering. Despite fabrications attempted to displace me, I stood true as any patriarch. People knew of my importance. Leonard knew, and Leonard knew I knew.

Alexander. A month of his absence passed while I worked on my career, alone. I waited for him to return and correct the town's misplaced gossip, alone. I knew he would clear the scandalous air like spring-felt sunshine and let the world know of our inevitable engagement. Alexander was the only one who could do it—he and he alone.

One day Leonard saw him strolling the streets as if nothing had happened, as if he and Leonard's sister had not spent prior weeks in loving conversations. Alexander. He sauntered as if we had not decided to spend the rest of our lives in love. Alexander. Leonard interrupted his arrogant, youthful swagger to ask of his marital intentions.

Leonard later reported to me Alexander's surprise, accusing me, loving sister, of lying through my eyes. Leonard's face peeled into waves of rage. He described how he made Alexander promise to make certain on his proposal, threatening a future of bringing congregations to their knees from the powerful position of the pulpit. Leonard told Alexander not to make me lie. Leonard said Alexander shrugged, said nothing, and carried on moving like ephemeral weather.

"Either you or he are a liar, Delia, and I trust the falsity can not come from my own flesh and blood. We are too piously Christian and wanting to suffer at the hands of some young rogue. He has used his way to the top. Leave him to me. I shall see to his decline." Poor Alexander. Leonard muttered, and I barely heard through broken breath: "That is the last time at our meetings he displays such grotesque intricacies as my sister's heart."

This was when I understood that perhaps I was involved in something strange, unseen, unsurfaced. I already knew about the prominent men gathering forbidden discussions. In New Haven, the Skull and Bones. In England, Fraternity, Rosy Cross. They talked together of wooing and wanting. They revealed every intimate detail to one another, recorded everything in a thick black book. Brothers, patriarchs, they shared their interests. They were their own best penetrations.

I could not help but ask my brother, my patriarch, my fraternal bond: "Leonard? Do you go to those secret society meetings? On Sundays after church?"

Leonard's eyes hazed over.

"Keep your interests to yourself. I will hear of them no longer. If you are wanting, ask your brother. Only then can I save you." Condescension and pity plumped his fleshy lips: "Remember this: I don't want to know every confidential facet of your heart. I have listened long enough. I know your every curve, more than you would ever like to know. Rules are rules and I refuse." Leonard rose and began to pace, inwardly arguing. With each step his skin peeled, exposing skeletal truths.

"I do not fear the vastness of your knowledge nor the rattling of your skull and bones." After I said those words, he vanished. Leonard and Alexander were both members. Say the name and they evaporate like water.

I needed to contemplate. Who was who and who worked against me? Alexander said he loved me. Leonard saved my soul. Brothers? Which was which? Truth? I loved Leonard. I loved Alexander. I waited, seeking a sure and uncontested proof. But who was who?

A few days after our conversation, Leonard told me of a plan to ensure that Alexander never preached again. He spoke of Alexander's devilish chameleon skin, not fit for the Lord or loving. The only part of his scheme with which I did not agree was the requirement that I never speak to Alexander again. Because I saw the way the storms brewed danger across Leonard's brow forming bilious clouds of murky consternation, with uncertainty, I vowed preliminary consent.

I spent time in solitude away from the gossip of the town thinking, studying. I was conscious of my love nearby but possibly no longer near. Not once did Alexander try to reach me. Through infrequent interactions with the grocer and people on the street, I heard rumors of trouble that shook and rattled our worlds divided.

One of my cousins came to visit and brought news of Alexander displaying my side of our intimate correspondence to every man around—every friend he had with a mouth to hee and haw like unsympathetic asses. I was advised by my cousin to get my half of our letters back, regardless of what I had to do. I became desperate.

I extricated myself from solitude to tell as many people as I could about my certainty of Alexander's marriage proposal. If Alexander chose to expose my letters, this wasn't too terrible. While Alexander's disregard for our privacy was distressing, as my future husband, I had to believe he was using his discretion. Once married, I was certain everything would work. I needed to speak with Alexander directly, but he seemed always busy with other activities.

Soon after I began to tell everyone of our deep and trusted love, an acquaintance informed me that Alexander was flatly denying his marriage proposal. Alexander was composing me as despicable, unforgivable, and calling me a liar. He said my mind wasn't properly working, that I believed secret societies were conspiring against my success as a writer and using him as a pawn. He joked about the way I read Shakespeare, he blasphemed everything of our love. He told people he couldn't understand why so many women desired to listen to the ramblings of a loon.

My heart turned volcanic liquid and coursed. I could not concentrate from a heat so intense I could not bear it. I was hurt and confused. I turned into a hell from a liquid heart that threatened to spill and purge.

It was imperative for me to retrieve my letters. I wrote to him and told him my love was finished now, gone. I told him I didn't want to believe what wasn't true. I did not want him for a friend or companion or brother or lover. I suggested he burn his hateful ash heart into the mouth of loneliness. I imagined shoving the pen he gave, false token, undeniable symbol, into his throat so when he spoke ink would splatter everything with the words: *I shall never be forgiven.* I returned his theological essays. I broke his pen, surprised at how easily it shattered.

He wrote to tell me he was still my faithful. He said I was in too brittle of a position, asking if I newly hurt.

Are the birds back? he asked, insisting I knew of our love's proof. He said I shouldn't listen to harping mouths full of jealousy. *How can you be so childish and subjective, Delia, to believe these other untruths?*

I wrote back: *For good, farewell.* I couldn't understand the contradictions speaking, but I understood Leonard's rage consistently on the verge.

Apparently Alexander received my final letter surrounded by friends. He laughed. He passed it around, enjoying the attentions of his circle. Everyone chuckled, exposing muscles. He said I was the one who proposed. He prattled and said I tried to seduce him, I was desperate, in love, I believed I had birds in my head, I was full of fevers. He said the worst for what was true.

Then Mr. Robert told Miss. Jane told Mr. Eleazar told Mrs. Thomas and this returned. In circular fashion, the intimacies of personal letters were made known to me via Mrs. Thomas, Mr. Eleazar, Miss. Jane, Mr. Robert that only Alexander could have known. He had betrayed me. I hated his many-hearted leanings. I despised him so much I once again burned his words.

My reputation was fizzling. People were beginning to wonder at me confused. I got sick again with slight fever and felt I could no longer stand. All of the beneficial effects of the water cure drowned in me after a few weeks and I was as sickly as before. I decided I must spare my reputation at all costs. I consulted with Leonard, uncertain of what he wanted us to do.

He planned an official investigation because, he said, it was imperative we clear our name. I asked Harriet to help, but she stayed far away from the mess of my molten heart. I wrote down in excruciating detail everything that happened with and under the water and how it once cured my beating, bird-bound body.

I came to the conclusion that Alexander was the one who must be mad. We couldn't both be lying. We couldn't both have told the truth. No one would act first the lover, then unreasonably shift and turn. He must have lost his reason in the last weeks of water. He must have feared drowning from the taking of his mother. His hands shook lunatic. He was confused. This was the truth.

In court we would determine nothing but the truth. Leonard, loving brother, on my right side. Alexander must not be able to preach because he'd lost his sight. Leonard would fight, saving my speech. Leonard had my true whole heart in mind. No sinner should preach the vicissitudes of love.

There was an official trial, and Alexander and I were to be judged.

———

A list of the members of the Skull and Bones society is now available online for public perusal. You are familiar with at least two former members: Leonard Bacon and Alexander MacWhorter. However, there is another historical Leonard Bacon and Alexander MacWhorter who were also public figures and well known. Both Alexanders happened to be preachers. One attended Yale. One didn't. The Alexander that Delia falls in love with attended Yale. He is the other Alexander's grandson.

The two Leonard Bacons are both Yale Alums; one was a preacher famous for his hymns who graduated in 1820, and the other was a well-known poet who completed school in 1909. In the list of Skull and Bones, there is surprisingly no date of membership listed next to Leonard Bacon's name. However, there are dates for almost every other member presented. This is a mysterious omission. Alexander MacWhorter's date is listed: 1842. He met Delia Bacon in 1844.

It is difficult to figure out which Leonard Bacon may have been a Skull. Consider, for example, Leonard Bacon's 1820 classmate and later president of Yale, Theodore Dwight Woolsey. Officially, he couldn't have been a Skull. He, like Leonard, graduated in 1820 before the Skulls' commencement in 1832. It is a society whose members are usually chosen from the senior class.

But hold your horses, dear reader, hold your bones. There is a Theodore *White* Woolsey on the roster of Skull and Bones who is also listed, like Leonard, mysteriously without a date of membership.

Consider this: the Skull and Bones were established by a Yale student named William H Russell after he traveled to Germany and befriended the leader of a secret society there. Theodore Dwight Woolsey is known to have studied Greek in Leipzig, Bonn and Berlin before he began his professorship and subsequent presidency at Yale. Maybe the supposed founder, William H Russell, didn't exist. Maybe he was a prop for the mysterious Theodore *White* Woolsey (a.k.a. Theodore Dwight Woolsey), who was the true originator of the Skull and Bones? Maybe "White" was a typo. Maybe not. Maybe so. But alas, William H Russell did exist. I've seen portraits of him looking down his distinguished nose.

Eminent members of the Yale faculty were often invited to become members of the Skull and Bones after its initial inauguration. These older, honored men were called "patriarchs". I've recently discovered that Theodore Dwight Woolsey was indeed a patriarch and that he planted a garden on the grounds of the Skull and Bones tomb that today is still in use.

Maybe Delia Bacon's brother Reverend Leonard Bacon was also a patriarch of the Skull and Bones? Maybe Leonard Bacon and Alexander MacWhorter's membership in the Skull and Bones is crucial evidence to explain Delia Bacon's slow descent into madness? Maybe her discovery of the Skull and Bones was integral to her theory that a secret society was responsible for the authorship of the Shakespearean cannon? Maybe the Skull and Bones are truly an innocuous group who just enjoy an occasional romp dressed in black robes while chanting to a goddess named Eulogia? Maybe it's simply a matter of harmless, amateur theatrics? Maybe not, maybe so...

Sunday hauled itself over the mountains and Rebecca knew she should go to church, but John still hadn't returned, and she was embarrassed. She didn't want to tell the other worshipers that for days John would leave her while she stared at light fixtures alone and prayed. They were a team. They worked together and could not be seen apart. She decided she would later tell her congregation she had been ill. She got into her car to drive around, looking for something to do.

She drove for over an hour. She decided to visit a national park to climb the tallest peak in the state to look down from above this tiny earth. She parked her car as close as she could so the people who lived in the houses at the foot would not come out with shotguns. She stepped out of her car and up. She saw brown all around in the rubble of rocks. She thought of Elaine. She invoked her on the dirt.

She first met Elaine when she was tormented by demons. Elaine worshiped with devils and would howl at night like the wolf at the moon. Rebecca loved Elaine, who would tell stories of frog crackle and lizard tongue. She was a witch like in storybooks. She sacrificed babies and lambs and covered herself in blood and chanted and called to the devil. Elaine was Rebecca's best and most interesting fictional friend. She and John decided one day to make her up, to make an example of her in Rebecca's books, but now Rebecca could not live without her. Elaine was as imaginary as dust, but she and John needed something for their followers; they needed evidence for them to believe in. With the invention of Elaine, Rebecca found someone to conjure the truth from readers' hearts so they would profess their love to Jesus. She needed Elaine for creating the belief that she had the power to dispossess even the worst of women from sins. Elaine had become more real than the mountain and Rebecca needed her.

Elaine walked with her through the trees and rocks and dirt. Branches and brambles sunk through the atmospheres of Elaine's air-made skin. Elaine asked her about John.

Start from the beginning, she said. *Tell me about how you came to know your place into this heaven here on earth.* Elaine looked at Rebecca and trees glistened through her teeth.

John worked at a bowling alley in Fort Smith and fixed the machines that set the pins if they ever broke. Rebecca went there occasionally to throw a ball down the lane because she liked the sounds of the rumble and crack. It reminded her of God stomping through the lightning flickered nights. One day she decided to see where the ball went after it hit the pins. She saw a man in a brown suit walk through a small door at the side of the alley, so she decided to follow him. Behind the door was all metal and gadget. The machines cracked and grinded like people that chew and lose their teeth. John noticed her and snuck up behind. He grabbed her waist and she jumped.

"You don't belong back here. Where are you going?"

"I just wanted to see the machines."

"Let me give you a tour." He led and Rebecca followed. They walked while he pointed at the metal contraptions. He told her what each part was for and she listened, even though she couldn't hear over the crash and ramble of the jawbones that crunched. When they reached the end of the alley, he took her into an office. He picked her up and set her on a desk. Jesus and his bleeding heart lined the walls in calendars, posters, busts.

"Do you pray?" He asked, and Rebecca nodded. "Then I don't have to ask you to join us." John lifted up her shirt.

At the middle of the mountain Rebecca realized she had to stop. She was tired. She looked for Elaine. She had disappeared during the story to return to the places of babbling brooks. Perhaps Rebecca needed to invent another woman who would not leave her in these times of need. Perhaps she needed to find another character who she could make an example of, locked behind walls until she saw the rights of her wrongs and could be forgiven.

Rebecca looked down. She thought she might be able to see as far as a coast, so she strained to look. Everything was rocky brown or congested green and hot. From this distance, the trees below looked like mangled figures twisted from a hellish heat.

After that day at the bowling alley, John had soon brought his shirts, underwear and bibles to Rebecca's house and began requiring her to make soup. Rebecca did what he wanted, because she was tired of being alone. John reminded her of how important it was to pray and always think of God. He told her if she was good, she would hear him, if she would listen, he would speak. Rebecca believed him. John told her to stay inside and think about her sins. He told her to study the bible and prepare for war on earth. Shortly after, they began to write her books.

Plants scratched at her legs like the dead. She knew she must go home to try to write something soon or they would all fall down.

———

Rebecca's phone rang and she jumped. She must have fallen asleep. The morning sun seeped into the window and warmed her legs and feet. Sophia drooled and stared at her like a stranger. Rebecca's stomach had smoothed out. She attempted to shake the incomprehensibility of her dreams and rolled from the couch, practically crushing Sophia. Rebecca moved across the floor with rapid, rubbery kicks. She slithered to answer the phone, trying to soothe out the hisses in her voice. She picked up the receiver with what she realized must be an overly-obsessive "Elaine?"

"Hello, my darling serpentine. You must miss me."

"God, Elaine. When are you coming back? What are you doing? Did you get the poems I sent you? How's the research?"

"Jesus, Rebecca. Slow down. I'm fine. Research is fine. I still don't know when I'll be able to come home. Swami Vivakananda? What's gotten into you? It's just not like you at all. '*In the roaring, whirling wind are the souls of a million lunatics just loosed from the prison-house, wrenching trees by the roots, sweeping all from the path?*' Are you okay?"

"I thought you'd like him. He was instrumental in bringing that whole 'we are one' universal consciousness stuff to the States. I don't know."

"Speaking of consciousness...how's writing?"

"Good. I mean, not good. I'm not actually writing anything. Just thinking a lot, as usual. But Elaine, I am twisted and fucked without you. This is not right."

"We talked about this. You need me; I need this time. Patience. My work comes first right now. Why don't you go for a walk? Cook some soup? Learn how to sew or something? Keep yourself busy. What about your students?"

"They are not you."

"What's wrong? Are you eating meat again? I told you about beef and depression. You've got to eat more vegetables. They have enzymes. Meat equals melancholy."

"No. I don't know. Maybe. That's not it. That's not it at all. There's no one around except Sophia. I'm just...alone. Suffering. Lethargic. Anxious. You choose."

"Remember. Learn to be uncomfortable. Micromanage your ennui. How is Sophia?"

"Drooling."

"Well. I'm not sure what else I can say. You've got to take care of this on your own. I've really got to go. I've found a new bin in the archives with some particularly interesting diaries written by women who were once committed here. I have so much work now…But Rebecca?"

"Yes?"

"I love you."

"I love you, too. Please come home."

"Soon. I'll call you again soon."

Rebecca listened to the high-pitched buzz before hanging up. In it, she heard the distance spread between them filled with wastes of time. She thought:

breathing with passion anew, and wound with many a river, i find old mail addressed to you. you are a terrible girl. you are some demon's mistress, or the demon's self.

you leave me full of silver moons as i howl like a wolf, interwreathed luster with gloomier tapestries. maybe you've found something new. how are you living with the living barely living? i stare at vacant places. i am touched with misery without you.

By the time she finishes, she is furious with her discomfort. She has had to deal with it most of her life—from the time she was split in two. She wishes she had something to strangle and strike, but she realizes the familiar consolation of historical repetitions would not relieve her ancient wounds.

Rebecca knew the best thing to do was to get out of the house. She decided to spend the rest of the day in her office, and she hoped she would not run into anyone who might see uneasiness flushing her skin scarlet with those memories.

SEVEN

O God, let not Passion lead me now. The centre beaming truth,
not passion's narrow ray, must light me here! But am I not his?
Delia Bacon

NURSE ELAINE SAYS I am becoming stronger. She stands in the corner of my room and stares with eyes nicely lustrous. I can see the outside reflected in trees that green themselves with the wind waving their vegetable heads back and forth in hypnotic comfort. She wears a white smock spotted with yellow. When I ask her what the yellow is, she blinks her head nodding back and says help from beams of sunray. She looks with a sanguine smile between it placed with tiny teeth. Her hair is wire like brown. She holds my hand while I sleep.

When I dream, she tells me Leonard loves me. She hands me papers, books and pens, and says how good. She is always there, more real than I remember. She whispers my only friend. She holds me while I take my stand.

*

I took the witness stand against my once and only love Alexander. I had to save myself from drowning in all of the arms that would gladly push me into the water just to see me not afloat, determined of my flailing. They tried to submerge me, floundering witch with hair spread out like frogs' legs. I would fight to deny them.

I hadn't seen Alexander eye to eye since I knew he had betrayed me. Time and a thousand ghastly rumors helped control my urging. He shifted away from me how the amoeba hides its flagellation beneath the black eye of the microscopic lens.

Leonard initially arranged for a lawyer to represent me, but then decided he would do most of the speaking, the sort of man who set them reeling. He believed we had Yale President Theodore Dwight Woolsey on our side, and Mr. Woolsey planned to sit behind me in the newly-fashioned ecclesiastical courtroom of Mr. Jeremiah Day's parlor. Leonard thought Mr. Woolsey would remind the community who to believe, a gentle patriarch strong and overlooking.

Alexander's ability to preach as a sober man of right constitution was to be determined, and everyone from the New Haven West Association and Yale's Theological Department had an interest in the case. I was the prime witness against his malevolence. To show he wronged me was to illustrate he was not seated on the right side of the Lord and could not speak spiritually uplifting true Christian followers because of the wavering lilts of hypocrisy.

Some men tried to protect him. They wanted to keep Yale orders concretized; they wished to protect their institutions. Leonard did not desire to tear down those standing brick by brick, he being situated comfortably between; instead, he had personal problems with Alexander. Because Alexander humiliated me, because he spread disgrace like ripples to everyone he touched, Leonard wished to defeat him. Leonard said our once love contaminated everyone.

Although I didn't wish to risk a display of vulnerability, Leonard told me I must take the stand despite a face fraught with fragile dispositions. I did not want to sit in front of all of those gasping people, their leering picking clean like worms did skeletons. Despite my pleading, Leonard told me that I must. He told me to remain firm and solid, a pillar of his community.

These were Alexander's counts:

Calumny, Falsehood, and Disgraceful Conduct, as a man, a Christian, and especially as a candidate for the Christian ministry.

I was the main witness that would provide key evidence of his devastating fabrications. Leonard also asked Miss. Catharine to testify, but she wanted no part in this condemnation. After Leonard requested her presence at my side, she replied to him by letter. He read her sentences aloud:

Reverend: You are represented as a man that will crush and cut and slash and sympathy is awakened for a young novice—fallen into the hands of an artful woman—with such a brother to back her.

Apparently Miss. Catherine believed I was "artful", a rough-limbed doll made out of parts twined and plied with a needle. Apparently she believed my brother some sort of shear. Did her sympathies lie with the poor, naïve, novice Alexander? Leonard's duty in the trial was to convince the jury my truths were not fictitious, that I was not contrived as a pieced together graft. Although she would not take the stand in my defense, Miss. Catharine did agree to sit in the courtroom nearby to listen. She was given permission to hover and compile notes on the situation. She decided to use the dalliances of the courtroom to work on the draft of a new manuscript.

When the trial finally began, and Mr. Day's parlor was aswarm with men judging and discerning, I was conscious of the sound of Miss. Catharine's small hands scuffing pen to paper, inking every tear and facial twitch. Although her presence was mildly comforting (she was often the only other woman in the room), she also made me dizzy with her attention. I wondered if she were working to support me, or if she was merely assisting herself with the building of a new book.

Although tediously extensive (two weeks, ninety six hours), the trial was a windstorm. So much stirred uncontrollable while words spun like scraps of paper I once pinned to twirl on my skirts. People who testified against me said I was some sort of witch with magical influence who could charm young boys into submission. They cited my affects as a teacher. They said during my lectures ladies' eyes lustered, as if drawn by magnets toward earth. They believed I had a geometric attraction to the ground like some sorceress luring loves into her nightgown. Witnesses said there was power in my voice lower than the average woman's and that I unnaturally convinced masculinic. They insinuated at night I turned myself into a man and roamed the streets arguing intoxicated in a state that was and was not me. These people said Alexander was innocent, just a boy, wrongly taken advantage of by someone older and controlling who robbed him of desire. They said I fed him magical sweets that turned his tongue red and illuminated his throbbing heart. They said I slipped him asleep while I breathed in his breath to steal his youthful innocence. They said I was on fire from devil doings. I never blinked or bulged or turned furious under the scrutiny of these accusations. If there were those that tried to condemn me, I had my brother piously fervent to convince them the light of my soul was protected by a God who knew I was wanting. Leonard lied my Christian spirit: *reputation, reputation, reputation.*

The most painful accusations came from Miss. Hattie Blake, one of my former students who once listened to my lectures while I encouraged her to daydream. She wanted to sail on ships across oceans to merchant as only men could. I had once told her she might do anything she set herself towards because a dream was like a compass. She excelled in my class and studied harder than any other girl in order to impress me. Imagine my disappointment as she took the stand.

Miss. Blake would look in my direction guiltily as if I were a thief, but it is futile to condemn the unimaginative. She had met Alexander after he returned from Brattleboro and instantly fell into his void. Miss. Catharine saw Miss. Blake often following wherever he went, Alexander's Shadow. She became the fins of his coattails that swam continent to continent gathering sea muck. Her hair turned to seaweed as she latched upon his wavelets and she wouldn't let go until he drowned beneath her dragging. Attached like that, she would never recognize herself for dreaming.

As far as I knew, Alexander did not return Miss. Blake's affections, but I also realized I knew nothing about this supposed and surreptitious Alexander. He had communicated secretly a cipher I could not read, and didn't know existed. What I knew was I had lost friends and associates in our lovelorn schism; people took sides and turned affections. In this respect, Alexander and I were still similarly divided. We shared a reflection twinned by parallel partitions.

During the trial, Alexander sat patiently while his witnesses counter-testified and were cross-examined. He sat parallel to me perpendicular so I could barely make out the shapes of his hands occasionally on his head leaning his fate hopefully innocent. He never looked in my direction. This was the first time we were in the same space since we were both submerged in Brattleboro water. I felt slight heart flutter nothing magnificent nor beating as the baby birds that once brained themselves against the ribs of my cage. I began to believe in Leonard. I abhorred Alexander's physical closeness far away in the courtroom, knowing I now knew nothing. I detested how he troubled me, how he challenged my certainty. There will never be anyone else like him. I will never tell the truth to those who profess their love.

At some time during the drawn-out hours when Leonard raged and fumed and cut and slashed those who would question my character into the spindly finger pricking mechanics of a sorceress, I had to speak in my own defense. I walked toward the front of the room, and could feel my heart pounding through the fabric of my dress that strangled from the inside. The drapery of my skin bled and ornamented my body like a massacre. My mind pulsed. I could see the muscles of my toes as they tightened over my shoes reluctantly pacing to the front of the room. I sat down and looked out upon faces concealed and controlled. I could not become them. Everyone was together inside in and I was splayed into bareness like a body that had burst. Alexander looked wooden and puppeteered, most especially collected. Leonard was like a god sculpting fury through the clay.

"Sister Delia," Leonard began to cast coats of stone, "tell us of your acquaintance with Mr. Alexander MacWhorter."

I looked at my brother and felt myself turn from flesh to fluid. I could not control my body's burgeon. The courtroom began to fill with papers eddied at my ankles. I was at Brattleboro while Alexander helped me enter a deep pit of the river, and this time he was not scared. He held his hand out and waited while I lifted my skirt. I felt the freeze from toe to ankle, my body electric, weaving its way to my thighbone. Alexander looked into my eyes as I sank. He did not look below my neck as I felt the fullness around me, rising. Miniscule fish swam through my legs, but I was not afraid.

Once was once and now was now and the seas dried up vast and desiccated. I was in Mr. Jeremiah Day's parlor. I had been asked a question. Sacks of people impatiently awaited. The air was voluminous and heavy, bags of sand.

"Miss. Bacon? Compose yourself, sister. Can you answer?" Leonard spoke as if comforting the little lambs of his flock, but in his eyes I could see he would not be easy for long. Acute as a compass needle, he steeled me back to obedience. Alexander was just behind Leonard looking, and this made everything worse. If I were to notice his eyes, oceans would drown out the desert.

"Yes. The question. Please repeat it." I felt my face swelling cloud storms. Hot rank wind blew over. Leonard began to shift a little, then a little more, rocking back and forth. He moved, and Alexander was visible in front of me. I felt his eyes. They were terrified.

"Please explain the nature of your relationship to Mr. MacWhorter."

Clouds gathered tight as pits in my cheekbones that condensed the inside in.

"I can not," strangled the words. Every syllable took a breath. The emptiness of language parched me.

"Obviously we must continue questioning another day." Leonard looked me into infanthood and turned to address the court. "The witness is unable to provide her testimony at this time."

Rain. My face released a barrage.

Alexander stood and left, shifting through moving streams to the door where he could save himself from drowning. If he had stayed the length of my testimony, I could not have carried on.

Moments passed. The air cleared of cloud but still remained thick.

"I can answer. Please, let's resume."

"What were the circumstances behind your introduction to Mr. MacWhorter?"

"We met at the Tontine Hotel. I was a boarder. I was studying and working, and hadn't had much contact with the outside world. Another boarder invited me to supper and I noticed Mr. MacWhorter eavesdropping on our conversation. He introduced himself and I invited him to meet with me for future discussion."

"Did he accept your invitation?"

"Yes. He visited my room that very same day."

"And you didn't send him away?"

"No."

"Why not? Miss. Bacon, surely you would want to give an enterprising young man time for individual contemplations?"

I could not explain why I did not discount him. I could not talk about the way he held his hand with longing and I unknowingly shook, impossible to relay Alexander as my only brother, lover, husband.

I summoned my manners. I consulted my memory. I pooled myself from river to rain to cloud to birds beating to before language scrawled my hands into meaning, before I was Alexander.

"Your honorable Reverend Bacon. I am a teacher, a respectable woman, as some of the members in this room shall testify. I have never led my students astray when it came to knowledge and learning. I have taught them to look beyond surface appearances, discerning their own truths within history. I have never turned a student away from my door, nor have I denied the opportunity to discuss knowledge with fellow scholars. I knew Alexander to be a budding student of divinity. He asked that we might discuss our intellectual interests, and for this I could not refuse. He was ripe for learning, and I had no intentions of being anything other than a respected colleague. Perhaps, in some ways, a muse."

The lies came easily enough, each syllable reduced to a thick and authoritative sound. I pronounced every sentence as if it were the last to leave me. These were the first lies I ever told. I focused on rendering Alexander shape-shifter, everything deceptive. I behaved like Leonard. I followed the patterns of his motions and mirrored his convictions with a strength rarely before known. One day the others would see Alexander for what he truly was. He would end up in his own forgettable histories. This was no fault of my own.

*

For now, I must be done. Lights that attempt to escape from the hallway blink out while Elaine shifts unpleasantly near. Rain plies the windows, attempting to get in. I sleep beneath the fact of this ever-present water.

———

Now you must determine who is guilty. Determine what is true.

I once served on the jury for a trial where a man stole a pile of designer jeans from a department store by walking in, stacking them in his arms, and casually walking out the door. He had unfortunately stolen one pair too many to make his crime a felony instead of a misdemeanor for a third strike and was caught on camera, head turning left to right, loading up his arms, and leaving. The man on the video was clearly the same man sitting across from me in the courtroom. He was guilty beyond a shadow of a doubt.

As I waited through the proceedings, which lasted a few hours too many, I wondered why I was sitting there in the first place. It was bothersome for me to be paid five dollars a day to watch middle-aged people flirt with one another in the selection room. I was angry I had been chosen. The prosecuting attorney compiled charts and graphs. The arguments went back and forth like an unexciting tennis match. This is not my client. This is your client. That is not my client. That is your client.

When our jury left to deliberate, one man decided the defendant was not necessarily guilty because the videotape could have been tampered with. I thought about this for two minutes. I considered agreeing with the annoying, contentious juror and realized I could not tell the truth. Our jury split. The man could have been another man. He could not have been himself. Although there was a video, there was no solid proof. The case went to retrial.

I was once almost chosen to be a prosecutor on *Judge Judy*. I was suing a man who had accidentally pulled the bumper off of my car while trying to back out of a parking lot while drunk in Tijuana. The parking lot attendants fortunately saw this accident and made the man wait for my inebriated return. We exchanged contact information, and I asked him and his buddies to pose for a picture with their forty-ounce bottles of malt liquor raised in perpetual toast to the damaged bumper of my car. They complied. Because of the photographic evidence, the interviewer for *Judge Judy* said the defendant did not have a case and therefore we were not going to appear on the show. I have never quite forgiven him for this missed opportunity of celebrity. When I called to collect payment he said, "I don't know what you are talking about. That isn't me. Who are you?" He told me he wasn't the man for whom I was asking, but it was him, I am certain, not telling the truth.

I once considered suing the hospital because Satanists tried to poison my food. During my clinicals, I noticed every lunch hour that certain members of the staff would stare at me to see if I would swallow my cafeteria peas. Often God would stop me just before with a shout. I tried to gather evidence to prove I was a victim of the Satanists' plots and taped tiny hairs to my locker to see if anyone attempted a break in. They did, yet I could not tell who. I asked the security guard for copies of the surveillance videos in order to expose those planning my demise. He would not comply. I considered suing him for conspiracy. I thought about purchasing a miniature camera equipped for my clipboard; I couldn't rely on the justice system and had to fight these demons with my own truths.

Here is the proof:
Rebecca Brown is a Christian fundamentalist, concerned with saving people's souls. She writes books that warn people about demonic possession. Rebecca believes she can deliver the word. She and her husband John are inspired by their distorted versions of the truth.
Rebecca Brown is a fiction writer fighting the tyranny of a snaking depression. She is desirous, wanting. Her lover Elaine searches through the

archives of The Institute for Living and discovers manuscripts written by many well-known women. Rebecca hasn't been feeling very inspired because of her absent lover, yet she believes in the power of emotional truth.

Rebbecca Brown is a struggling poet. She is elusive, a liar, completely untrue.

Delia Bacon has been glossed over historically except for as a lunatic who created a theory of secretive authorial circles. During her lifetime, she was considered brilliant. Both Nathaniel Hawthorne and Ralph Waldo Emerson respected her scholarly determination, but now she has been almost forgotten. Which Delia presented in the historical records is true?

And, then, there is you. Who are you? Who are you? Who are you?

———

When she arrived back at home, Rebecca noticed that some of John's shirts were gone. Sometimes he left for a few hours, sometimes a few days, but he never left a note, and she knew not to ask him. The first time she questioned him about where he was going, he made her write the following a hundred times in a row:

Who are you to judge someone else's servant? To his own master he stands or falls.

She wrote and wrote until her hand was numb. John had taped it to their refrigerator to remind her of what she'd done. When she was young, her mother would tape up Rebecca's drawings of circles stacked on top of each other like masses of faces or balls.

She once had a favorite red ball. The ball was plastic and larger than her head. She first saw the ball in a metal basket at the supermarket and stared at it until she was lost. Her mother left her staring. Rebecca could not stop looking at the bright red ball. When she had finished shopping, her mother came back to the basket and unburied the red orb from the blues and greens. She put the ball in the cart and Rebecca followed the ball to the counter and all the way home.

She loved her ball and could not help but follow it wherever it might go. It bounced higher than the roof, higher than the blue of sky. It bounced in the dust and made clouds full of animals, heaven, and prophets. It bounced against the house and exploded through the walls. It bounced across streets and turned into a chariot led by horses with nostrils puffing fire. It bounced and sometimes Rebecca was not there to bounce it. Sometimes it bounced on its own.

Sometimes the ball turned into people she knew and said things she did not understand. It was the first nonhuman thing that spoke to her. Mostly it said things like "dloop dloop dloop" or "shlip shlip dloop" and since sometimes she did not understand she made the meaning up. Once the ball told her through bouncing syllables she was going to be a dancer. It told her she would bounce like the ball up through the air and when at the top, she would explode like a firework. The ball told her Francis liked the taste of spaghetti. The ball also told her she might be famous. It said one day she might save the entire world.

The ball talked for weeks and she followed, listening. One day it told her it was getting tired of bouncing and telling secrets with a plastic bouncing tongue. It bounced far across the dust and landed in a tree. She saw a family of crows that did not love the ball because they began to peck at it until it popped. Sometimes late at night, she thought she still heard the ball's voice flattened and slurring. Sometimes she still listens for the ball's thoughts in other things.

Rebecca looks out the window to see if there is any evidence of John leaving or returning. There are no new tire tracks or secret messages in the trees. She sees the mailman pull to the edge of their dirt driveway and drop letters inside. Carefully, she makes her way down to check. She does not want to attract the attention of any demons that might be floating by. She has to make sure there are no bombs or anthrax in her letters.

All she receives are a few Christian catalogues. She is in luck. She says a silent "thanks be to God", but knows he is still not in the mood to speak or listen. In one catalogue, men and women smile in white robes bedecked with threads and crosses. They are clean like doctors and surgeons. Their teeth are straight in a row like posts. Rebecca sticks her finger in her mouth and touches her teeth. They feel like unorganized stones.

In the catalogue, slightly wrinkled inside her crimson hands, she sees a blood red crucifix lined with cubic zirconium and plated with gold for two hundred dollars. Rebecca wonders how she might afford it. If she didn't donate as much to the congregation this month, she could save for the crucifix, and this would count as another type of devotion. Or, she could use some of the money she earned from the sale of her books, which were doing especially well now in the south. She needed to ask John when he returned. She flipped through the pages and stared at the people. They were models of the Lord.

She thinks:

Hello. Hello. Hello. God? Do you think I should buy it?

No response. She thought of lashing herself with a nylon filled with stones from the driveway and bearing pain in an obvious display of devotion, but she didn't feel like gathering rocks. She considered trying to talk to John to see if he might answer, but if she did, he might be angry she was disturbing his peace and place. Rebecca wandered into her room again and stared at the ceiling, trying not to sleep so she would be awake in case anyone, someday, somewhere, might want to listen or talk.

———

Rebecca walked through the main campus to the English Department, careful to avoid the Biology building. She did not want to run into Dr. Leonard, a herpetologist who once followed her around for a year with plastic baggies and tweezers, hoping to catch wayward flakes of her skin. Dr. Leonard became interested in the scale of her legs when he sat next to her at a graduation ceremony. It was a particularly humid spring, and Rebecca's squirm and scratch drew his attention. He stared at the bottom of her gown with no attempts to deny it. She hissed, he winked, and she fought for years to avoid him.

Dr. Leonard was a beetle-like man who peered through too small lenses with eyes too large to be anything other than licentious. One of Rebecca's graduate students told her he liked to call his female students "fucking dimwits" if they did poorly on his test about amphibian bones. Dr. Leonard was frequently in trouble with the administration for displaying twittering fears of women through random expulsions of profanity and disgust. Rebecca also heard rumors of his attempts to seduce some of the more timid female undergraduates, and sometimes as she walked by his office window she would see him leaning over their shoulders close, too close for them to muster a modicum of comfort. These girls sat rigid, apparently afraid to move or breathe lest they happen to brush a muscle. Rebecca didn't know what bothered her the most, girls without backbones or men covert with outrageous compulsions for unrequited lust.

Rebecca arrived at her office and had to move piles of papers from her desk to clear space enough to work. The room was filled with books and projects former students had left throughout the years. There were collages with pictures of lipsticked lips uttering words like "écriture féminine," "transcendental signifier," "differánce," paintings of many armed women and abstract expressions of crotch, a mobile of dangling ideological state apparati, and sculptures of bulging masses of god knows what. A former student who moved on to study at a prestigious Ph.D. program somewhere in the Midwest made these clay abominations to represent something about language, confusion, and loss. Rebecca remembered her student's presentation, how she talked of monuments and mythology, language constituting itself into oft-incoherent lumps. Her student had taken these hunks of clay and thrown them at the classroom wall in order to shatter them at the penultimate moment in her presentation, but the chunks had cloddishly bounced off in solid thumps—codified, knobbed. Rebecca's student had been shattered herself, upset to the point of tears at her failure to destroy the unique "language" she had created with her own hands. Points earned and point taken: Rebecca gave her an "A".

Rebecca sat squeezing a water weenie painted like an eel one of her students had given her as a thank-you-for-a-wonderful-semester gift. She let the plastic coolly slip from palm to palm, palm to palm, never tiring of the sleek and boneless bulkiness slithering over her fingers. When she wasn't sure how to proceed, the repetition of the eel's slosh often helped her clear her thoughts.

She wondered if she should read some of her students' stories. She had plenty of time to get to them; their workshop met once a week for three hours and it had only been a few days since they last saw each other in a class slightly lackluster because of end of the semester fatigue. It was about that time when no matter how engaging the class, students gazed through windows dreaming of outside worlds chimerical and fabled. Rebecca looked at the story on top of the stack to see if it would pique her interest.

Julia's hands were itching again and she couldn't stand it.

An all right start, she supposed, but when she scanned the following paragraphs and found sentences like *"the thought of hell sometimes bored her"* and *"washing dishes made her think about the comforts up in heaven"*, she hoped she would not have to read another exposition on the benefits of rapture. Sometimes there were students in Rebecca's workshop like that: devout, dedicated, pathological, nuts. Rebecca hadn't pinned this student for a fundamentalist, but you never could tell when their fear and derision would strike and you'd get a twenty-page manuscript on how one gay-bashes their path into the Promised Land. She'd save this story for last.

Rebecca stared at the digital clock and watched the red numbers slick into one another smoothly electrical and stimulating. She thought of Elaine and their earlier conversation. There was nothing she could do to get Elaine to come home sooner; Elaine had a basement full of material she would have to rummage through. There was too much, and Rebecca knew Elaine needed time to sort and start a career that was just beginning. She missed Elaine's encouragement, however; she missed how she sometimes was inspired to write just from hearing Elaine talk. All Rebecca could do was wait, counting down or up. The clock motioned time in relative patterns of organization: 10:09, 12:34, 1:00, 2:34, 3:22. Numbers that meant nothing without the magnitude of lives willing to sustain them.

EIGHT

If they were but human, I could move them—and yet it is the human in them that is so dreadful. To die were sad enough—to die by violence, by the power of the innocent elements, were dreadful, or to be torn of beasts; to meet the wild, fierce eye, with its fixed and deadly purpose, more dreadful; but ah, to see the human soul, from the murderer's eye glaring on you, to encounter the human will in its wickedness, amid that wild struggle—Oh God! spare me.

Delia Bacon

NURSE ELAINE AND I mock trial. She is Miss. Catharine and she props herself up. Her eyes lie upon my back and her pen scratches. She frightens me with her particular kind of glassy knowing.

Sometimes I am Leonard. I stand and pace and glare and slash. The leaves outside the window tremble when I look and sometimes shake themselves free. The fall colors rest from green to burnt orange reds in the plant life; soon it will be another season. Piles of browns and yellows stack themselves like dead skin sheaves and churn with gusts often icy. Clouds blow gray lips quiet and this land becomes chilled with a winter arriving.

In the middle of my story, I move slowly through this time. I grow musty as a book.

I am worried for Nurse Elaine. My story might surpass her. She will disappear into the earth and I will walk endlessly wanting and writing. The dead shall be raised, they say. The dead shall be raised.

Each day she is more like a game or plaything. Her hands as cold as the ice outside that brushes the panes in the morning. She is unable to bend at the knee or the elbow. She still speaks, tells me to continue, but sometimes her mouth doesn't move and her lips have lost their fleshly apples.

I miss her delicate tissues of skin. She looks at my back during trial. I can hear her like rats scuttling through the walls.

*

The trial concluded to a jury divided. The evidence presented to the judge, his stories and her stories, were often contradicting. Some testified Alexander and I were to be married, some not. Some said I was admirable, a woman to believe and remember, some not. Mr. John Lord, phlegmatic wooly mammoth, testified to my eagerness for fame and advancement. He agitated the room lice-like with accusations of my wanting to crush, my desire for distinction and fortune. So many I once trusted tried to somehow defeat me. I couldn't believe how easily these former friends shifted their affections, all Alexander.

When the testimonies were over, the jury fasted and prayed and asked God to show them the facts so they could effectively come to a conclusion. They looked heavenward and asked for Him to speak a verdict. They lined themselves kneeling with heads bowed, hair white static. Through Mr. Jeremiah Day's window I watched them in their row of contemplation. Finally, they came to not exactly an agreement. They broke their symmetrical prayer line and invited the public in.

They couldn't make Alexander's counts figure specifically against him, could not find him guilty of calumny or falsehood. They scratched their heads and pulled their moustaches into twisted confluences of confusion when they argued over ideas of disgraceful conduct. They agreed they would no longer think and fast and pray over the truth or falsity of the situation.

Their verdict: this story is finished. Let us leave it all alone. Drop the subject. Close the case. Let Delia lecture. Let Alexander preach and move on. The vote was twelve to one. They agreed they couldn't come to an agreement.

Soon Alexander's reputation was reestablished. As a man, he was able to put trite affairs of the heart behind him. The Yale Theological Society showed their support by back-patting him into a profession, a position in the pastorate.

I, however, did not have the help of the men who met in the evenings and spoke secretly in their tombs. Each member of their society swore in secrecy to protect one another from professional devastation, and I had no such group working to defend me. The same men who decoyed Shakespeare into authorship worked their traces westward. Leonard was outnumbered by the other members of the Skull and Bones who would not protect officious women above their blue-blooded members.

I knew my reputation might suffer, but I also knew that I had the ability to lift myself from the wreck of almost every devastation. I could overcome anything as tried and tiny as the breaking of a woman heart, and knew I was not in danger of losing my audiences; more women wanted to attend my lectures who knew the bend and breach of fragility that can't keep itself safe from those who wish to destroy it.

While angry and disappointed, there was nothing I couldn't do. I felt folded and fooled into myself like an envelope sagging against the weight of a seal's external fastening, but I would surmount my own disappointment. I would forget fish babies that swam through my thighs at Brattleboro. I was not that kind of woman. I was a scholar, true only to words that would become me. This time it was certain: I would never see Alexander again. I would work to expose the lies history set forth in a stage too grand for mediocre actors.

I left New Haven. I was disappointed in former friends who looked at me and pooled their disparagement. I needed to be away from those who did not understand my work and its critical import. I was beautiful, respected. I was evil, condemned.

I traveled to New York where I could ramble the grey laden streets without the eyes that murdered me into disbelief. On one of my wanders from shop to shop, I met a woman as wistful as I. I introduced myself, but she already knew me. She had heard of my straits with Alexander—the trial spread from town to town all over New England—and my new friend expressed her wish to help. This woman was Mrs. Myra Clark Gaines and she once had the distressful pleasure of an introduction to Alexander. She said the minute he looked at her yawning and dangerous, she knew he would trouble someone's heart into irreconcilable beatings. Mrs. Gaines became my closest companion during the weeks I spent drifting my woes away in New York. We would often take tea together. We talked of everything except Alexander.

Mrs. Gaines soon invited me to take a trip with her and her husband to Washington and New Orleans because she knew it would help me forget how my foes had accused me to pieces. She was married to a well-known general, Mr. Edmund Pendleton Gaines, who had progressed through politics easily. We prepared for the trip by sharing ideas on what to do when in contact with important men and women who made decisions that affect the turns of history.

Of course, I could not refuse to join them, as I wanted to traverse a wilderness I had not yet known. It would be a dangerous journey, with perils that presented themselves in the wastelands of an overgrown nation.

I had to ask Leonard for money for the passage, but he was determined to keep me. He believed I should stay close to home so he could protect me from the future influence of others. He said I should hold my head high and walk through New Haven proud, a Bacon, unaffected. He said if he were I he would easily forget Alexander. Yet, it had come time again to deny him, so I borrowed money from Mrs. Gaines. As my new and faithful friend, she saw to my healing and happiness.

After insinuating he was no true brother of mine, I convinced Leonard to send me five dollars, at least, to purchase a new hat. Mrs. Gaines took me to a prominent New York hatter that fashioned me such a cap that made me newly distinguished. I wanted something that would show the world the burgeoning flora of my ideas. I covered former devastations with new fauna that grew: delphiunium decorum, trillium erectum, langloisia pectada, lupinous obtusilobus. With a new green hat that sloped towards the heavens, I had the help of sunlight to sustain me.

When Mrs. Gaines and I arrived in Washington, I was introduced to the President and his wife. I thought the experience would be one to remember always, but alas, I cannot hide the truth. It was tired, forgettable. Mr. Polk was mildly charming in his perfectly postured way, but he could not come up with anything of interest to talk about except weather, the simplest and most banal of conversations, unless there were presence of windstorms where livestock churned and tossed while people hovered in terror from what possible Gods stirred up to destroy them, of which in Washington at present there were none. Mr. Polk was terribly substandard. He fidgeted back and forth and had the uninteresting habit of looking more engaged than he really was. I hoped he had more zest when he spoke to ministers of the states. In our meetings I felt he was always on the verge of sleeping.

The White House itself wasn't sensational either. In fact, there was more elegance in my lack of fury. The rooms were insufficiently lit with candles that spilled their wax sloppily over tables. The heat caused the walls to swelter with the weight of issues that were lazily delayed from the making.

The president's wife, Mrs. Polk, wore tasteless short-sleeved dresses. She exposed the white of her arms for anyone who would stare at the minute hairs that swathed them in whorls of indecency. She frumped to and fro entertaining by shifting the air she moved through ever so slightly. When she spoke, she had the tendency to spray spittle on the recipient of her dreary discussions. President Polk and his marriage made for a disappointing foray into future decisions considering the verve of this country. While the West and our woods were heaving with life full of expansion and vigor, our capitol sat stationary, unimpressive and secure with its own inane protections. There is no joy in the commons.

The trip downriver was a thousand times more electrifying. The wild folded onto itself and crawled over its own skin because of thickness and no room for moving. Vines crept close to the river in dangerous choking configurations, and at night you could hear devilish chants from natives or phantoms lingering their way through the evening light. I often thought of my character Helen Gray, heart-broken and dedraggled to death. I often feared for the saving of my scalp, and always tried to keep my bright green hat tightly pressed down whenever I was on deck doing my lackadaisical dreaming and Alexander forgetting. I shouldn't have worried so much about the natives, who by this time of course were mostly dying and converting. They were not as much of a danger as when they roamed with deathly spears and tomahawks slashing anyone who would rightfully adopt them from their doings, as my poor father had tried when I was a child. I should not have worried about what treacherously attacked and maneuvered yesterday so much into today. I should have paid more attention to the present and other passengers.

I should have noticed some of the women on the boat sweat their hair unflattering their faces although the heat did not determine it, and I should have seen how some of the children and their grubbed-up hands were producing dirt and phlegm from a sickness. I should have noticed those around who could not contain cleanliness enough to prevent a disease from fleshly proliferation.

On the boat there was an outbreak of cholera and I caught it. Imagine. There were always invisible tidings sent to fight me. The bug that bit still ravaged its malarial fluid through my veins and now I had another imperceptible infection that wracked me sick like our boat's occasional pass through water that slicked its tongue against us to keep loquaciously moving. Cholera influenced my body into a new sort of submission. I spewed forth as voluminous as the river and I couldn't hold anymore my body water.

I was emptying myself of Alexander. I was drying up with his ejection, a necessarily relieving sort of pain. His words poured and pained—*I love you my sister my mirror my wife*—drained and eddied in pools of mucous until the last of his eye gleams left me. Various deaths from all sides coursed my veins and tried to break me, but I did not let them. I kept moving downriver, sick and tossing to New Orleans. I was one of the lucky. I would survive. Six other passengers could not keep their life's blood from leaking into heaven on rivers that drained them. Three children, two women and a man arrived at port stiff and expelled from this very life. Mrs. Gaines and I arrived with our spirits still in us.

I had never seen a city quite like New Orleans, a city I had to explore with frailness unlike the women there who collected lizard skin and chicken bladder to concoct various potions. I couldn't move as quick as when I first boarded the boat and had to be careful of the ebb and flow of illness that might spoil me seasick even if on land I was standing. I toughly maneuvered these streets that mysteriously assaulted my senses with garish contusions. The wrought iron porches and balconies of the French Quarter tilted against my vision as I wandered through the metallic music with Mrs. Gaines looking at all of the exotic offerings. Tinkling and brass-built things gleamed from every corner, and I wondered if it was the heat that made everything, even metal, seem as if it were sweating. It could have been my body.

In New Orleans, women dressed in layers of fabric that swept against their skins in such a way as to suggest showy displays of antiquated elegance. They wandered languorously here and there fanning themselves down streets that would not dare unruffle them. The colors of their dresses luridly merged and swirled, tided up with the muck of the Mississippi, on the shoreline loamy monuments. The men had bellies full of interest, fat with expansion. They were swollen with economic and objectionable passions. Their slaves were brought in and out of the streets grouped one against the other huddled in, tired, poor masses. They were taken and auctioned. I tried to avoid the deep contours of their unfamiliar eyes. I looked away or just in front of most everything about them.

Leonard asked that I pay attention to how Southerners dealt with the problem of these dark tides of involuntary invasions. We both believed in abolition, as did many of my New England contemporaries, and Leonard was working on political tracts that would steadily deny the necessity Southerners claimed for it. Most Northerners I associated with wished for slavery's quick extermination, yet we could not find a fitting end. Leonard's solution: send all slaves currently in America to a distant continent where we would not encounter them any longer. He didn't care for the ways in which they were treated. He was not concerned about their dignity or safeguarding Christian values in this particular situation.

Harriet, on the other hand, was interested in how it was possible on this earth for Christians to mistreat one another. She believed we should spend our lives working toward conversion. She was writing a book she thought might make a difference in the current state of affairs. What I saw was vicious: scars branding a nation—I would return and tell others to fight for abolition, although I had other work with which to focus my attentions. The falsity of the Shakespearean works was my primary obsession.

Southerners were definitely unusual. They swayed the avenues as if they owned the air where everyone else was not entitled. They spoke in a lilt I found emblematic of a heavy heat, as if they required more air in their lungs to pronounce each word, air filled with the fullness of cotton, air filled with others' sweat and blood. The women held everything close to them, especially emotions. They were women not completely unlike my own, however, I had no desire to befriend them. I examined them as an objective science from a distance, and watched how they treated one another with polite disdain.

Mrs. Gaines and I spent two weeks among the energetic avenues of New Orleans, exploring shops and eating dishes made with sea-like creatures that put a spice on your tongue like nothing in the North. I was beginning to wonder what went on in other parts of the world. I thought of large oceans and crossing by boat. I thought I could make it to reaches unknown if I were not sent another body-scrapping sickness. I knew I could make it, as I had finally forgotten Alexander. When we left, despite my alienation from most things Southern, I was sad to go.

When we returned home, I reluctantly said goodbye to Mrs. Gaines. I had no desire to go directly to New Haven and went to visit my sister Julia, now living in Michigan. When I arrived, she told me Miss. Catharine was searching for me. She had sent Julia numerous letters asking of my whereabouts, insisting I intentionally disappeared to avoid her. Apparently no one would tell her where I was for good reason. Miss. Catharine had completed her manuscript about her perception of the truth in my and Alexander's trial. Julia shared with me a letter Miss. Catharine had written while I was exploring the South. Miss. Catharine wrote:

I feel a great veneration for all that your resilient sister has had to behold. I can proudly say I am the only woman who can faithfully restore her suffering reputation. Although this may weaken her, I feel when time passes it can only make her strong. Where is she now? You must let me know.

Julia ignored Miss. Catherine's pleas because she knew I wanted the Alexander ordeal over with. I did not wish to reopen the wound in the air for everyone to peer at and re-contaminate. The cholera and New Orleans had helped ease in a new era of forgetting, and I did not want to visit a recently treacherous past. I worked at putting these things beside me, and Miss. Catharine wished to display me again to the public. She wanted to continue to mourn the loss of my sea lover. She was determined and righteous. I tried as long as I might to ignore her.

I stayed with Julia for a blissfully peaceful week and she showed me her various paintings and talked about an unhappy marriage to a man who wanted to take her brushes and canvases and turn them into more domesticated tools like needles to patch holes and mend work clothes. He worked in the field rigorously farming, and although she loved him, she wished to retain her former life of artistically making. She said she often snuck into her attic to complete work she once passionately started. She told me I should be glad nothing had come of my relationship with Alexander, because you never knew how through loving you would inevitably have to choose. While I felt sorry for her travails with a man who would submit her, I could only listen and console, my duty as her loving sister. After rest and relaxation and talks about men goings-on inside of each heart, I had to return to New Haven.

Before I left, I wrote to Leonard:

I have rested and dreamed and slept—my conscience tells me, and now, if I am not mistaken, the time has come to work.

I wanted to ensure a place for history's referring and was ready to put everything into words and books.

The ride home quickly passed and I planned to commence to my desk the minute I arrived. Unfortunately, Miss. Catharine was waiting for me as soon as I stepped off the coach. How she could specifically track me, I do not know. She had in her hands a heavy tome, impatient and waiting. She held the book out as if her arm might break from the magnitude of its importance. She glanced at me with eyes full of coins. Her pupils, the size of diamonds.

"I think you'll be quite pleased with me," she said. "I plan on vindicating you from your dire situation."

She was as pious and dew-eyed as a gold-plated Madonna. She imaginatively glowed and flushed. Although my hands were busy rearranging my self from the coach, I reluctantly took from her this book. I set my bag down, pulled my green hat powerfully over my head and flipped through. I thought this was the only way to keep her from stealthily following me when all I wanted to do was forget, remember, discover, work.

Her book was strangely constructed and had nothing to do with me, everything with her, although I saw myself on trial on each and every page. Unraveling, I read myself threaded through someone else's eyes. This me I would not want to meet and was not who I am or would be. I am referred to as "DB". Alexander: "AM". The poorly disguised letters and simple descriptions displayed who in fact was not whom by supposing they were who was whom. It was terribly written and false.

"I'm going to get it published. Then you shall be redeemed! Read it. You will thank me." Miss. Catharine gloated against my reaction, floating on her own importance in a cloud of gold-covered dust. She waited while I flipped the pages. She waited while I read and reread parts of not myself.

DB suppressed tears and valiantly listened to testimonies of those who would venerate AM. She was aghast as HR took the stand and confessed her former teacher's drive for fame, success and fortune. And yet, HR was not the only one.

It was true. DB wanted to conquer the world with her knowledge, and she suggested to any who'd listen how you might find her on a library's shelf. DB had the arrogance and pride of any man, and yet AM was not a man worth half her attentions. He was guilty of calumny and falsehoods, true, but she was intelligent and mature enough to restrain him.

I threw the book at her feet.

"I will never consent to have these words published. Take your manuscript. I wish to be alone. You are opening up old wounds."

"But, please, don't be hasty. It is what has gotten you in trouble in the past. Trust me. Read the work in its entirety. I'll ask you about it soon." With that, she left. She would not let the dead lie steady. She wanted to dredge up the past and use it to her advantage.

I couldn't meet with her again after I cast down the heavy handedness of her book. I couldn't bear to see her gloat and gloam, so I relayed my thoughts through letters. I also wanted to let her know, covertly, of my superior literary style.

this is not me I am not DB and you cannot write me who are you? you and AM are both two thirds villian and the other third fool.

Miss. Catharine responded:

DB, to disguise your identity. We must stand together as women in this cause. If your reputation is not redeemed, all women should as easily falter.

Do not analyze me alive, I replied.

After I expressed my wishes not to be subject to exposure as some scientific experiment splaying on a table, she began advertising a sensational release of her book, although I never consented to its publication.

I would again be bothered by the inevitable overabundance of unfair, subjective looks. Again the dead would be present in the living. With a title like *Truth Stranger Than Fiction*, people might mistake what she said for truth. It wasn't a problem if in death my words were picked shallow from my bones by vultures who pined my flesh with hungry, insatiable violence. The dead shall be raised. As long as I couldn't feel the pressure of their beaks pecking like the eyes of the wrongly accused, I wouldn't mind. Alive I could feel every threat upon me. It clamored my skin like sin.

Miss. Catharine and I inevitably crossed paths one day in New Haven while wandering through the Green.

"Miss. Bacon!" She waved a gloved hand in promenade, and shouted across a million open ears. "I have planned to save your feelings," she said, as if my feelings could be saved by the light and promise of Miss. Catherine's warm true Christian heart. When she got close enough to whisper, she buzzed beelike into the center of my thoughts, "if you will but return to the fealty of your childhood."

The nerve! I found it stranger than fiction how Miss. Catharine became Leonard. She wished to transform me infant, incapacitated doll needing care and cultivation. Why would I want to return? She continued, wrapping her gloved hand around my arm as if to imprison me by possession: "Obey me as you did then."

I couldn't remember obeying Miss. Catharine. I do remember the cries of girls when she wrongly awarded Harriet for my best composition. I remember Miss. Catharine's apology, her mistaken insult. I pulled my arm free from her grasping and gloved presumptions and brushed off her touch as if shaking a flea from a coat. I looked deep into her gloating, ghost-like eyes and pronounced as surely as a bell will toll, "No."

I turned away and began my walk home. Through the prying ears now all attuned around us, I heard Miss. Catharine's righteous preach-like calls: "This monstrous outrage will all be turned on me. Let it come. I cannot suffer in a better cause! I am no villain and I am no fool!"

There was no convincing her. She martyred in a female call, took the brunt of my misfortunes to rescue what she perceived as a weak and wilting soul. It was not just DB she wished to absolve, but every wrongly accused woman throughout history coursing the past into present and futures to come. Every woman now, then, forever would have recourse because of our liberator. Right! Wrong!

She pursued literary fanaticism under any unfortunately sensitive cause. She spoke from her place on high, taking liberties with her words. A crowd of female listeners had now gathered around her.

Miss. Catharine continued to call, "I dwell in the secret place of the Most High, and abide under the shadow of the Almighty!"

I wondered and worried about Miss. Catharine's book while I prepared for my later life without her. I wasn't sure how to prevent her from moving forward without the consent of her living heroine. She offered me one last flashing hope. She offered to pay for my visit to another water cure. I was frail from the malaria-Alexander-cholera-Miss. Catharine-Leonard-New Haven dilemma, and agreed. There was one stipulation: to save her money, we would share a room on Paradise Row.

We left for Brattleboro once more, and while it was wonderful to be submerged again beneath the chill and heat of water, it was not the same without Alexander. I had no desire to walk the country hunting wolves or watching rivers with men that manipulated through. I wanted to spend most of the time alone in my room, but this proved a problem with Miss. Catharine. She was always there, always wanting to talk about her book. She made sure to bring an extra copy for me and in case of a passage of dispute, she always knew the exact page and section with which to find it. She even carried her work to the special curing sessions. I found my arms tired from lugging always the thing around and intentionally left it in our room.

At the end of the day, Miss. Catharine would comb her wavy hair from its curled-up slickness and ask how I felt, if the water was helping my sickness and headaches, if chapter three was a bit too long? She would not wait for an answer before moving to another textual question. It didn't matter my response. This water cure was not, as it had been in the not-so-distant-times freezing to bone unrequited, rejuvenating. I was exhausted from wanting to speak but not speaking, entire lengthy conversations occurred with myself in my done-in head. Although I wished to stay and feel relief, I went home early under the guise of an upcoming lecture. Because she would not stop asking even as I stepped into the coach, questioning without end without stop, I told her I supposed I would not be entirely outraged to see the publication of her book. I was tired of her unrelenting.

A month after I returned to a somewhat steady life of study in New Haven, Miss. Catherine released her book. I was worried about the effect on Leonard, whose skin had grown reptilian from age and the preliminary annoyances of defeat. When he stood against certain light he was almost translucent. His eyelids became clear and embryonic, his pulse beating blue-veined traumas beyond the coat of his skin.

After he read Miss. Catharine's book, he scaled, Paleolithic. Immediate and ancient, Leonard considered the ordeal a scandal. He spoke of treachery. He promised he would never again support Miss. Catharine. Perhaps he did not like the way he was represented.

In her writing he covets attention, as if instead of pulpits he was made for stages and performance, not to be inspirationally heard. While Leonard raged and fumed, I, however, stopped caring. I came to believe people would not actually read her book because the story had been much more exciting during its own time. Finally, with passage, people were tired of a tale long-winded ending familiar and predicted.

My mother wrote to me late in a summer that was lukewarm with old-new gossip rehashed from Miss. Catharine's book. She told me she was ill and I should come at once. She did not own a copy of *Truth Stranger Than Fiction*, but wished to be familiar with this work, so I spent money I couldn't afford to purchase this soon to be unimportant, literary effort.

I hoped it would be a short visit. Her room was dim and smelled of a tinged metallic pestilence. Few sunrays wafted in through congested light coughed from windows swathing the place with sick. My mother was unable to use the broom or clean the crannies she once could.

Her grey hair hung in greasy strands plastered to her head as she sweat streaks skin drenched. She lay in bed covered with damp quilts that stank of sweet smelling mushrooms feverously sleeping. She was unaware of my entrance. Something rattled her chest as if attempting escape.

Before I could touch her shoulder to gently roll her awake from her hopefully honeyed dream, she opened her eyes and shook, surprised as if stirring from an ocular prison. I knew from the boat to New Orleans what it was that blighted her. It was cholera, and she looked to be suffering more than I ever could. I had a reason to fight fiends that demeaned me, but my mother, aged and done with a life spent scouring, had none. Her only role and benefit was to now lay to rest.

"Delia. Have you spoken to Leonard?" I wasn't sure to what she was referring.

"Yes, mother. Always. What for?" The blacks of her eyes skittered as if full of the shake of a sickened dog flexing against mange.

"He spoke to me of Miss. Beecher's book. Did you bring it?"

"Yes, mother." I handed her the manuscript and let its weight crush her graying fingers as she flipped from page to page groaning mucous sighs.

"This is good. Miss. Beecher is dignified and gracious. You would do well to follow her ways." She gazed into the corner as if finding other moments. "Leonard will take care of you." I couldn't tell if she was crying or sweating sickness from her skin in agonizing perspirations. I had never seen her tears. I looked at these almost tender drops to see if they were like my own.

"Mother. I can take care of myself."

She nodded, bobbing, diving, her movement unintended. She was on a watercourse not of her own making.

"Delia. Do not forget to admire your brother. I am very proud of him. He has done the most for this family since your father died. Your sisters and you must obey and not create tragedy. This ordeal with Alexander has left me defeated. Do you think of anyone except yourself?" She coughed again. A mass of something amoebic strew its slick substance across the backs of her fingers. "Leonard told me you wished I was not your mother. He said you believed I couldn't keep proper house or care in such a way befitting for a mother. He told me you were glad to be left with Miss. Williams. Is this true?"

"Mother! I said nothing. Please don't let Leonard speak for me."

"I forgive you." She rolled her back to face me. Her breathing deepened. I couldn't think of anything to say. I stared at her tenuous form for moments that lengthened into the frets of her sallow skin, her face resting right beneath the window.

I do not know how long I sat. Once, I took her hand. It dripped through my fingers. There was nothing left for me to hold. I shall never forgive her for leaving.

My mother died a week after my visit. She is deeply punctured in the ground. I do not like the words left just above it:

Her children shall rise up and call her blessed.

Why did she define her life as thus? Why motherhood guilt and resentment? It is impossible to figure answers to these questions. People court the ground into one day disappearing. The dead shall be raised.

Nurse Elaine plays hide and seek. She crawls under the bed and makes tapping sounds on the underside. I hear her clicking and I lay with hands covering my eyes so I won't cheat and see. She says: don't peek don't peek.

Sometimes when I am waiting she touches my arm and the ice-cold shock sends me into quivers. Her voice, glasses tinkling.

I tell Nurse Elaine my mother has died. She tells me there are more mothers than any girl can imagine. She says she is my mother, asks me to change her yellow frock. I dress her however I like; I hold her and we rock.

She wants me to write her poems. Shh, shh, mother is sleeping.

The other morning I looked for her and she was not underneath the bed hiding and tapping. I called Mother! Mother!, but there was nobody there to listen. Another woman behind the wall responded. Her No No No No No No staccatoed the hospital awake with her hopeless repetitions. It was her. It was not her. It will never be her. I've written you a poem, mother. If only you were here:

She carries body in body for months unfailing
until the sea breaks loose then roiling. Out
she becomes and is as always has been, fails.
Starts from one make another, out cries sharp
as sirens. Hush she sings—I can give you only diamonds.
Out she begins to give though unable.
She tries despite warrings of age old from in and out
of darklight tunnels. Speak to her carried away
years filling arms' slow recede as a shrivel. She isn't
or could not unneeded she isn't. Later learn
shades of own night where the heart lonely pump
puts an end to itself like all the other little lambs bleating.

Nurse Elaine has come from hiding. She takes my hand and we pretend we are mother and daughter and cycles repeating.

———

When I introduced you to my mother, I asked that you not pay attention to her appearance. She was sick and saw things not exactly there. Her favorite hallucinations were spiders crawling up corners of the living room to build secret webs in the attic to nest baby furry legs that crept on her at night when she tried through the drugs to elicit comfortable sleep. You were polite. You chose to sit quietly and listen.

You might not have noticed my mother's hands dry, red and cracked, or that she sang songs while washing dishes. She hated it when my father worked late cursing loudly underneath the truck. When she became sick, she sweat herself through a fever that unpredictably killed her. You may remember.

Poor mother, may we all rise up and call her blessed.

———

Rebecca lay in bed for what seemed like days or weeks or hours. When she spent time sleeping or not sleeping she was able to think simultaneously about everything and nothing. She was waiting for someone to call or God to talk to or Satanists to peep through her windows at her sleeping or not sleeping or thinking of everything or nothing. John never came home and maybe he would never come home although she doubted it because he always came home and she was always there listening and waiting and thinking of everything and nothing. She needed John to help carry out their work. Maybe he would return with presents from his journey like freshly printed Bibles or stories of demons seeping through the skin of lusty women.

Rebecca grew more and more sentimental. She thought about the crash and rumble of pins when her and John first began. She does not miss the rumble of his hands when she does not have soup for him on time. These are things she uneasily lives with. She wished he were there for them to kneel and pray and speak together in tongues of love for the Lord. Where was he? There wasn't much she could think of except God and with him inevitable thoughts of John. There must be some sort of work she could do, some sort of writing to fill the pages with abandonment.

She looked to the height of her closet and noticed a piece of dusty metal staring at her like a murky eye. It was her typewriter. She thought about how exciting it might be to hear the satisfying clicks.

God? she asked, *wouldn't it be nice if I wrote another book? Maybe on my own this time? I am a great author. You told me so. You told me so. Maybe a mystery? A story about merciless women with ambition beyond their dreams? God? Hello?*

There were always demons mucking about who made perfect topics for the written word, and with so much sin, Rebecca should never have writer's block, but without John to inspire her, she was often lost. She wondered if there was anyone specific with whom to make an example. Elaine was getting to be a bore. Nobody immediately came to mind, and God was still apparently in no mood to tell her. Rebecca ran through a brief list of people she knew: the guy who sold cigarettes at the Crash&Burn, Eliza her high school friend who liked lighting trashcans on fire, her mother.

Her mother was not someone Rebecca thought of often. Her mother was one of those Christians who acted as a homing device for demons to temporarily dwell in from the underworld. Rebecca could write a whole book just about her.

At the end of her life, when Rebecca's mother spoke, she was confusing or confused or staring off. When she was young, she was thin and wiry and filled with an electricity that coursed her into exhilarating spasms of silence. Her hair was curly as a seahorse and just as brown and jagged. She often wore form-fitting bodysuits that molded her into an athlete ready for marathons of running away or through woods breathing as heavily silent as a mute. Her mother would occasionally jump back and forth as if exercising. Her eyes would spark off currents and she would weave around the room as if running from trails of dynamite.

Rebecca's mother soon stopped moving around and jerking much. She spent more time at the oven cooking and baking and wearing an apron. These things did not become her. She filled out like bread she would knead for dough. She could not wear bodysuits any longer because she splurged and bulged from them packed with her body to overfull. Her mouth was sewn shut and she began to stare at the spaces before spaces as if there was nothing everywhere. She paced through the house vague and unassuming. She would move things that did not belong in certain places. She might make tiny peeping noises like a furry baby chick out of quietude, but inevitably she returned to shush like someone who has buried themselves within themselves covered by earth awkward with contemplation. Rebecca knew when she started communing with God that her mother was possessed with death.

The last time Rebecca spoke to her, her mother did not answer back. Rebecca told her she needed to be saved. Her mother looked herself into a corner and stayed like a punished little girl. Her mother was a ghost. You can't save everyone. Some you have to let live and burn.

Rebecca stared out her bedroom window and noticed a plant that once thrived was now dead. Its alien head bent toward the ground and its large stalk seeped with a retching brown mold. Rebecca knew she must do something about it. She decided to get out of the house because she did not know how long she had been there. Her memories took up too much room.

She must forget about John and her mother. A plant was dead and she was the one who killed it. Rebecca stood up and felt the ache and pull of unresponsive muscles. She stretched. She must leave without being gone for long. She mustn't anger John if he decides to come home.

———

Rebecca must have dozed off. She spent the late spring and summer so often sleeping, something innate in her blood. Early evening pinkness coursed through the window and she could hear the sounds of a janitor sloshing the hall with bleach and water. She had read through half of her class's stories and hadn't found anything too impressive.

One girl wrote an interesting experimental piece about a father who takes his daughter hunting for wolves deep in the woods. The story was punctuated with repetition of the phrase: *You are gonna skin me. You will do what you are told*, which provided a nice refrain for a particular kind of violence. At the end of the story when the father disappears, the reader can't help but feel terror. Harriet was a good writer, but she spent too much time biting her fingernails in class to pay attention when Rebecca discussed the crux of her best work.

Rebecca must have began dreaming shortly after she finished Harriet's story because she recalled hazy images of falling into a ravine somewhere in thick woods. In the dream, she had scratched herself terribly with twigs and brambles. Rebecca realizes from the chaotic ink doodlings on her arm she must have been twitching and twisting around too close to her grading pens.

Rebecca decided to check her email before she made her way back home.

Her inbox was filled with advertisements for cheap prescriptions for Viagra and the latest stock about to drop. She noticed requests from princes in Africa whose associates died constricted in jungles who needed to unload a few million dollars on some helpful soul. She deleted and deleted, punctuating and exaggerating each click. She clutched the mouse, infuriated with the unending electronic junk. The plastic cracked. Rebecca has to replace her mice every other month.

Disturbed, Rebecca noticed another email advertising greeting cards in honor of one's mother.

Rebecca often wondered what life would have been like had her mother survived her birth. In photographs she was beautiful, stately, enough to make gods or kings fall into her arms. Her dark hair tumbled around her shoulders like tides spilling foam across the ends of the earth. Rebecca knew her father fell deeply in love the first time he ran his fingers through her locks. He once told Rebecca her mother's hair smelled like the deep, barnacled blue, filled with life teeming through the thick of it. Although Rebecca never knew her, sometimes she believed she could hear her mother sighing across windstorms pregnant with danger.

Perhaps because of her distressing birth, Rebecca detested hospitals. While she has no memories of the surgeon's slice and slit that were a part of her initiation into this world, hospitals cause her inevitable grief over her mother. Her father has told her numerous times it was not her fault. Being snake-like, it was an easy birth. According to her dad, Rebecca slithered out comfortably smooth and adorably looped. It was the doctors' fault; they confused her mother's medication, sending her into shock. She was dead before she held Rebecca with her two new legs bending back and forth.

Rebecca once told Elaine she would never allow herself to be checked into a hospital. *If I'm dying or bleeding or my arms get severed off, shoot me dead as a dog,* Rebecca told her. *Or if my mind goes loose and flanked with amnesia let me wander the streets and occasionally have the compassion to feed me. I won't be confined and captive, locked behind those walls. Doctors turn people into ghosts,* Rebecca insisted.

Rebecca could not bear the memory of a mother she only knew through photograph and invented recollections. She would work to forget the painful stories she created when she was young. Rebecca decided she would forget about her mother's inevitable sacrifice and move on, keep moving on.

NINE

*I think when Heaven deserts a cause, it's time for us
poor mortals to begin to think about it.*
Delia Bacon

NURSE ELAINE HID under my bed for days in the corner gathering dust
and her hair turned chalk like a specter. I hope she speaks again. I do not talk
about my mother, unresisting under the earth.

I pulled Elaine from underneath the bed and propped her elbows up with
pillows and continued my story as if it were a lecture. She watched me, arms
across her chest like an audience inspired, judicious. My audiences love the
light electric current, some magnetism, some animal in possession.

Nurse Elaine loves me too when full of passion rolling my tongue around
topics of Egyptology, The Vedas, the slurp and slime of historic ancient rivers. I
miss her hands caressing me through the water.

Leonard came and would not see me. He asked for Nurse Elaine. I heard
him speaking through the walls from woman to woman where we carry
messages from the outside. He has plans and may let me out. I must pretend I
am finished. I promise Leonard I will never hold the pen again. I deny myself
of my own making.

I saw him walk away whistling as he avoided the look from my window.

Where are you, Nurse Elaine? I wish she were through with her rigamortial
hiding. I must write it down. I must.

*

I finally left New Haven for what I wished was forever. I planned never to return except to be placed deep in the dirt of the worm-soiled earth. Leonard told me not to go, not to do it, he said if I left I wouldn't be able to stand on my own, that I would surely sicken.

Delia, you're too frail. Delia, you'll get headaches again. Delia, the work is none for a woman. Delia, bend your knees and pray. Delia, be my helpmate. Delia, you don't have children. Delia, I told you so. I am telling you it is so.

Despite Leonard's demands, I would compose my Shakespearean theory and make my life my book. I gathered my small reserve of manuscripts and clothing, packed everything in a trunk and left for the bustling hub of Boston. I was excited to carouse these lanes with anyone with a mind active with ideas. There were men interested in Eastern philosophies: souls being reborn into animals and new lifelines. There were women discussing the energetic pull and fields of magnetic force unapparent until we tapped and encountered it rapt-like. In Boston, life was unencumbered by the staunch and conservatism of established belief and churchmen who pointed their fingers accusatory at anyone who would deny their antediluvian authority. A man named Ralph Waldo Emerson was leading a revolution.

I would be welcomed into Boston's intellectual arms. There, I had something of value – a mind that worked like an ocean frothing to inflict its ancient maritime present into opening coves of historicity. I knew how to curdle the waves of enthusiasm and watch intellect row through thoughtful waters that fluttered with awareness; everything as historical metaphor, everything delivered with purposeful water-filled shocks.

Despite my forty odd years battered by disease and let down of love and a brother who would not release me for my own, despite everything against me, I would survive. This was my new beginning, as certain as a spiritualist conjuring ghosts from curtains gestured by the lost. Everything converged with the nothing that is one. I gathered information with hands woven with age, my usefully collecting, thick-veined baskets.

I planned the logistics of my lectures. I would charge enough to pay off my debts—five dollars for a series of twelve with at least twenty people in attendance. This would solve a fix. If I were to pay off all of the money I owed, I would never have to appeal to the pickled clean fingers of Leonard always anxious for asking. I could live on my own. I had never been able to do so, always relying on the gratitude of others. I only had myself to give.

Miss. Catharine had recently rescinded her offer to pay for my water cure. She made it a point not to directly inform me. A post arrived with a bill written from an accusing, tautly-rounded hand. She had used my love for the water to weaken our now dying friendship.

I lodged at a hotel downtown and spent hours increasing my knowledge so I might astonish crowds with as much luminosity as the late Miss. Margaret Fuller. I heard often of Miss. Fuller, how she hosted brilliant conversations with intellectuals, a self-educated and prolific lecturer who set thoughts spooling, often criticized for her brash and mercurial emotions. From what I learned, she was a woman of my own intentions. She had been intimate with the most important thinkers.

Unfortunately, I was unable to meet Miss. Fuller in the flesh. Three months prior, when I was traversing the wild Mississippi and comforting Julia from suppressive loves, Miss. Fuller gave her life, choking and sputtering underneath the bulk of the sea. She was on a return journey across the Atlantic with a new young husband, recently born boy, and a host of papers that comprised her latest work teeming with revolutionary experiences. A captain gave over in deaththroes to an inexperienced sailor who pummeled the ship into rocks close to New York's harbor, and the early lives of the passengers were taken to their knees in front of the Lord.

Miss. Fuller and her family had drowned. The city was still blighted with this unfortunate disaster, covered with calcified sadness, washed away with oceans, tears. Miss. Fuller and her boat had been tossed. Henry David Thoreau was sent to comb the sands for her body or work. He searched for days and could not find them. Miss. Fuller's friendship with Emerson and other famous men of letters outlived her, watering her way into lifetimes forever pressed by the flow of an oceanic current. If only she were living.

I knew of a bookstore where most of the intellectuals shopped, and it was there one day I was looking for charts and graphs when I first met the helpful and self-sacrificing Miss. Elizabeth Peabody. She manipulated confidently through the stacks, head held high as the bookshelves. I noticed as she passed, smelling of oak and jasmine, she had within her arms a copy of Miss. Catharine's book. I couldn't resist.

"Have you heard of such a book? What do you think of its author?" I questioned, accidentally assaulting. Miss. Peabody turned and glared at the inappropriateness of such an outward asking.

"Who has not heard of this book?" She looked me up and down and seemed to pin me against the wall with exasperation. "Who cares about the author if the content is not worthy of heightened attention? One day the author will surely be dead. Before such a time, I'm glad there are works that make for a pleasurable read." She blew a steam of hot air from her nose and stomped her foot as if to tromp away. As she was turning, I could not help but continue.

"The pleasure you are afforded from that meager book, madam, is at my own expense. I am Miss. Delia Bacon."

"*The* Miss. Delia Bacon? What unfortunate events! That Mr. MacWhorter! What a scoundrel! I hope you never meet anyone like him again." She searched me for missing information, looking for sadness on the sly. I couldn't help but weigh a visible sagging. Miss. Peabody could tell the affair was slightly near my forgotten heart.

"I'm sorry, dear. What can I do for you during your stay in Boston? Anything you need, I'd be willing to provide."

With that, we began our friendship. Miss. Peabody knew many literary and high-minded men and women with whom to put me into contact. I needed supporters for my lectures, and she was just the woman to introduce me to those who could graciously help. Men signed their names next to mine: Fredrick, George, Robert, Edward, Ralph, Choate, Hillard, Winthrop, Huntington, Emerson. The advertisement bills I printed daring those to attend my lectures had lists of names that helped to pack the rooms with eager listeners.

Julia sent me a black velvet dress she had poured her domestic heart delicately into. More often than not, she was unable to sneak to her paintings, and her husband, she wrote, watched over her like a hungry dog. He wouldn't let her out of sight as long as he was around her. He sniffed at her heels and knew every scent. He would often snuffle and suck the air and ask:

Is that oil I smell? Thinner on your breath? Chemicals for your painting my dear wife, Julia? Is the landscape coming along? I wouldn't want to see it quickly completed. How might you occupy your abundantly free time? Don't forget your husband.

While he had problems with her painting, he didn't mind her sewing, and my sister learned to insert landscapes into secretly fashionable stitches. My black dress was beautifully gathered at the shoulders into mountains, sunsets. She put her eye into each design under the guise of practicality. Julia's masterpieces were my customary lecturing attire and I wore the beauty of her artistry through the folds of slick black velvet.

All went perfectly as if planned. People listened to my lectures and called me prophet. They called me seer. They said I made the past present. I would say things like:

We are living monuments. There is no mistaking those who come from the past. We go spinning like tops uphill and down and fancy ourselves made of feathers. In myself I am wholly undone, clothed in the pure righteousness of Christ.

I connected everything appealingly to Christ and the story of him walking into the desert to become the man made of the future. By bringing in the Lord, people believed most everything I told them. When I arrived we were delivered.

Some believed I was the reincarnation of the great Miss. Margaret Fuller, willingly walking in waterlogged shoes. Somehow with my dress velveting pictures of sea snake and sleek eel, I was oracle, a sibyl. The Unitarians, the Transcendentalists, the Whigs and Conservatives admired the way I spoke pasts into the future, and they willingly spent their money to hear me. They heeded my advice to read what interested them. Like myself, they followed the course of their own decisions.

I must admit, I was truly impressive. I used no notes, no books. Often I would point to multi-colored maps, the latest fashion of the pedagogical season, or I would recite a poem I composed directly on the spot just for expression. On the subject of people crossing oceans:

The buoyant slick of moments slides by floating on a wave fins find beautiful. We wait when the water rolls to sway away from shores of sand and dryness. Our mouths move slowly into tighter tighter O's.

One day after a particularly rousing lecture, I was approached by a woman twenty years my senior. It was Miss. Eliza Farrar, whose book I once read for advice on how to grow into a proper woman without flirting or sinning. She seemed to fold inside of herself except for bright greenish eyes that sparked with a long life of decorum. We became immediate friends, and she invited me to take afternoon teas in her apartments.

Miss. Farrar and I loved each other quick as sisters and did many things in our leisure time together. She was interested in animal magnetism and spiritual rappings and would invite me to these full-mooned meetings. One night we went to a woman's house who summoned spirits from the middle air to make a mess of her table and everyone's nerves. She called to a demon and spoke in babbledeegook knocking on walls as we held hands. The voice awe-strikingly said:

What's in a name? Is it nobler in the mind to suffer outrageous fortune or take arms against a sea of troubles and oppose them?

This voice was speaking to me, reinforcing my theory. Shakespeare was not a man, but a name. What's in his name? That which we call by any other name would smell as sour I suppose.

A painting of a ship storming dangerous rocks slid down the wall to land with a crashing near my backbone. The woman who was summoning the spirits had hair made of chameleon tongue and she shook like walls rambled with ghosts who spoke in garbled, deep-voiced talking. Ghosts and deaths of the wrongly departed mingled with the upper air to do bidding for women like the one at the head of the table. Devils planned invisibilities I could through mediums become aware of. Something from the underworld must have been sent to conquer me, to deter me from making my theory public, a certainty.

Miss. Farrar sat through these gatherings as still as a steamer as the wind galed and blew around her. Sometimes we wondered after we attended these spiritual summonings if we had encountered the late Miss. Fuller. Eliza said she could see her through me, looking out of my eyes at the table the spirits shook with hands trying to wake us. I wondered if it were not the ghost of the fictitious William Shakespeare haggling lines from the mouths of mediums quick enough to speak them. Miss. Farrar and I scared each other through evenings as we walked home for a night of restless retirement afraid of spirits. We saw things too odd not to consider.

While my leisure time was spent hobnobbing with ghostly spooks, these callings did not deter me from my work. I told Miss. Farrar and a few friends about my ideas because I was confident they would not share this information with others or pass it off as their own. Some found my theory outlandish, but I culled evidence with which to convince them, for years now forming this truth. I began to notice that when I visited their houses, my friends would hide their Shakespearean plays so I wouldn't talk endlessly on the subject. Once I asked Miss. Farrar,

Dear, where have you put your Corolianus?

She lied and told me she did not own that volume. I glanced around the corners of the room and noticed it on top of a cupboard. I invented a new game to locate the hidden Shakespeare whenever I visited and said nothing. Their lack of belief to me was amusing.

The story of my brightness spread through Boston, and my life would not be complete without mention of a friend invaluable for my future. I introduced myself to Ralph Waldo Emerson via letter, and he enthusiastically agreed to help in whatever intellectual endeavor I might embark upon. His friends were Miss. Fuller's friends, thus my friends, thus Miss. Peabody's friends, thus Miss. Farrar's friends, and they told him what a wonderful woman I was. Although I never met him physically for more than a moment, I cannot mention a life spent without him. Mr. Emerson promised to help disseminate my work with his worldly influence, an invaluable supporter.

The sprawl of my theory was often the only motivation for my occasionally frail body to keep fleetingly breathing. I successfully paid off my debts but still did not have enough money for comfortable living. I limited myself to two meals a day and did not sleep so I could spend more hours at study. I became more Leonard-like in body, my skin rapturing on angular bones. When I looked at portraits or lithographs, I saw the dead living into the present day. Sometimes the slick of oil through the canvas was real and I couldn't tell likeness from what was authentic.

I needed to garner more evidence for my book, and I knew that I would eventually have to sail across the ocean to confront the third-rate play actor moldering in his dust. I would have to stare at his monument, eyes joking with pun and derision. There was no way to avoid it. I would leave Boston to cross the sea and hoped I wouldn't turn to ghosts that haunt from sunken shipwrecks.

I read an average of ten hours a day. Overall, my theory was quite simple, even for those who shied away from specific facts. All could be connected through the birth of Christ, a date at zero everyone could remember. From the point of zero, everything divided. History was only six thousand years old, with a few events worth remembering. I displayed charts of war and ideas that put us as people into this room on earth. The rest was up to my audience and their personal investment. If someone found a pharaoh or watershed of particular interest, I encouraged them to pursue their line of thought and read for the joy of it. Look how the Egyptians invented poetic sensibilities as meaningful as their great and pointed temples. They were not heathens, I reported, but neighborly ancestors. Everything was placed on earth for us to mentally engage with and discern for ourselves the one and only consciousness. Look at texts and examples. Look at the monuments and temples. We are books of our own making. They become us.

Sometimes I was too controversial. Because I spoke mostly extemporaneous from the heart, at one lecture my tongue was ahead of my thought and I did not will the words as I wanted. Some of the audience inferred jaw-shocked and blasphemous I did not believe in God. I then professed:

Christianity is the central fact of history. I will show you divinity as the beginning and end of all history.

Of course they surmised what I already knew, time was an arbitrary system of dating used to situate a beginning, middle, end. Of course I lied like a good Christian, wanting. I wouldn't publicly dare defy Leonard or the Lord.

I was famous and successful, and soon I moved from Boston to conquer New York. When I wasn't spinning the heads of the intellectuals with my treatise on Hinduism and the promise of new birth, I liked to ride the quick-ice slickening with sleighs. I would not go to theatre, as was fashionable, because of my former life's distress and obvious fictions. Instead I fancied the freezing Fifth Avenue air whizzing through my hair as children giddied themselves with winter. I also enjoyed examining the ships with their bulk and immigrating masses. Leonard could not deter a life traveling to other lands to see for its self.

I searched for someone who might publish my theory in book or essay form, almost ready to release the full scope of my literary intentions onto the world. Emerson would be the perfect literary agent, as we both believed in my brilliance. I wrote to him:

My life was finished a long time ago and this is the world's work, not mine. What I am doing I suppose the expense of it will have to be paid in some way. So if you could procure someone to pay passage to England, I will gather more evidence. I will complete my work in a land not my own. You know how much the world needs this to tear the veil from blindness and let the truth illumine through. Yours, Miss. Delia Bacon.

Emerson promised to be both my dear friend and agent.

Miss. Farrar knew most of all my deep desire to venture overseas and she introduced me to Mr. Charles Butler, who agreed to fund a study abroad for six months in England. With the help of my new benefactor, I was finally to visit a land I might one day call home. The water awakened, calling.

I wrote to Leonard informing him of my immanent departure, and did not leave an address for him to find me. I would do it on my own. *I told him so. I told him so.* I did not supply any indication of who supported me morally, financially, without his approval; he distrusted the revolutionary ideas of the Transcendentalists. I wrote:

I have ample means at my disposal and shall go supported as to be able to command whatever attention I need.

I was finally in command. Leonard, no longer. Emerson, new brother, supportive father, wrote letters for my arrival to the best of his friends. I was to set sail alone, in control of my own mastery, ready for a life lived writing. No one would be able to stop me.

*

I show Nurse Elaine how on the journey we rocked back and forth. I sway like a mast with sails underneath wind in my bedclothes. She has surfaced again fluid and malleable as fish I saw jumping from the water with pips and squeaks chattering with passengers, strange creatures. Nurse Elaine is no longer still and glass. She makes references to the window by tilting her head and opening her mouth with tiny sounds that echo like the creatures I saw call.

Leonard came to see her and that is why she disappeared for so long. He took her and set her on a shelf behind glass, as quiet as a doll. Nurse Elaine tells me Leonard has asked her to contain my writing and not allow further notations unless for him. She does not want to hand me over. I do not deserve to be hidden deep in the earth, untouched and unread and rotting all the secrets safe with me.

Nurse Elaine says she gave him a few of my latest pages. He would not be satisfied. I nod. I would rather it wasn't this way.

I let her because my friends are abandoned. When the book was published, gone, they believed it was my writing. They did not know my words were spread like Miss. Margaret Fuller's, bloated and skimming on an inconsistent sea. They did not know the men took my work, placed it into their collections. They wrote my book to make me. This is insanity.

Nurse Elaine may be the only one to help. Once I asked Miss. Peabody or Miss. Farrar to complete my work, sensing the danger, but they would not agree. They did not know what would become me.

On my journey, I swayed back and forth across the sea and died in it. This is how one day you will find me. You must complete my work. You must dig up the bones and write me. The dead, as they say, shall be raised.

———

One day I was in need of inspiration, so I looked to a tried and true source, a *Choose Your Own Adventure* written by Edward Packard and entitled *Hyperspace*. It is the only *Choose Your Own Adventure* where the author appears in his own text. To my vexation, however, I no longer found this book engaging. I had run the gamut of those rapidly ending adventures and needed unfamiliar material for contemplation. I live in a town where there are two used bookstores located directly next to one another. I decided to visit these stores in order to find other books that might help me figure out how to proceed through the story.

I entered the first bookstore, which I had never visited before. I generally don't go out in public unless I absolutely have to. The town I live in is small, and I wish to avoid the awkward glances and accusatory "how are you todays" sure to bombard me. The bookstore was filled floor to ceiling with books I had never even heard of, written by unfamiliar authors like the likes of: Dayana Stetco, Jeremy and Jason VanWinkle, Rebecca Baroma, Katharine Haake, David Greening, Anjali Goyal, Michele Garza, Sonya Elliot, Nicole Farah, Heather Momyer, Tony Okopnik, Shem Byron, Robert Lopez, Jerry McGuire, Bo Chung, Peter Thomason, Gavin Hollis, Christopher Lopez, Cristina Alfar, Stephen Wetta. The list goes on and on. Don't get me wrong, I'm no Harold Bloom, but I do believe I have read enough to at least recognize some of the literary greats. This chockfull, junked-up bookstore contained absolutely none of them. Rest in peace beautiful, forgotten, ghostly books.

Of course I could not find anything of use in this first store, so I ventured next door, which was mostly full of undesirable junk. I couldn't understand who would want to purchase any of this dust-covered, dirt-smothered, chipped and rusted rubbish. I wandered towards the rear and found myself slightly more at ease because at least now I was surrounded by recognizable authors, as the owner had acquired a respectable blend of pulp and classic. What is a bookstore without Stephen King and Joyce Carol Oates happily joined at their best-selling sides?

After an unsuccessful attempt to locate a desirable text, I decided to ask the proprietor if he had any recommendations. He informed me that he thought he might have something that might help me, but he wasn't certain. He raised his arthritic body from behind the counter amongst clouds of puff and dust, and muttered despondently about knowing exactly where to look. He led me through meandering aisles to the furthest reaches of the store. He paused at a salient juncture between heaps of *Sweet Valley High* and *Animorphs*. He reached up.

His fingers scrabbled to the back of the shelf like trilobites staunched against the onrushing of time. One of his eyes cocked at me from the corner of the horror section. *I think I've got one,* he garbled.

He drew the book back. He brought it down with fingers fraught with overexertion.

It was *Hyperspace.*

I know this may not sound that strange, but in case you are not aware, the *Choose Your Own Adventure* series contains almost two hundred titles. I happened to walk into a used bookstore that had the only one I currently own, the one I have been using as fodder for adventure; this was the only book capable of filling my clichéd and abstract soul with superstition.

The lower half of my body seemed to drag against the floor as I ran out of the bookstore, hoping the mad professor/antique dealer/author/Satanist/cult leader/Transcendentalist/secret society member would not follow me home. I've since barred my doors. I shall never go outside again. If I need any more books, I'll order them online with a stolen identity.

Don't tell anyone, but I believe they're after me. You might be the only one who can save us. Help me. We need you.

Who are they? What did they do? What did you do to Delia?

Rebecca is disappointed she has killed her plant. She thought about it weeping and browning and going straight to hell. It might make a nice decoration on Satan's desk. She envisioned it next to file folders and a red smoldering stapler.

Rebecca still did not know what to do while she waited for John. She thought about medical school, in which she had spent many years of her life only to have some ridiculous board take her license away for something as innocuous as a little praying and malpractice. It wasn't her fault the Lord didn't want to cure her patients. It wasn't her fault Darviset was easily accessible or that she listened when God told her to take her medicine. Rebecca didn't want to pay for another pointless degree, anyway. She could make one on her own.

When she was little she used to play a game with Francis called office. Office consisted of shuffling around a lot of make-believe documents, stamping each other's hands, drawing pictures of Jesus leading his flock on the walls and using tape to stick papers to each other's foreheads like a blessing. Her and Francis would sit together on the floor and play this game for hours.

"Francis take this package fast to the dogs. They need this envelope or they won't get food tonight and you will have to feed them instead of me. If I have to feed them we will not end up in heaven."

"Ok." Francis ran while Rebecca stamped the paper so the dogs could have food and not fall down dead from wanting and jumping on the wooden door because they are hungry, hungry. Their claws picked and scratched because they needed to eat. Their bones poked from their ribs like jaws. Francis needed to hurry or they wouldn't eat and they would fall down dead like those God liked to smite.

Rebecca heard a wailing *Yow* from a dog or her brother. She ran through the hall on the oily carpet careful not to slide. In the living room, she saw Francis wedged in the door with paper stuck on his cheek staring like a prophet *yow yow yowing* while the dogs licked and nipped his fleshy hand.

"Francis, give the dogs their delivery right away. They are hungry."

Francis squeezed inside the house and poked his hands in and out of the door thrusting papers. The dogs grabbed the paper and tore. They ripped everything shredded and bit at pieces around the yard. The paper flowed with breezes and dogs tossing dirt and dust while Francis and Rebecca laughed. They went back to Rebecca's room to write messages that would soon be delivered.

Rebecca liked offices because they were a nice comfortable temperature and people visit. Offices usually had green healthy plants, music that made you want to close your eyes, Christians, women who smiled and wore nylons, and paintings of ships on water. Rebecca liked offices because they contained people she could speak with about God and his ever-present messages. In offices, she saw God's word on Post-its, pop-up screens and halls. She saw God in motivational pictures with soaring birds, glaciers, and the words "Teamwork," "Decision" and "Jesus". Rebecca believed offices holy, reverent spaces.

Rebecca decided she would try to work in an office. This would be the best way for her to come into contact with God and directly encounter his ignoring. This way she could pass time pleasantly stamping and stapling while waiting for John. She drove to the Crash&Burn to buy a newspaper. She decided if she was successful finding a job, she could spread God's word with other efficient typists. There were plenty of quick-collating, Christian soldiers she could enlist to fight the side of right in the impending, apocalyptic war. If she found five more like her, the word of God would be distributed in no time. Maybe she could rally a group of pure-hearted typists to help write her next few books. Rebecca loved the satisfying click and clack with which information was recorded.

Rebecca first learned to type in high school. A girl named Eliza in her class typed the quickest because of her incredibly long, acrylic fingernails. Eliza decided one day she would be a secretary to prove that her mother, who once told her she wouldn't be good at anything except flipping burgers, was wrong. Eliza currently worked the grill and fry station at Lardys and didn't particularly like it.

Rebecca admired the way Eliza's nails would dazzle as she skillfully hit each key. She told Rebecca her nails were cemented in a special shop by ladies who wore masks and knew how to dexterously manipulate mechanical filing machines. The cement nails made Eliza's hands fast like birds' wings. Brilliant blues, reds and sometimes golds ringed through her fingertips and would sparkle qwerty into an incandescent alphabet. On special occasions, Eliza had the ladies detail her nails properly for the season. During Christmas time, Rebecca noticed snowmen or jingling bells. The fourth of July always brought fireworks and explosions.

"You know you could go a lot faster with acrylics," Eliza told her over deafening keys and bubble gum pops.

"Really? Why?"

"I don't know why, you just can. Plus my boyfriend likes it when I scratch his back. I'm going after school. Come with me."

"To your boyfriend's house? My mother told me I can't date until I'm married." Rebecca flushed.

"Not there, you idiot. To the nail salon."

Rebecca skipped her youth group and went with Eliza after school. She sat at one of the tables with a woman who kneaded her hands. The woman pushed and prodded her nails and covered them with glue. After what seemed like eternity, Rebecca had nails attached as if they were her very own. She could not tell the difference between what was real and what had been artificially added. Rebecca decided to have her fingertips colored silver because that was the color of the typing teacher's ties. She was proud of how she extended. She made sure to hide them from her parents, which wasn't difficult because they were too busy to notice.

The next day in class she finished her exercise immediately after Eliza. Their teacher Mr. Hacking smiled from behind his desk and gave Rebecca thumbs-up. She returned his gesture and noticed the light from the classroom that glared from her fingertips like brilliant stars guiding the three wise men to Jesus. Rebecca smiled at Eliza and felt satisfied. Rebecca often remembered Eliza's elaborate fingernails with joy: the quickness of silver, red and blue birds.

Rebecca scanned the columns and noticed there were plenty of jobs to choose from. It was a matter of finding the perfect place to type. One ad in particular sounded promising. It read:

Do you like working with friendly people in a relaxed atmosphere? Can you type over 30 wpm? Are you good at talking to people? If so, we need you. If not, we might need you anyway. Call for a good time.

Rebecca dialed the number.

"PS Supplies, how can I help you?"

"I'm calling about the ad in the paper for someone who likes to type and work for friendly people and I like to have a good time. For example, I think reading the Bible is fun. I also like washing dishes. That's pretty fun. There's so much fun if we look, just like the Lord. Do you agree? Can I have an interview?"

The woman on the other end took no time to respond.

"Not a problem. Just bring a resume to our office tomorrow at 9 a.m. The address is listed under the ad. Do you need directions?"

Rebecca scribbled the information and hung up. She was ecstatic to have an interview. It had been a long time since she had been in one of those awkward situations. She thought of a job she had as a teenager as a waitress serving steaks and beer. That interview was the best she ever had.

When she met with the manager she was so nervous she spilled half a latte down the front of her dress. There was not enough time for her to change into different clothes, so she went dripping wet and smelling like java. When the owner saw her, he laughed and asked if she had an accident. She told him she was driving and hit a bump. He told her she was brave.

"What makes you think you would make a satisfactory addition to our team?"

Rebecca had an answer. "I like to sing songs. If something makes me angry, I sing. Plus I like food and walking back and forth. I like balancing plates on my arms. When I was young I liked to pretend I was an acrobat, crossing the high wire to spread the word of Jesus. Working here would be a dream come true."

"You read the Bible?" he asked, and hired her on the spot.

She worked at Billy's Beef Barn for a year until she accidentally dropped five steak dinners on the floor. She enjoyed working at Billy's and sometimes missed it. She especially missed the cooks who would talk to her in languages she couldn't understand. She could relate well to those who talked in tongues.

Rebecca was excited about meeting the woman on the phone. She thought of the nylons in her sock drawer she hadn't worn in years because John didn't like them. Rebecca thought about what color she might have a masked woman paint her nails. She hadn't had acrylics since her brief typing class friendship with Eliza. Rebecca was excited to bring some strength back into her life while she waited, no longer bored, for her lost mute Lord.

———

The janitor, who liked to refer to himself as "Charles the Pink" for some reason, sloshed his way across the hallway, stopping to wave at Rebecca who was gathering her things to leave.

"Evening, Rebecca. I didn't want to wake or bother you or else I would have come by earlier."

"Hello, Pink. Any new kittens this month?"

Charles looked at Rebecca suspiciously. He was a member of an insurgent group of campus employees who regularly fed the feral cats that lived and reproduced underneath the Economics building in droves. Charles and about fifteen other faculty and staff religiously pooled their money and interests to buy these cats food and proper play things. There was currently a debate on campus between the Physical Plant and the group quirkily entitled "Coo-Coo-For-Cats"—Physical Plant wanted to exterminate the strays because of potential hazards to student body health. They argued that the cats brought dirt and disease (and Rebecca agreed), while the Coo-Coos believed the cats helped rid the campus of unwanted pests. As far as Rebecca could see, and because of the rate the repulsive, straggly felines reproduced, the debate would never end.

"They're killing them again. De-con. They take the Tender Vittles and dump in some De-con. Assholes. Excuse me. Treating them just like rats. A guy from the paint shop said he climbed under the building and came out covered in fleas and that was why they killed them. I haven't seen Pebbles

153

since." Charles sloshed and lowered his head. "Have you seen Pebbles? The brown one with the black ring around his tail?"

Rebecca had, in fact, seen Pebbles. Was perhaps the last to see Pebbles, late in the evening the day she sent Elaine off to the airport. She could not explain the magnitude of her late night hunger, her archaic desire to penetrate the flesh. Rebecca could not verbalize the feeling of the last life's breath, how it pulses steadily waning under a twisting mass. Rebecca believed cats were distrustful and had no guilt about occasionally squeezing life from the unwanted.

"No, I haven't." Rebecca lied. "Sorry about that."

When she was a teenager, she accidentally slammed her neighbor's kitten in a door, killing it with unexpected force. Rebecca had been in a hurry to smoke cigarettes in the park, and hadn't noticed her neighbor's kitten racing inside of her house. Rebecca slammed and the kitten was squashed, spasming uncontrollably in fits and thrusts. At first Rebecca thought it was funny, until she realized the gravity of what she had done. Rebecca looked at the kitten lying stiff, it's eye bulging a bit. Her father was listening to a baseball game on the radio and had no idea what had just happened.

Rebecca stood awhile, contemplating. There was no way she was going to confess to her neighbor. Other kids at school would call her a murderer, and most of them already avoided her vertical gaze with fear and stunned surprise. Realizing her only option, and certain she could effectively feign ignorance of the "missing kitten" signs soon to appear on every telephone pole in the neighborhood, Rebecca swallowed, and the evidence was gone.

"Did I tell you about my cousin Ralph's cats?" Rebecca asked Charles.

"You said he would be great in the Coo-Coos. You told me his whole room is decorated with carpet mazes and walkways. How many did you say he had? Fifteen?"

Rebecca nodded. Charles didn't seem to notice that she also rolled her eyes.

"Yeah, yeah. You said he barely had enough room for them under one roof. He must be a great father to all those kitties."

"That's him," Rebecca said, gathering her things and turning her key in the lock. Unable to speak any more of the creatures she believed nauseating, she waved as she walked away. Rebecca moved down the hall careful to avoid the spots Charles had mopped.

She thought about writing a satirical novel entitled *Cats* that would make a nice sequel to one of her previous works but decided there were too many potential problems with copyright infringement because of the well-known musical. She also didn't want to spend so much time with those mewling, needy beasts.

Rebecca knew that for her next novel, she must come up with something soon. Her publisher would hound her if she didn't give her at least an outline in the upcoming month. Unfortunately, nothing had struck her long enough to move her into the throes of a book's new language. She composed defiantly as she moved through the bleached cleanliness of the English Department. She was conscious of beauty in compulsive repetitions:

words fight like moths flitter. underneath their wings are threads holding and fastening geometric histories. we build their bonds then burn them with light from the cinders. we become our own simple symmetry. our wing span is small like a sentence.

you are where people walk with hands tied to their throats flat across their chests. madness perfects you. their mouths open Os and they gasp the air that they breathe in, as wide as an open jaw. this becomes you.

you once held me too tranquil and i couldn't move except for everywhere i saw you. you tell stories i believe in.

who are you and what did you do? tell me, what did you do? what did you do?

TEN

There is an immeasurable power about us, a foreign and strange thing,
that answers not to the soul, that seems to know or to heed nothing of the living suffering,
rejoicing being of the spirit. Why should I struggle with it any longer?
Delia Bacon

NURSE ELAINE TELLS with secrets in her lips. Leonard wants to know about England, but I can't explain the pleasant solitude of my room, or those poor, slight creatures, how I bent over pages sitting in bed each night and ducked as they swooped and nuzzled their thin wings.

I can't tell him how I couldn't eat and how I watched my skin ripple about my bones while I listened to my pens shush across the page because I couldn't stop the writing, not ever, not then.

Nurse Elaine cannot say his name, knowing it sends me silent. To heal I must speak in low voices, do not disturb. Like the men, I make a mouthpiece of her so others might believe I am someone I am not. This is uncomfortable, like the forcing of my arms backwards through tight cotton shirts sometimes pulled constricting over. She says: *Write, here, write. If you want to get out, you must write.*

The story now lies beneath me.

*

After weeks at sea, I arrived in England to a swagger of parade with cadenced marches down soot-coated lanes in honor of the Queen Miss. Victoria's birthday. People rejoiced and cheered while the ship swooned near, and as I looked at faces making merriment I swore the celebration just for me. Explosions of music coupled in the air to birth shouts in my honor: *Delia. This ends. Delia. Celebration. Delia. Her day. Birthed. Commemoration.* Women pasted the docks sighing skyward while I waited for delivery amongst them. When the water reflected their faces, I knew where I had come from. I searched under the hat brims of men moustached and suited more properly than the shabby that lived among the American wilderness. No Leonard. No eyes looked me back into a little girl like his. I scanned again. No Alexander. I was in no danger. I had finally arrived.

One of Mr. Emerson's friends, also a Unitarian minister, waited on the docks to meet me. He was calm and warmly waiting to please. I wished to explore the old countryside as soon as plausible and go to Stratford to see the topography that birthed the meager man who so plagued me. I asked that my friend take me to where Shakespeare had been paid to place his grave.

In the quietude of Stratford, cottages dumped around veins of green and the sky bundled up with history. At Holy Trinity, I was awed by the way the church loomed with ancient proceedings and how the past insisted its place in the present, just as my theory. These buildings were hundreds of years older than what America constructed to mark its recent beginnings, and I was impressed.

My ministerial tour guide steered through a path of lime trees all the while talking. He proudly pomped us to the entrance where I might individually take a look. I noticed the stone arches that balanced God through the roof and the wooden pews old enough to father years of devotees. I noted where the original church had stood before new brick and mortar. People in the past gathered and crowded with people presently anxious for a glimpse. There was no room for me to do any obvious or dangerous explorations, so I had to suffice my first visit by looking superficially at the famous sepulcher. I noticed the old curse:

Good friend for jesus sake forbeare, to digg the dust encloased heare. Bleste be ye man yt spares thes stones, and curst be he yt moves my bones.

I noticed the newness. As one tour after another hobbled boringly away, I stayed behind to ask questions about renovations and replacements.

"Why does new mortar surround Shakespeare's grave?" I gestured at fresh grey among fading brick while an antique organ piped a somber melody. Old William must have been smirking ungentlemanly underneath. I glared at his bust and imagined his earth-eaten expression.

"Some of the stones were replaced in 1830. Unknown benefactors paid for this refurbishment. The moneys were also used to add to the church's glorious expansion. I'm sure you know of the contention surrounding his memorial statue?" He looked at me as if informing me of some mystery. "In the original bust, Shakespeare was holding a sack of wheat. In this memorial, however, created sometime between his death and the publication of the first folio, the sack of wheat was replaced by a quill. There have been many beautifications of the original bust. We really have no idea what the man actually looked like. Isn't it curious?"

I looked at my escort and feigned interest. Of course I knew why it was important for a wheat sack to turn to pen and replace it. Of course I knew why the unattractive visage had been prettied to withhold the literature of a republic. "Interesting," was all I had heart to say.

I needed more time to think about the replacement of the grave. I hoped old Will had not already been completely unearthed and searched. When men were mucking with the old player's tomb, it must have been the time a bug bit my fevered sleep in Queens. Perhaps the mysterious benefactors were the very same Skull and Bones? It must have been around the same time the men moved their meetings to New Haven.

Actions wrinkled forwards, backwards. Maybe a spirit was released and sunk into my skin to fill me full of what I needed to know to uncover the real authors. Maybe the false rogue was prematurely disturbed when I rocked feverously through sleep calling for the absence of my brother. I thought about what wasn't coincidence: my visions of boats crossing water and writing with hands made of memories I couldn't have fathomed. Prophetess. Sibyl. I was desecrated so he might be a writer. I was fated.

I listened as the packs of visitors entered and left, a constant stream of coming and going. My companion was now outside impatiently pacing the grounds. In between the godly humming of the organ, I heard shushes of slow waters. Voices long gone hallowed from death echoed. The Avon slipped sleekishly near bringing boats and bodies to eternity. I was on unstable ground that might one day slither between me. I went outside to find my companion. I needed time for reflection.

"I'm sorry to be in a rush, but I must get to my new home. I am to introduce myself to Mr. and Mrs. Thomas Carlyle. If you could help coordinate my travel, I've secured a place in London." I reluctantly left the body of the old, withering joke.

Within days, I was arranged and comfortable in my new apartments. I sent the Carlyles an introductory letter penned by Mr. Emerson and waited for a formal invitation to meet them. I desired to share my theory with Mr. Carlyle, not having any doubts he would support me. Mr. Emerson spoke of Mr. Carlyle's kindness and eloquent, judicious manner, assuring me that we would get along spectacular. Truly, I did not wish to cultivate a friendship with the great thinker, but needed to secure access to museums and archives necessary for my research.

Soon enough, I was invited for evening tea and given directions to locate the Carlyle home. I wondered if the Carlyles thought me ignorant; the instructions were so precise as to guide the brainless. Mr. Carlyle also made mention that he and his wife were ill equipped to receive me. They had some sickness that prevented them from visiting for very long. It was a terrible excuse for their obvious lack of hospitality.

I rode a steamer to their neighborhood and passed time examining the buildings blackening under a technologically advancing era. Men and children scrambled the streets like crabs, calling to each other laboring shouts of loud-lunged advertisements. Wealthier women fanned themselves indifferent with velveteen-hooped skirts surrounding their skin. Moneyed men tipped top hats to every lady with a look and tapped canes as if bred by intellectuals. These were the images peopling the place.

At the Carlyles, I was shown to the drawing room where books lined shelves and piled comfortably in corners. A fire burned, though the weather was not yet extreme in the evenings. Maybe the Carlyles had not lied about their illness; it was possible I misjudged them. The only sight I noticed with scorn was a whole shelf piously devoted to Shakespeare, the blatant counterfeit. His works were reverently displayed, and this perturbed my spirits. Yet, I patiently waited, hands folded like messages, to be prompted by Mr. Carlyle.

When Mr. and Mrs. Carlyle entered, I was surprisingly filled with a warmth that did not emanate from the silently burning coals. The Carlyles were gracious and welcoming, with Mrs. Carlyle plain enough to serve the obviously superior Mr. Carlyle. I sensed an animosity seething from her frosty fingers when she shook my larger, stronger hand, but it was not her I wished to commune with. She left untrustingly as her husband and I were introduced, and I noticed a backward glance of suspicion that looped my security like a wasp. She did not want her husband near me, but did not have that right to choose.

"Miss. Bacon. It's a pleasure to meet you. Mr. Emerson spoke highly of your ability for public speech in addition to your fascinating intellectual pursuits. He says I might be able to help accommodate you. I support others with keen and industrious minds." Mr. Carlyle scanned his rows of books to punctuate this thought. The room seemed glazed as a dream. "Why exactly have you come? Emerson mentioned it had something to do with our national playwright."

I began to explain in detail the theory I had for years been forming, careful to avoid discussions of Alexander, Leonard, or the meetings of the men. This recent coterie was not quite ripe for revealing, and I did not know where Mr. Carlyle might stand on these current developments. I discussed Sir Francis Bacon, the perfect seed, and the others eligible to disseminate dangerous critiques through the new learning. I spoke of these men's superior work for well over an hour, using my techniques of rousing to charm Mr. Carlyle into belief. When I finished, the clock was heard ticking ravenous echoes and emptying words into the hearth. A log fell from the fire onto wasted embers with a resigned thump. Ashes flurried excitedly up the chimney. Mr. Carlyle searched my face for signs of breaking or hoax or weakness. I stood stolid and met him eye for eye.

Something rumbled the depths of him. Something tumultuous resounded from his chest surfacing, dangerously surfacing. Pitch and tones deep erupted as he opened his mouth and guffawed. It was a laugh as such as I have never heard the likes of. He must have eaten thunder. It sounded as if the walls of the house would come tumbling down to find within its bowels a man mixed with volcanic mountains. He laughed while I flushed as red as embers. The fire flicked uncomfortably while he calmed himself from the torrents of his private joke.

"Oh, Miss. Bacon. That's quite a wallop. You really are amusing."

"I am quite serious." I continued as assured as I could. "I have come to England and don't need permission to prove it. I've already begun a series of drafts for a manuscript. I've no doubt I will eventually secure a publisher."

He searched and saw that I, unlike other earths he may have shattered, was not ready for this continental demolition. He blinked through the after shudders of his entrail erupting laugh. The air silenced itself, timid and waiting.

"Dear girl. You are serious, aren't you?" He searched me once again. "You are the woman to prove wrong decades of England's most brilliant scholars? You are honestly going to prove that one William Shakespeare did not write those exceptional works?" I returned his scrutiny with the steadfastness of my look. "Old Emerson was right. No deterring you. I suppose one must admire your determination and spirit. Personally, I am unconvinced of your ideas, but if you are so committed..."

"I am convinced," I interrupted.

"...if you must, I suppose. If nothing will persuade you this world will not take you seriously, I might support..."

"...I will find proof..." I insisted.

"You are quite correct! Proof must be wrested from the vaults of the best libraries and archives of this country. I shall write letters informing the curators of your research. You will be given access to it all! The best of luck, Miss. Bacon. I find your quest charmingly Quixotic!"

There was nothing more to say. Despite his tumultuous guffaw, I had his support. Mr. Carlyle promised to send letters of introduction to the librarians and curators, and we said our hasty goodbyes. In the face of a laugh that shook trees down to their timbers, I could not help but to like Mr. Carlyle. While Mrs. Carlyle was wifely and uncomforting, nothing matched the impressive detonations of Mr. Carlyle's laugh. I almost admired him for it. Mrs. Jane Carlyle I would simply have to put up with.

The next few months studiously slid by. My first summer from laugh to finish is somewhat blurred by the sputtered and furious movements of my fingers, eager at my life's text. I made little time for sightseeing not necessary for the development of my book. I worked, pages building, the only indication of time passing. Calendars became unimportant, imposed by someone else—my miserly benefactor, for example, paid for my overseas visit only one hastening summer long.

After the acclimations of my first summer, I found the bustle and stench of my first residence unbearable and made plans to move nearer to landscapes providing lifeblood to my work. I moved from the distraction of London to the northern peace of St. Albans where Sir Francis Bacon once honed his know.

In my new home, I spent my time in blissful writerly seclusion, waking each morning to bells calling history forth for my perusal. Birds swooped and landed in nearby trees, but did not come so near to me. My head was clear, and I found a perfect spot to stretch my intellect.

My new house was cheaper than paying for the dirt and creak of cart's wheel or urchin call that interrupted me in London. My new lodging consisted of two rooms in the front of a house, a bedroom, a veranda, a striking view, and a parlor to receive guests I did not wish to entertain. Although the rent was inexpensive, I had to be frugal in order to make my money last longer than the close of a quickening summer. I wished to stay in England as long as I could, and had to cut expenses. Again, I stopped eating, limiting myself to as few meals as possible, and allowed myself only a few shillings to spend on mending dresses or acquiring books. I tried not to visit or make acquaintances because I didn't wish to waste money keeping myself alive.

I turned down numerous invitations to the Carlyles, who now seemed always in the spirit to entertain, and while I wished to be connected to Mr. Carlyle's thundering mind, I could not allow myself the idleness of those social visits. Besides, I had to avoid leaving things absentmindedly at the Carlyle home. Each time I went, I always left something behind, and would inevitably have to return to retrieve it. On my first visit, I left an embroidered handkerchief given to me by my now dead mother. On the third, for a chat and cup of tea, I left an umbrella and later got caught in a rainstorm. I didn't want to buy another, but couldn't retrieve the first when that harsh weather tossed. The best course of action was to remain at home to avoid inattentiveness, although the more I knew of Mr. Carlyle, the more I liked him.

Mr. Carlyle and I found we had more in common than I once thought. For example, I discovered he did not care much for Harriet's recent publishing successes. She had caused quite a sensation in England. We agreed *Uncle Tom's Cabin* was poorly written, an example of sorry sensationalist propaganda. We discussed our disgust at this book being sold in prominent and noteworthy shops. I told Mr. Carlyle I was certain Harriet's opinion of herself had gotten larger than the sales of her work; I told him of my belief that her towering sense of self arrived via boat two weeks before her feet first hit English shores. Mr. Carlyle let loose his laughing thunder.

Harriet was roaming around England on a book tour, paid for by a generous patron, but I was unable to visit her when she passed through penning autographs on each title page of her book; besides, she didn't search for me as enthusiastic as any friend should. She sent no letter asking of my health or desiring to meet at her ridiculously crowded signings. My landlady saw her, and said Harriet paraded the American wilderness with its social shortcomings as her own. I no longer wished to claim the red white and blue ablaze like Harriet, and understood the tenuousness of where you place the heart. Harriet used my former nation's turmoil to her own literary benefit and Mr. Carlyle, too, understood it.

"All she's capable of writing is Yankee Governess romance." He laughed again, certain to rupture a lung.

He discussed how Harriet's work was one example of how women with flimsy constitutions produce even flimsier written works. Her book, he snickered, hadn't been properly researched! I did not tell him that I had yet to visit any archives.

My most pleasant days were spent in seclusion writing. I dared not venture out of the house until evening after I determined I had written sufficient sentences. Pages piled; words linking line to line—soon I had a volume that contained the seeds, the germs, the child's first timid steps of walk. I nurtured the word efficiently into what would be as apparent as another women's blush. My book grew on its own and soon did not need my encouraging.

I had to obtain a publisher, and I was uncertain how to proceed. There were discrepancies regarding copyright that disallowed me to publish simultaneously in both America and Britain. Time, money, and literary information were what I needed most. I wrote my patron for more funds, which he abruptly declined. I was appalled but not deterred—it was not his place to determine when and where I should work. A year passed and I was not yet finished. Although the pages were frequent, multiplying, I promised myself I would not leave this new land until I saw my project's completion. This was my new home. These were the best of years, the worst of years without writing.

I asked Mr. Emerson for advice on procuring a publisher and told him about my dire financial situation. He returned my notes with hints of worry:

Miss. Bacon you have spent a long time across the sea. I hope you have not tipped over its edge! Do send me some of your recent chapters, and I will act as your agent. I might find you a publisher.

I wrote to assuage his anxiety with the only words I could:

I am done harvesting my toils with weeping. The spirit that has brought me here, covered with words and demanding, perturbed and unrested until I should satisfy its ancient cries at last, has somewhat ceased its rattling. My work is no longer burdensome to me. I find in it a rest such as no one else can know except in heaven.

This was true.

I explained how I could not send my manuscript because I could not afford the time spent copying. I was now without a secretary, although my landlady offered her hand. If she had been more than minutely literate, I might have accepted.

Mr. Emerson replied: *Fare well and fare gloriously!*

I promised him I would.

I remained by myself writing, just writing. Sometimes I saw my landlady hang her wash, and I would wave my hand from the window, and she would return with a maladroit, boisterous fluttering, but aside from the bells I heard sounding olden tones through an increasingly unburdensome sky, I relished in a long-awaited solitude.

Sometimes when I revised or added length to the book's increasing hulk, I would hold pages in front of the glare of a candle close enough so individual letters burned the thin films of my eyesight. They would imprint as if branded. Often I would take pages newly wet and soft with ink and press them on my skin so I became covered in language, as I once was in childhood. Words spread their characters across me. I looked back and dreamt of becoming. Inscriptions coated my arms and legs under the guise of moonlight and I looked at my sentences reflected in perfect sense as I gazed through a looking glass back. There I was, able to read myself. Covered in words and peacefully dreaming, this was how the world might find me.

Mr. Emerson soon found a publisher, and told me I should send a few chapters to Dix and Edwards. He congratulated me on a life dedicated and hard won, and replied that these men were advanced enough to print me. When I told Mr. Carlyle the news, he congratulated me on near completion, and asked that I might one day personally deliver a copy of my book. I almost expressed a varied kind of love.

A few days were wasted copying the first two chapters. I sent these pages with an introductory note to Dix and Edwards, awaiting their reply. I did not wait for long.

Because of Emerson's introduction, they were excitedly waiting. They would publish my book chapter by chapter in *Putnam's*, and I was to be paid handsomely in return. Dix and Edwards believed they were helping spread the new learning—on this basis alone they were willing to see my ideas in print. They were as thrilled as I to see my theories dispersed to a public ready for grand disturbances of thought. They agreed we needed an intellectual revolution and expressed relief that they were given the opportunity to obtain my material before the British presses, as the British might erroneously think my theory sacrilegious. I was proud to know there were good men across oceans that supported illumination.

I worked readying chapter after chapter. Because my handwriting left meaning to be desired, I had to reproduce slowly to clarify every thought. I only ventured away from my house after the dawn of dusk, and couldn't stay outside to wander farther than a block because I was often too preoccupied to tell by landmark where I was. If I became too misplaced, I would have to pay someone to take me home and I could not afford it. I couldn't leave my book because of an increasingly wandering mind.

Because the book was almost completed, I wrote letters to my sister Julia, who I hadn't seen now for years:

I seem to be in danger of going down in sight of land, too tired to care much for living on my own account, but I should be glad to live till the work is finished. It seems very sad, but those who live on and struggle still have perhaps the hardest of it. I have been doing the best thing I could, the most honorable. I am not going to abase myself because I have done my duty. I am not afraid to die in the way of it; when the road comes fairly to an end, I shall stop.

This, too, was the truth. There ceased to be anything aside from the life I was writing.

As I awaited publication of the first chapter, when I became tired of copying sentences neatly line for line, I composed personal notes. More often than not I would burn them to keep them close to a heart needing warmth. I was nervous with anticipation. Soon I received a copy of my first article.

My first chapter is well-written, concise, well-informed, clever, composed of sentences such as:

We are, indeed, by no means insensible to the difference between this Shakespeare drama, and that on which it is based, and that which surrounds it. We do, indeed, already pronounce that difference, and not faintly, in our word 'Shakespeare'; for that is what the word now means with us, though we received it with no such significance. Its historical development is but the next step in our progress.

These are lovely sentences, yet the beauty of these words and thoughts were lost on a boorish public. The ignoble, dull-witted constituents of my nation were not ready for another revolution. They wished to remain navel gazers as long as they could.

Not only the ill-bred public, but scholars—who are supposedly receptive to progressive thoughts—scoffed disbelief while cowering behind their stacks of Shakespearean works. They wrote angry, condemning letters to *Putnam's* demanding proof. They accused me of nay-saying the bard in order to further my own writerly agenda. I hoped knowledgeable men might sway to my side and understand the necessity for Shakespeare to tumble from the privilege of unknowing—he had no right to iconography. America needn't buy the antiquated past when it had new literary foundations to build. These men, scholars, Gloucester, my brother, Alexander, men all blind and wrong.

My article made the conspiracy apparent. Here are the ideas I presume:

1. There no copies of the plays or notes written in Shakespeare's hand. Was he that much of a genius he decided not to write down any of his own words? If he was such a man of brilliance, why not also avail the use of scribes?

2. He was a poorly actor mouthing the words of the intelligentsia in exchange for a coat of arms and a privileged place of burial. He commissioned patronage in exchange for the unimportance of his death.

3. The Folios were written second, third, and fourth hand by ignorant mnemonics years after William's timely death. Like the New Testament, these histories were recorded through shoddy, misspelled, second-hand accounts. All dim Will did was sign a will (the only record known in his own hand).

4. For this are we to believe his infinite wisdom?

5. Where is the proof of genius in the body of William Shakespeare?

6. Unknown benefactors changed the sack of wheat to pen that stands teasingly above his tampered grave. If he were so intelligent and revered, why do no likenesses exist assuredly illuminating his visage?

7. Who is William Shakespeare? Does anyone have a clue? He is a mesh of men, parts of lives lived with lack of proof. Prankster. Hock. Insignificant. That's who. It is words that have become him.

My final question:
If I am mad, why should I be asked to justify myself or provide the truth?

Presumably disheartened by the public's response, Dix and Edwards asked the next chapter be edited to include a narrow definition of evidence. Scholars laughed me asunder because I shattered familiarity, boring convention. If someone cannot understand at first, why repeat when they are not ready to listen? Most are unable to believe a history other than the one they unknowingly inherit.

When I sent *Putnam's* chapter two, they said I still had not provided proof. I heard of parodies that presented me with magnifying glass looking for ciphered clues: a letter here, a formula there, spelling names through code. I was not so unlearned or absurd. Leonard must have seen my article and shared it at his meetings. Who knows how many times he corroborated with the men in order to mute me? They had known of my theory for years now, drawn from my body and explained during Alexander's initiation.

Putnam's paid me meagerly for my pages, and asked no other chapters be sent. I ceased copying. I would have to find someone gracious to help me, someone not afraid of the men and what they might do.

My headaches returned. The beating wings beat back. The birds that roosted in the bell tower fluttered when they were supposed to be sleeping. They battered around the bells that wouldn't stop clanging, banging. I tried to ignore them and continue, but they flew from tower to room. I watched them enter and scatter. When they came close, I saw their eyes bead like drops of blood and knew. They were not birds. They were bats. The sky filled with dusk from their skin-like wings and I couldn't leave without them beating me back. They turned upside down and hung from the ceiling in disorderly groups.

I might need a doctor, but I couldn't leave or the bats disturbingly glided. I wasn't finished. I needed proof. A publisher. Food. My landlady brought me soup and overlooked the rent. She cared for me like my once mother. Her hair curled around her face in friendly knitted whorls and she tended me as nurse. She knew if I did not find money, I might have to beg among the light of moon.

My dreams were vivid. I woke to Leonard hovering over with bone fingers pointing his pursed lips shut. He moved about in circles dancing with brides, their white dresses made of dead birds' feathers swirling. Leonard's brides pushed their corpsey bodies into mine because I did not want to listen to him shout about the Lord. Sometimes Francis stood bruised beneath a coach, and he'd run behind a tree to seek. Julia painted him into a landscape made of eyes that blinked from his head like dolls. Through my weary sleep sometimes the howling. There were rumors in St. Albans of a newly-discovered wolf that prowled through eating cats and children. I thought Alexander dead. Nothing except my book was right, and despite these warnings, I kept writing deep into the night.

Leonard wanted to send money for my passage home. I would not accept his offer. My book was my new home and I did not wish to see him. My book and I exchanged news and lay together gazing at bats sighing on the ceiling. It was a lively book. It liked to spread its pages like arms waiting for embrace and grab lightly onto legs when I walked from room to room. My book and I were happy, but I knew one day, I would have to let it loose. It began to take up too much room.

*

I tell Nurse Elaine my story is almost finished. She motions arms cradling and crinkles her lips. Her mouth is made of shuffling pages, fingers creased and stained with ink. She folds my manuscript into a dress of paper that skims her shins down halls she wanders back and forth nightly. She moves toward Leonard, fluttering. He waits behind a vault. I look in corners, nowhere else to look. My pens are missing. Leonard has replaced them. My room is rising, sacks of wheat.

———

I have spent too much time in my room, writing, staring at corners, nowhere else to look. I listen to rain, mumbling made in mass, trains in the distance, sirens, and women who move in and out of passageways. Sometimes I watch the sun drown itself in settings while bats flee trees to catch it as it sinks. Poor creatures.

Of strange coincidences, there are many. The end is near and nigh, drawing closer to the truth.

I recently saw a film on late night television where the main character one day hears a strange voice in his head. The voice this man hears turns out to be "the narrator" who is writing his life in her books. The man goes on a quest to find his author, because she is about to kill him. She is at her wits end and can no longer write these books. The man must find her before she destroys him. The title: *Stranger than Fiction*, like Catharine Beecher's book.

The other day I was at a prison (I have, as do we all, an interesting uncle) perusing the handicrafts at their annual fair. My uncle had discovered a newfound fondness for woodwork, and spent his free time joyfully carving horses out of cedar. I admired his intricate figurines, informed him of a few personal tidbits about the family, bought one of his impressively detailed Clydesdales, and took his advice on inspecting his inmate chum's wares. I introduced myself to my uncle's friend, who invented board games about prison life and deliverance. After acknowledging my interest in his creative work, he gave me a flyer describing his life's sentence and his subsequent inventive pursuits. I noticed that he had previously spent time in Connecticut's Institute for Living. His board game was called *They Detain Him*.

I took a vacation to the San Francisco Bay area to visit some writer friends, and told them excitedly about the near completion of my book. When they asked what it was about, I mentioned the *Choose Your Own Adventure* series we all had read as kids, and noted its indelible influence. Each writer pal of mine coincidentally expressed the desire to somehow reinvent these works. How strange, we thought, that we had similar thoughts about this compelling genre. We laughed and joked, encouraging each other in our writerly pursuits.

While in the area, I also decided to look up a particularly annoying ex to ensure I was happier and more accomplished than him. When I brought up *Choose Your Own Adventures* and their influence to this irksome man, he had the nerve to ask if I remembered an idea he had for a book twelve years prior when we were up late one night on psychedelic mushrooms. I briefly wondered why he thought his intellect had more of an impact on me at the time than the putrid smell of his feet, and told him I did not appreciate him accusing me of stealing his idea. He then mentioned something about his beautiful brainchild getting planted in my subconscious, asked if my cat still had leukemia, and left without another word.

I Googled the sentence *"when my father left, I found myself in a fretful fire for Jesus"* to see what the cyber world would produce. All blogs. All websites honoring lineage. All uninteresting. Not one website mentioned *They Become Her*. Apparently no one had written it yet.

I have written myself into a quandary. It seems every time I contemplate the situations of this book, they are evoked. This would not be so difficult if this were a light-hearted romp filled with romance. I am thinking of writing a new work. The pain and complications of this piece are wreaking havoc, almost ruining my usually stable, often humdrum and mystery-free, romantically-lackluster life. I wonder about Rebecca. Maybe she has gotten lost in a bookstore. Maybe she has been pursued by Satanists. Maybe she has been locked up.

I have not provided any verifiable proof, and yet I swear I am telling the truth. My father lost an eye. My brother decided to become a Reverend. Letters form on my skin, and the dermatologist says they are the most unusual eczemic markings. When I read myself, I can faintly make out the words: *Let me out*. I swear to God, this is the truth.

———

Rebecca was happy because she finally had something to do. She had an interview at an office with shiny staplers and tape and motivational sayings professing the word of God. She knew something new would happen. She decided to purchase acrylic fingernails for faster typing and to look nice on her interview. Her nails have not been long since high school because she developed a slight suspicion God would not approve. Since he still was not speaking, she thought she would ask the women at the nail salon to paint crosses and angels on the tips to let Him know she was still anxiously awaiting his communication. John told her not to waste money on frivolous things, but Rebecca knew these new nails would increase her typing speed, and the luster of cross and angel might cause the other office girls to believe. On her way into town, Rebecca promised God that with these new extensions, she would compose a new work on the perils of wicked women.

There were many salons to choose from but she parked at the first she saw. Three women with masks pulled around their necks were inside. Echoes of muffled *Hello Hello Hello* greeted her over Satanic disco, and Rebecca tried to recognize other signs of the devil's presence. Except for the music and an enlarged photograph of a woman's red blood lips, she noticed none. She could avoid staring at the lascivious picture. As for the music, she would have to recite hymns:

O God, beneath Thy guiding hand our exiled fathers crossed the sea.
Rebecca approached.
"Can I help you?" The mask muffled the woman.

"Nails. Can you cover them with crosses? Silver, red, blue?"

And when they trod the wintry strand, with prayer and psalm they worshipped Thee.

"Sit." The woman began working while Rebecca watched.

Thou heardest, well pleased, the song, the prayer: Thy blessing came; and still its power shall onward, through all ages, bear the memory of that holy hour.

The woman rubbed her hands with soaps and oils, and used different tools for filing and shaping. Rebecca fell entranced with the buzz of the machines and was almost lulled into sleep. She repeated lines of the hymn over and over:

And here Thy Name, O God of love, their children's children still adore, till these eternal hills remove, and spring adorns the earth no more.

In an hour, the woman was finished and Rebecca's hands looked impressive despite the slight redness that surrounded the new nails protruding from her fingers. The crosses glistened, glinted.

When Rebecca was young, she went to see a Thanksgiving parade tromp down main street in the town she was a girl in. She went with her mother, who donned her spandex suit especially for the occasion. Francis and her father stayed home, uninterested in the repetition of this small-town celebration. Motorized vehicles pulled cars of waving cheerleaders covered with metallic fringe and sparkle. Rebecca was impressed with those who rode on horses.

There was a group of horsemen called "Redemption Riders" decked in gold and bearing flags that said "Fight for Jesus," "God Bless America," and "Only He Will Save You". They wore beige chaps bedazzled with sequins spelling words like "GLORY" down their thighs. Their cowboy hats were covered with cubic zirconium shimmering like suns. One man galloped close, and Rebecca pressed herself against her mother's leg to avoid being trampled by the horse's brutal stomp. Her mother shoved her forward, almost pushing her through the wire that marked the parade's route.

"He's waving to you, honey. You'd better wave back. There goes your prince in shining armor." Her mother laughed. Rebecca watched the man ignore her to wave at teenaged girls shrieking through their lip gloss. Her mother blew him far away kisses.

"I'll pray for that. Don't tell your father!" Rebecca watched her mother gazing off at the riders disappearing into dusk. A marching band was next to pass, and it blared through Rebecca's ears with adolescent triumph.

Rebecca dried her nails underneath a miniature fan. Her crosses were glorious. She hoped to make a good impression at the interview. When the woman behind the mask shooed her like a fly, Rebecca knew it was time to leave. She wondered what John would think when he saw her fingers.

Once home, she tried to go to bed, although it was only 5:30 and she was too exalted. Unable to fall, she brewed a pot of coffee and pulled the television down once more from her closet. Rebecca stayed awake late. The last thing she remembered was a glittering Cher selling makeup, surrounded by gibbering girls as dazzling and provocative as the Redemption Riders.

Soon it was the morning and Rebecca had to hurry. She showered. While the water ran, she sang. Birds chirped along: *Dear God. Give me a job. Dear God. Give me a job.* Over and over, she sang.

Rebecca searched her drawer for old nylons. They were nice to the touch, like the downy soft hair on the head of infant Jesus, and she was too excited to put them on one leg at a time. She ripped long lines down her thighs but left them on. She searched underneath cotton pajamas covered with doves and found a jean skirt buried in the bottom she hadn't worn since high school. She pulled it over her running legs. The skirt barely covered her, and if she dropped something and picked it up, someone might see her underwear. She had no other office clothes, just conservative Sunday service wear, so she left it on. She found a white silk blouse. Her pumps had scratches she did not have time to polish. Back in the bathroom, she searched for an aging can of Aqua Net. Rebecca had enough aerosol to style her hair exactly how she wanted. She took a piece of her bangs, pulled it away from her forehead and stuck the end into a brush. She sprayed, counted to five, blow-drying her hair straight up. She did the same to the sides of her hair. When she finished, she teased everything into fluff. She thought her attention to style would make a lasting impression. She was ready to leave. She grabbed her purse, making sure not to forget a few pamphlets detailing the war. She wanted to give one to her new boss. When she opened the door, her heart nearly burst. All hell was breaking loose.

John was home, stomping up the dirt driveway and swinging a heavy book in each hand. His eyes gazed fire and fury straight into her heart. Rebecca fell to her knees. An acrylic nail broke and seemed to float midair like a spirit before it landed in the dust. The silver cross gleamed glorious, shining in a light as cracked as her bones.

———

Rebecca noticed a light coming from the office of one of her colleagues and decided to say hello.

"Hey Jane. How's work?" Rebecca leaned into the doorway, startling her friend from her computer screen and causing a cascade of books. A fern sprawled the length of a window behind her. Jane named her plant Hattie because she liked to name most everything: her stapler, John; her computer, Thomas; her coffee mug, Beau. Sometimes Jane stared out her window and gave ephemeral names to the changing landscape of clouds. Rebecca would often walk by Jane's office listening for echoes of Romper Room like roll call: *I see Jason and Heather and Tony and Katharine.* Rebecca shared Jane's passion for invention.

"Rebecca! You scared the bees and Jesus knees out of me. What are you doing here so late?"

"You know. Working. Reading. I fell asleep. I couldn't read another sentence. I kept rereading the same one over and over. *Shining in a light as cracked as her bones. Shining in a light as cracked as her bones.* I'm having one of those weeks where everything seems to repeat itself. Know what I mean?"

"I know what you mean. I know what you mean." She laughed, jerking herself into spasms. "Did I tell you I heard from Elaine? She emailed me wanting information about Catherine Beecher. Did she tell you?"

"No." Rebecca smoldered with jealousy. "Why would she do that? Not tell me, I mean. We don't tell each other everything. We trust each other. With our work. You know. With everything. What did she want?"

"Calm down. I think she's planning to tell you. I've probably ruined the surprise, in fact. She found some particularly interesting manuscripts, that's all. Diaries and letters written by an American woman. Mid-eighteen hundreds. Connected with Catharine Beecher somehow. She said I might have heard of her but the name didn't resonate." Jane stared at the empty spaces behind Rebecca's shoulder. People who didn't know her often thought she was gazing at something specific behind them, and they would inevitably turn around to look. They found nothing. Jane usually took that opportunity to joke about forming a society filled with lazy-eyed beings who could see in more than one direction at once.

"What's her name?" Rebecca looked into Jane's face to find evidence of another in Elaine's potentially wandering eye. She held her breath to keep from slithering across Jane's desk.

"Doris? That's not it. Dolly? No. Damn. Dementia? Pamela? Fuck. I've forgotten. I think she was also a friend of Margaret Fuller's. Did you know Fuller was the first woman to translate *The Lotus Sutra* into English? Imagine all of those women back then dallying with ideas of reincarnation and universal consciousness! It's no surprise most of them were locked up. I accidentally deleted the email or else I would tell you who Elaine had mentioned. You could always Google something."

"I can't Google anything if I don't know what I'm looking for."

"Catherine Beecher and a book. A fiction strange and true? Maybe that's backwards. I don't believe it's in print anyway, and I doubt our library has it. You might check the store in town that's got those unfamiliar used books. Really, I have no idea what Elaine was talking about. If it isn't real, I'm lost. Ha! That isn't true!" Jane gazed off. Rebecca's venom settled into vessels just beneath her teeth.

"Well, thanks, Jane. Now I'm confused."

"Just remember—we're all in this together! One day at a time..."

"Fuck you." Rebecca imagined her legs entwined around Jane's throbbing, leathery throat.

"Hey! Fuck you, too!" Jane waved and Rebecca slunk away.

The streets were deserted. People were in their beds and bodies, peacefully dreaming. Rebecca decided as soon as she got home, she would write no matter what. She would find a story, remembered in fits and suffocations, and finally place it on a page beyond mere mental associations. There were too many words to fight and fret with. She would make them her lovers.

She was livid with Elaine for not sharing whatever information she possessed. Rebecca wondered what it would be like if she could turn Elaine into a doll, pulling strings to make her talk. She would set her in the corners, staring faraway and beautiful, and Rebecca would be the one who was in control.

ELEVEN

In an hour more you would be the only living thing in all this solitude...
How strangely any voice sounds amid this loneliness. I am glad you are here.
Delia Bacon

THE WALLS CLOSE TIGHTER, coffins made of rot. The pages pulse, binding. Words echo as if welled. Let me out! Let me out! What have you done to Delia? Soil forms my face and language worms.

I am soon to be released, freed, the end of living in these fictions. I am to wake in a world underneath, flesh falling from my sides. I smuggle pages to those who hide them. I push into crevices of crumbling brick.

When I go home, I will rest my head on Leonard's lap. I will be delivered. The dead shall be raised and ascend the language up. I will enter night and join the constellations.

The men will not subject me to their endless examinations. Now there is no use. I am their joke, fourth-rate play actor, their fraud.

My last days will be alone, aware of the recede and stutter of an almost extinguished heart. I will wait silent until the days when I will not be forgotten.

*

I grew thin because history had me surrounded. England continued to fabricate stories. Buildings stacked up, and bodies crumpled down. I remained in my lodging and did not want to leave. I could never go back home.

Sometimes I would wander through the parlor and trace my hand along the wall. I had to keep from falling. Something was wrong, and I only knew of one person who might be kind enough to listen.

With faltering faith I contacted him, a man of letters, the current consulate in Liverpool. He was a man I knew from stories, famous for romance and books. I appealed to him pleading the difficulty of living with the secrets of my work. My manuscript grew heavy, weighing my hips to a slant when I'd haul it. It bent my back like a question when I heaved it to and fro. Almost tendrils laid pages on me and I could barely breathe. They devoured and I pleaded:

My Dear Sir Mr. Nathaniel Hawthorne,

You are the only one I know of in this hemisphere able to appreciate the position I find myself in, and I know of no one else fully qualified to judge the claims of a work not hemispherical. I tried to publish it myself, but I did not succeed. I lost years in the endeavor. It is a science the world is waiting for, a work I have cast into it not only all the living that I had, but my life also. I need literary counsel such as no Englishman is able to give. The Atlantic Ocean and the English nation were too mighty for me. I was not a writer when I began, I despaired of ever being able to write it; I had to keep my secret for many years, because I did not know how to tell it. The honor of the country is at stake. Please help. I have nowhere else to turn.

This paragraph turned to twenty pages, writing cramming and shoving into every free space of margin, writing frivolously a danger because I had to conserve what paper I could afford for my consumptive, greedy book. I had more words than I could get my hands through. They would rattle the pages writing and I could not make them stop. Sometimes I had to stack them heavy with books after regretfully signing my name to ensure an end to endless beginnings. This was how I finished the letter I composed to Hawthorne – pressed hands book bound to quash this delirious writing. I waited for his reply with flattened hands in a room full of the spreading of bat wings. My landlady burrowed through the filmy threads to bring me biscuits and blankets. I waited. I waited. I waited for his response.

Letters built bridges in my skin: *S* and *H* and *A* and *K* and *E* and *S*. Sometimes I sifted. My mind clattered.

I could not go much further on. I began to forget myself and remember I was not who I once had been. My book beckoned. I waited.

One day, I do not know the time, a letter arrived addressed from my new savior. Providence had found me once more and Mr. Hawthorne had listened. I read:

I feel you have done a thing that ought to be reverenced, in devoting yourself so entirely to this object, whatever it be, and whether right or wrong; and that, by so doing, you have acquired some of the privileges of an inspired person and a prophetess—and that the world is bound to hear you, if for nothing else, yet because you are so sure of your own mission. We find thoughts in all great writers that strike their roots far beneath the surface, and intertwine themselves with the roots of other writers' thoughts; so that when we pull up one, we stir the whole, and yet these writers have had no conscious society with one another.

A man of my own mind. He and I were rooted and connected. This encouraged me to compose a few phrases. I wrote:

To be me, William Shakespeare, is not to be. That question, who is not me. It is not noble a cause to be, but to BE. We are left in the west and not the east.

Some bats flew from their roost, whipping through the evening air high and pitching. I could almost see the ceiling. I began to see more than words encircling me from pages. I saw sheets and linens, chairs, a writing table. I saw books empty themselves of words. Language was leaving. My landlady may have cleared the rooms. Was she underneath my bed and hiding?

My apartments began to vacate from clutter until they were transparent. I could see the world outside through walls that had become clear. I heard the wind bellow, but it bawled against itself. The only thing besides dust was a mirror, and I looked at my dark eyes looking back and saw what had become of me.

I gathered what was left of my once powerful constitution to write back to Mr. Hawthorne telling him how much I had turned to ghost. I wished to meet him, but I was no longer the person who stood in a room's full view and talked of meeting pharaohs. I was not the same girl who marched through New Haven with love boiling the mind with desire. I was too wraithlike, a woman. I wrote to him that if he wished to visit, I would don my only best dress and meet him face to face as if living. I hoped he wouldn't mind conversing with ghosts. I hoped he would not mind the wind echoing out of my throat. I wrote:

I am nothing but this work, and don't wish to be. I would rather be this than anything else. I don't wish to return to the world. I shrink with the horror from the thought of it.

While waiting for his reply, I blustered through the empty rooms, grasping what I thought were objects and turning them into words.

Mr. Hawthorne soon promised me a visit, and I vowed to look through the grates of my wind-wound cell as pleasantly as possible to see him. I waited for him each day, peering through windows. I could hear the bats trembling with the lob of anticipatory nights.

One day, I watched him walk the path lined quaint with stones. His hair exploded around his face wildly and I couldn't see the extent of his expression. He walked with confidence yet slightly tilted groundward as if to shelter his midsection with lean arms swinging from his sides. He wore all black and hid mystery beneath the folds of his suit. I slightly shook, possibly older than I looked. I breathed a breath and turned the outside in, as concrete as it must have always been.

I opened the door before he knocked and mustered every spare bit of energy for this meeting. I had subsided the remaining bats by covering their wings with imaginary sheets draped lightly so as not to disturb them. I had a feeling they were not visible to anyone else but me, but I had to make the most appropriate impressions on Mr. Hawthorne, my final aspiration. When I swung the door wide with an exuberance I had not marshaled for years, Mr. Hawthorne jumped.

"Miss. Bacon, I presume." He searched me for danger or imbecility, but found none. His eyes were deep as Alexander's, except he prevented the world from seeping in through some intentional interference of his mind. He must have understood the cruelty of greedily drawing. Conscious of his capability, he looked at the shiny tips of his shoes respectfully not fetching me. I thrust my hand in front and he was inclined to take it.

"Please, come in. I've tried to tidy the place, but I've no time. We'll have to make do with the front parlor."

He looked without distress at the books and papers disorganized on the tables, and appeared comfortable amongst my scholastic mess.

"You are much different than I expected." He was looking at my stacks of books.

"What do you mean? I am not shriveled and bent over a caldron or calling women to the woods to prance? Is it because I've no veil to cover the face I choose to possess?"

He finally met my eye for the first time and I saw something undeniably somber. He gathered himself and stretched a smile despite the weight of his self-restraint.

"I just…I apologize. You are much younger than I imagined."

"You expected me elderly? Not every woman engaged with acts of the mind must sacrifice her body. I still have every tooth and wit to match." I smiled to prove this. He wrapped his arms around his chest.

"You are a surprise, Miss. Bacon. But for now we must avoid any unnecessary exchange of pleasantries. My position in England does not allow for superfluous activities. This dreary climate has affected me and I am unable to maintain a cheerful disposition. Would you mind telling me why you have so voraciously contacted me?" He met my gaze indirectly. If I were younger, I might feel sensation dissolving.

I told him of the horrors I suffered at the hands of foolish, mendacious publishers and complained of a public unable to progress. I spoke of lack of vision. Unlike Mr. Carlyle, Mr. Hawthorne did not laugh me into childhood, nor did he blink an eye at my authorial propositions. He understood, listening entranced. Occasionally I saw him reach into his jacket pocket to search for something apparently not there anymore. He seemed to be seeking out a pipe or stone with which to occupy his nervous fingers.

When I finished, he sat rocking, reflecting.

"You do understand *Putnam's* desire to be presented with evidence? I agree that vision is often stifled by an unripe public, but you must have a plan to locate empirical evidence?"

"I know I must provide proof of the secret society working in collusion to disseminate their works. I have made the men's motives clear through my examinations of the plays, and despite the existence of an offshoot of the society even now in New Haven, I understand I must find solid ground with which to rest my feet. It is this ground I must first disturb. I believe the only way I can locate the necessary documents is by unsettling the soil that surrounds us. William Shakespeare must be woken from his fictitious sleep."

"I'm afraid I do not understand your suggestion..."

"Not to worry, Mr. Hawthorne. I will find proof, and you will not be implicated in any action I choose. I have decided I must arrange an overnight visit to the actor's gravesite. He bought his resting place in that church. He doesn't belong there."

Somehow, he did not seem entirely shocked.

"If you think you might find something beneath the ground or above, I wish you luck. You are an admirable woman with as princely a spirit as Queen Elizabeth. It is a very singular phenomenon that you have constructed this entire system of philosophy within the depths of your mind. To have created these unconsciously elaborated details with fancy is almost as wonderful as to really have found it in the plays. I support you in your quest."

And that was that. When he left, the moon rose and I could hear dancing in the hollows.

I remained in communication with Mr. Hawthorne, and kept him abreast of my expansions. He introduced me via post to his wife Mrs. Sophia Peabody Hawthorne, and I was glad to finally be introduced to the sister of my old friend, Miss. Elizabeth Peabody. Mr. Hawthorne said his wife might provide me with encouragement while completing my work. This is what she had done for him, so I sent her some of my chapters. She enjoyed my progressive ideas with a zest I could not elicit in her husband. She wrote:

I feel so ignorant in the presence of your extraordinary learning, that it seems absurd to say what I think of your manuscripts, and yet I cannot help it; for I never read so profound and wonderful a criticism. I felt as if I wanted to take this manuscript and all the others and run off to some profound retreat and study it all over and reproduce it again with my own faculties.

It is not a wonder her husband was successful with such a wife to support him. She was too astute to ask for droll, empirical evidence and would not judge if I unearthed a body in order to discover what I already knew. This was a woman of my own mind, who would take and remake the language.

Time was passing, and if I wanted to finish, I had to make my move. I organized a visit to Holy Trinity. I would take my landlady, who was all too eager to assist. Everything was alive with the spirit of near completion.

I was to arrive before my landlady and obtain permission from the vicar to spend the night on the guise of a special pilgrimage for literary knowledge. If needed, I would show him my statements of character from Mr. Emerson and Mr. Carlyle. Once stationed and ready, my landlady would bring necessary tools wrapped and concealed in a blanket to unearth stones and lift heavy segments of soil. I would need only one evening, and with the proper scrutiny and enough candles lighting my way, I would be able to put all back in place after removing the confidential documents. I hoped the worms would not have eaten through them.

The night soon came when I was to dig up the Bard's unholy bones. The vicar did not regard me suspiciously because I greeted him with professional elegance. I elaborated vaguely on my holy, scholarly quest, interspersing my thoughts with prayers to the Lord and all those protected by His word. I gathered my former speaking habits to charm him into support without skepticism. Sooner than later I had him won. He was trusting and jovial and possibly part deaf and blind, unaware of most of my fabricated explanations. When the evening bells chimed in the tower, I heard him scratch his way along the walls to his resting place for the evening. I was alone, eternities reflecting.

I examined the grave while there was still light because I wished to conserve my candles. I figured the decrepit corpse was at the most nine feet below considering recent renovations, and I had to work quickly in order to have him replaced before morning.

I studied Shakespeare's false bust and quill. He glared at me mocking and I thought of Sir Francis and his perplexing tomb. I hoped I was exhuming the right remains. Maybe the manuscripts were buried with Marlowe or Sir Francis Bacon? The sun vanished, and I burned through candles growing meager and impatient. I became lost in the pitch of darkness without sight.

Every din or scratch, I thought rats might crawl up my legs to bite my chilly flesh. I lay down on a pew desperately. Behind all unexpected noises, the Avon continued in quietude.

Deep into the night, my landlady finally arrived. She brought the large blunt objects needed to uproot the author and more candles which I hoped weren't quick to burn. She was overzealous with help, excited by an adventure her domestic confinement could not afford.

I quickly regretted my decision to include her. She would not cease eagerly speaking and she reeked of strong consumptive substances. She was not much help, having to lean on a wall or recline in order to remain motionless. She battered me doubtful with questions:

"What if he is covered in worms? Are you afraid of what you might find in this wretched dark? What was that noise? Do you think we are haunted? Look, eyes, over there, peering through the light near Jesus!"

I asked her to leave so I might better be able to work. I could not think accordingly with her superstitious ramblings or the stench of fire that burned her breath out of fearlessness. After she had gone, the church hushed and I could commune. I thought I heard Shakespeare speaking, but couldn't understand those words. My landlady never returned. Her spirits finally put her to sleep. I was thankful for them, and set about determining the night's dwindling chance to finally finish my work.

I thought about Leonard and the other Skull and Bones. I thought of writing and the world unwilling. I thought of the deaf ears and eyes of the vicar making up meaning for a conversation only he alone heard. I thought I saw him motion through a doorway in the dark, too silent for certainty. My candles were again extinguished, and I hadn't removed a modicum of dust. The false and fixed Shakespeare continued to grin through the night's musk. I looked at the spaces in-between spaces and saw a million tiny lights of red, white and blue glowing, flying toward me.

I couldn't do it. I could not unearth the proof. If the world did not want me without dirt on my hands from the false rotten flesh, fine. I was through. I would wait for history to momentarily erase me.

I left the church when the sun rose on another day I had not yet completed. Birds woke from their nests and chattered through the sky with gossiping perpetuity. The stockings of my landlady stuck out sloppily from beneath a lime tree. A bell tolled.

I wrote to Mr. Hawthorne describing my night; how I found out from my landlady once she was not intoxicated that the vicar, not blind at all, kept constant watch over me. She watched him watching me watching Shakespeare's bust. His appearances in doorways were not hallucinations. The unexplained noises, the shuffling of his soft-soled shoes. He even brought my landlady a blanket to lay her head upon while she slept beneath that unfortunate tree. If I had dug the player up, I would have been stopped. I let his bones lie for the last time, never to return to this world again.

My book was finished. I had to get it out, with or without proof. I sent it to Mr. Hawthorne, and he promised to see it published. Eventually, he found an affable soul to print it. I was grateful for its final journey. It had taken years of becoming. I was tired. I was through. Finally, I was through.

The preface Mr. Hawthorne wrote contains indications of his disbelief in my theory. After reading his unkind words, it was him I shunned and avoided. We were never to speak again, despite his once sympathetic hand. Someone later told me they believed it was he who paid for its publication out of his own pocket, but I did not believe them. This could not have been the truth.

I did not receive money for my book's publication; Mr. Hawthorne may have been the one who ultimately wronged me. I suppose I will never know.

The public was not ready to believe but there is reason behind their unwillingness to face the truth. They are not prepared to be reborn in a thinking entirely new.

One day the world will open its welcoming arms. For now, I split at least in two. For now, I am finished. I am through.

My book is bound, yet I cannot read the writing. The words are not my words. I do not recognize myself. The men must have replaced it. The ramble long, incomprehensible, not my language. It is me as they beheld me. I am through. I am through.

I was put in an asylum by a man who found my landlady rocking me through an alley comforted from the inexplicable belittling of batwings. The man wrote of madness to my brother and said it was difficult to sustain me. He said I spoke of things mysterious, incomprehensible. I spoke too loudly, not a voice proper for the inside. The doctor said I moaned about Shakespeare killed in between pages of books and Leonard laying a hand on fevered heads for forgiveness. He told my brother my sentences wound in ways that wouldn't work. I was forced in a room where I wobbled and waited, wobbled and waited, muttering as low as I could so as not to reveal myself.

I stayed and I waited for someone to rest me on a ship before crossing finality drowning—pages bloated and floating to shipwrecked shores one day someone might search for. One day Leonard would pronounce me dead before living.

The doctors pushed and prodded and stuck my body with pins, their hands not smooth like water. They tied me in small cold rooms where dew dripped like the everlasting Avon. I told stories to keep occupied, unable to use my hands to find voices. Sometimes I began at beginnings:

Once there was a girl whose father fled. Her mother left her in a fret. Her father fled the wild. Her father fled.

My nephew came and promised to take me home. He looked with eyes made out of Leonard. I arrived on a once-familiar shore, and Leonard locked me where I watched myself wrest. I found Nurse Elaine, old friend.

He told me I wouldn't see him or his children or Julia or my former life until I confessed how I lied a life untrue. I had to write my own sentence, provide evidence of how I had been living, and it was good. It was good. I was through. I finished my book and was finally through.

*

Nurse Elaine prepares for my release. When I go home, I will fawn, fake and pray. I will thank Leonard for a new life lived and spend my days again forgetting. I will visit the last places.

I will be written from the living. The dead shall be raised. This is true. Finally, I had found my proof. This is true. This is true. This is true.

———

I've been here so long, wasting away while the world winds on. Lines of sight limiting, restricted. I am tired of meetings and picnics. I might embark upon a journey, anything to leave these grounds. I miss the outside, months since my brother came to visit. When we last walked, orange and red leaves were beginning to fall from the branches and crunch beneath our feet like the scattering of bones.

I told a friend I was almost finished. He knows people who might want to publish my book. I wrote:

Inside walls and tombs, buried beneath paved-up brick and stone, are sounds of singing. A woman hums about skin that is itched and blotched. Another moans through the after light about long distances of earth between bodies. They cant themselves through stories passed along lifelines not printed through page or book. On the air, ripples fan outward in effervescent motions of waves without final destination. The stories are true, needing no explanation. Names echo times past and present. We speak to those speaking. They become us. They become her, too.

I wrote these words, but they quickly disappeared. Someone had become them. Was it you? Was it you? Was it you?

———

Rebecca was glad John had come home. He had thoughtfully brought her gifts—angels for her collection—and she dusted them after their post-breakfast prayer. God was speaking to her again in muted tones she could barely make form words. She did not miss her former life without him. It was easier to have John there to tell her what to do.

Her wrist slowly healed and the skin underneath the cast itched. She found a thin twig while cleaning shards of television set from the backyard, and used it to get to the source. John had been warm and loving. He had often cooked her soup.

He told her stories of his journeys, how he met up with a group to examine and study hymns. John was planning to research the authors of these works and their families in order to discover if they led fine and pious Christian lives. He told Rebecca he had discovered men just like him.

Rebecca promised to help, and she was glad to write again. She planned to research the author of the hymn she sang while painting her nails red, silver, and blue.

Laws, freedom, and faith in God came with those exiles o'er the waves. And, where their pilgrim feet have trod, the God they trusted guards their graves.

Rebecca found out that the hymn was written in the 1800s by a man named Leonard Bacon. Rebecca believed he was a good man looking to spread the word so the worthy were prepared to fight upon this earth. She learned that Leonard Bacon led a holy, noble life. Although she was not supposed to, she was also gathering information about his sister, a woman who went mad because of dangerous thoughts. Her insanity and possession led her to self-destruction and her brother had made an example of her. Rebecca wanted to write about Leonard's sister Delia, who lived a life less righteous.

Rebecca convinced John that they must travel and research. Leonard Bacon's work was located in an archive at the Yale Library, and Rebecca would like to have a look. John planned for their trip. In secret, Rebecca turned over possible first sentences, but nothing, for a while, would work.

One morning, while John was dousing her with holy water, she woke up. Her room glowed with the light of god and she knew she had finally found it, or it finally had found her. He was once again clearly speaking to her. She rushed to the typewriter, vowing never again to be forgotten:

When my father left I found myself in a fretful fire for Jesus.

———

Sophia was waiting for Rebecca, drooling at the door. Although Rebecca furiously wanted to contact Elaine, she decided to prevent any unnecessary accidents by first taking Sophia out. She grabbed Sophia's leash and hooked it to her neck. They walked through a neighborhood once again eerily void of children playing. While her walks with Sophia were usually relaxing, Rebecca was pissed—every breath a huff and hiss. Sophia seemed worried that if

Rebecca pulled too hard, she would be choked.

Rebecca was furious with Elaine for a secrecy that was by this time characteristic. She wondered at her ability to keep things private for days, weeks, months, without any revelatory expressions. Rebecca questioned if perhaps, a long time ago, she should have told Elaine about her extraordinary birth. Maybe Rebecca was getting what she deserved.

Sophia tugged at her leash cautiously, stopping at every light post or bush. Rebecca's mind wound in ribbons of verse:

i seek you through pages packed tight. one day i might find you gurgling the words of your first breath, the womb that watered you bursting.

What did Elaine think she was doing? Asking Jane about mysterious, unusual work? Why wouldn't she share her ideas with Rebecca? Rebecca imagined Xeroxing a wanted poster with Elaine's photograph and stapling it along each telephone pole warning others of Elaine's secretive indiscretions. Rebecca's tongue flickered and flicked. She licked her lips.

i loved your faults and flows as if skin i could cling to. what useless flesh, what soul. what matter. what a husk.

What crap. Rebecca couldn't think of anything to connect worth keeping. She still hadn't written anything down.

Sophia pulled. They were almost to the corner where a liquor store gleamed its neon tackiness in spasms of seductive flash. Advertisements for cheap whiskey smothered the windows in enticing scribbles of future debilitations. Rebecca considered a moment. How long had it been since she'd had a drink? Six years? Seven? She wondered what would happen if she were to buy a fifth and finish it.

She unfolded the drama of Elaine searching, desperate, finally finding her, drunk and reeking in some ditch screaming to the stars about the incredible noise of her solitude. She would be surrounded by bottles, legs curled around the glass, and blood would drip from her pointed incisors to form red accusatory puddles. Elaine would cradle Rebecca's head in her arms and calm her until she sobered; she would lick her wounds.

Or maybe Elaine would find Rebecca lying across railroad tracks, wrapped into a coil, lights of a train approaching. The terrifying whistle would shatter the sky with danger encroaching. Elaine would lift her at just the last second and they would gallop into the sunset like real cowboys.

Rebecca's legs began to burn and itch. She could not resist the lure and decided there was no harm in purchasing a small nip of whiskey. She did not necessarily have to drink it. She could pour some of it down the sink and leave a half-empty bottle for Elaine's inevitable intervention. She could hide it somewhere Elaine would certainly find it. Rebecca paid for the whiskey. Rebecca decided she might make hints of drunkenness the next time Elaine called. She would add just enough slur to arouse Elaine's suspicions.

Sophia and Rebecca made it home with the whiskey. She sat at the table and unscrewed the bottle. The smell filled the room with the familiar scent of her old disease. There was a shuffling behind the front door. In haste and shock, Rebecca spilled the whiskey onto the floor. She ran, expecting a thief or Elaine or both. She opened the door quick enough to see the postman scurry off.

A package was on the ground. From Elaine.

Rebecca convulsed through the doorframe, tearing the box and ripping the cardboard with her teeth. Inside there was a note and jewelry sized box. Rebecca quivered with a surplus of forgiveness and devotion. She read:

Dear love: I found this for you. Thought you might be interested in a new project. Love, E.

Inside the box was a tiny spool of microfiche. Rebecca unrolled it and held it up to the light. Letters and dated entries written with a crowded, ancient hand collided with incomprehensible doodles and demarcations. Rebecca looked at the date. 1811-1859. She read the first sentence of the first document aloud and listened to the words:

When my father left I found myself in a fretful fire for Jesus.

POSTSCRIPT

I KNEW THAT I should visit the nearly departed, but I delayed this last adventure, uncertain of what I might find once I exhumed. Perhaps amongst the flesh and rotting, I might discover the new learning? I didn't have a clue, but I knew I needed proof.

I prepared myself mentally for an encounter with Leonard. I would ignore the fluttering pigeons of his hands, and set to work when the sun went down. I would use the night as my shelter; I would lie on the grass and let it shield me from his accusatory glances.

She lies in Grove Street, a few hundred yards from the Skull and Bones tomb. She has frequent visitors. In the guestbook, the initials RB are written multiple times, our inevitable collaborations.

I had to obtain permission from the groundskeeper. When I asked about the inscription above the Egyptian revival archway, "The Dead Shall Be Raised", he obliquely replied, "history has a way of changing the truth, depending on who's telling the story."

I walked along the fallen leaves, crushing their fragile stems underfoot while staring at the monuments for Theodore Dwight Woolsey, Lyman Beecher, Jeremiah Day, Noah Webster. I delivered as friendly a greeting as I could.

After wandering underneath the shedding trees, I saw her looming and sturdy, directly in front of Leonard so that he was nearly hidden. She was covered with minute lichens. She was as devastating and decorous as I had always imagined.

"Delia," I asked, "do you know who I am?"

Her mouth opened, and golden leaves hushed through. I looked closely, wondering if she was still covered with words. I studied her for a sentence, and noticed a crumbling smile that belied her age. Her hands were furiously groping patches of grass as if she were afraid of letting go. Her dress was churchly white. Near her knees hobbled and bent were the words:

In graceful remembrance this monument is erected by her former pupils.

Leonard sat smugly behind, jutting his chin to a setting sky. Someone had planted an American flag at his feet.

I watched Leonard ignore me.

When I began to remove pebbles from the soles of his sister's worn out boots, he spoke:

I have preached righteousness in the great congregation. Lo, I have not refrained my lips. O Lord thou knowest.

I lobbed some stones at him and continued with my consecratory homage to his sister.

She was looking lighter and lighter. Earthworms and roots squiggled around her feet. While she still would not speak, she began to swing and shift a bit, moving with the undulations of breeze in the trees. She seemed about to sweep herself off her feet, and I flung clods of dirt and soil onto Leonard so that she could move about more freely.

She knew I was looking for the truth.

She began to dramatically gesture behind her, and I could not help but to glance at what she needed me to see. I stopped my unearthing.

"Rebecca Bacon" curves like a fingernail at the top of the tombstone directly to Leonard's right. Next to it are the words:

Well reported for good works of whom the world was not worthy.

I gathered my tools and ran toward the archway that would have the dead raised. When I looked back, I noticed Delia drifting, finally released.

SOURCE TEXTS

MUCH OF THE INFORMATION in this book has generously depended on the following:

Bacon, Delia. *The Bride of Fort Edward*. Whitefish: Kessinger Publishing, 2004.

———. *The Philosophy of the Plays of Shakspere Unfolded*. New York: AMS Press, 1857.

Bacon, Theodore. *Delia Bacon: A Biographical Sketch*. Boston and New York: Houghton, Mifflin and Company, 1888.

Beecher, Catharine Esther. *Truth Stranger Than Fiction : A Narrative of Recent Transactions, Involving Inquiries In Regard to the Principles of Honor, Truth, and Justice, Which Obtain In a Distinguished American University*. Boston: Phillips, Sampson & co., 1850.

Bradley, Michael. *The Secret Societies Handbook*. New York: Gusto Company, 2004.

Brown, Rebecca. *Prepare for War*. Springdale: Whittaker House, 1992.

Brown, Rebecca. *Excerpts from a Family Medical Dictionary*. London: Granta Books, 2004.

―――. *The Dogs: A Modern Bestiary.* San Francisco: City Lights Books, 1998.

―――. *The Gifts of the Body.* New York: HarperCollins, 1994.

―――. *The Last Time I Saw You.* San Francisco: City Lights Books, 2006.

―――. *The Terrible Girls.* San Francisco: City Lights Books, 1990.

Cantwell, Robert. "Hawthorne and Delia Bacon." *American Quarterly* 1 (1949): 343-360.

Collins, Paul. *Banvard's Folly: Thirteen Tales of People Who Didn't Change the World.* New York: Picador, 2001.

Hawthorne, Nathaniel. "Recollections of a Gifted Woman". *Our Old Home: A Series of English Sketches.* Boston: Houghton and Mifflin and Co., 1883.

Hope, Warren and Kim Holston. *The Shakespeare Controversy.* North Carolina: McFarland and Company, 1992.

Hopkins, Vivian. *Prodigal Puritan: A Life of Delia Bacon.* Cambridge: Harvard University Press, 1959.

Packard, Edward. *Hyperspace.* New York: Bantam, 1983.

Robbins, Alexandra. *Secrets of the Tomb: Skull and Bones, The Ivy League, and the Hidden Paths of Power.* Boston: Little, Brown and Company, 2002.

Schoenbaum, S. *Shakespeare's Lives.* Oxford: Clarendon Press, 1991.

Ticknor, Caroline. *Hawthorne and His Publisher.* Port Washington: Kennikat Press, Inc., 1913.

REBBECCA BROWN received her Ph.D. in Creative Writing from the University of Louisiana at Lafayette in 2007. Her work has appeared in journals such as *American Literary Review, Confrontation, 88: A Journal of Contemporary American Poetry, Eclipse, Requited, H_ngm_n* and *Ekleksographia*. She received an Honorable Mention from the Academy of American Poets, the Rachel Sherwood Prize for Poetry, First Place in the LACC Writing Contest for Creative Nonfiction, and has taught as a Fulbright-Nehru Visiting Lecturer at Kannur University in Kerala, India. Her first novel, *They Become Her*, received Honorable Mention in the 2009-2010 Starcherone Innovative Fiction Contest. She lives in New York City and teaches at Hunter College.

TITLES FROM
WHAT BOOKS PRESS

POETRY

Molly Bendall & Gail Wronsky, *Bling & Fringe (The L.A. Poems)*

Laurie Blauner, *It Looks Worse Than I Am*

Kevin Cantwell, *One of Those Russian Novels*

Ramón García, *Other Countries*

Karen Kevorkian, *Lizard Dream*

Patty Seyburn, *Perfecta*

Judith Taylor, *Sex Libris*

Lynne Thompson, *Start with a Small Guitar*

Gail Wronsky, *So Quick Bright Things*
BILINGUAL, SPANISH TRANSLATED BY ALICIA PARTNOY

ART

Gronk, *A Giant Claw*
BILINGUAL, SPANISH

Chuck Rosenthal, Gail Wronsky, & Gronk,
Tomorrow You'll Be One of Us: Sci Fi Poems

PROSE

Rebbecca Brown, *They Become Her*

François Camoin, *April, May, and So On*

A.W. DeAnnuntis, *Master Siger's Dream*

A.W. DeAnnuntis, *The Final Death of Rock and Roll and Other Stories*

A.W. DeAnnuntis, *The Mermaid at the Americana Arms Motel*

Katharine Haake, *The Origin of Stars and Other Stories*

Katharine Haake, *The Time of Quarantine*

Mona Houghton, *Frottage & Even As We Speak: Two Novellas*

Rod Val Moore, *Brittle Star*

Chuck Rosenthal, *Are We Not There Yet?*
Travels in Nepal, North India, and Bhutan

Chuck Rosenthal, *Coyote O'Donohughe's History of Texas*

Chuck Rosenthal, *West of Eden: A Life in 21st Century Los Angeles*

WHAT
BOOKS
PRESS

LOS ANGELES

What Books Press books may be ordered from:
SPDBOOKS.ORG | ORDERS@SPDBOOKS.ORG | (800) 869 7553 | AMAZON.COM

Visit our website at
WHATBOOKSPRESS.COM

CPSIA information can be obtained
at www.ICGtesting.com
Printed in the USA
FFOW01n1653190914
7435FF

9 780988 924871